THE HAUNTING OF HATTIE HASTINGS

AUDREY DAVIS

TANZANITE BOOKS

For my Family. Bill, Euan and Callum. Thanks guys for always being there for me.

'Tis better to have loved and lost than never to have loved at all.

Alfred Lord Tennyson

THE HAUNTING OF HATTIE HASTINGS

PART ONE

CHAPTER 1

GARY GYRATED AROUND THE ROOM, pelvis thrusting in every possible direction, vocal cords strained to the max as he went for the big finale. He was performing one of his favourites, all about being naked apart from headwear. His adoring fans – ninety-three-year-old Agnes who was fortunately completely deaf, and barmaid Bertha, who wasn't renowned for her taste in music or men – whooped and cheered. At least, Bertha did while Agnes gave her walking frame an enthusiastic waggle. The rest of the audience clapped in that way that suggested they would much rather be somewhere else. Or be wearing industrial-strength earplugs.

Hattie drained her drink and sighed. Very heavily, like a worn-out old couch when someone sat on it. She'd kill for another but as she had to drive Joe Cocker home, it wasn't an option. She eyed the stage (a five-foot-square platform in the centre of The Nobody Inn) and saw he was revving up for an encore. Fan-bloody-tastic. If he even *attempted* 'American Pie,' she'd take him down with a home-made catapult comprising of a twenty-denier stocking and a pork pie purloined from the pre-party buffet.

Luck was on her side. The microphone was snatched from Gary's hand by a Diana Ross wannabe, sporting a wig that could have provided a hiding place for the other Supremes. As she – or was it a he? – launched into an enthusiastic rendition of 'Chain Reaction', sequins flew around, spattering the crowd and landing in a few disgruntled punters' pints.

'How's it going, babe?' A very sweaty Gary gave Hattie an enormous squeeze from behind. She wriggled free from his damp embrace and jangled her car keys pointedly.

'It's fine, but I think it's time we headed home, don't you?' It was already past midnight and Hattie had work in the morning. Gary was currently unemployed, or 'on a break', as he liked to put it. He worked as a long-haul lorry driver, but his company had recently implemented a cost-cutting exercise which involved asking employees to consider voluntary redundancy (or wait for the *axle* to fall). Gary had jumped at the offer (without consulting Hattie, much to her irritation), and now seemed intent on spending the pay-out at lightning speed. Nor did he appear to be in any rush to find another job.

'Give a man a break, Harriet!' he'd retorted the other morning when she'd asked if there was any chance he might extract himself from under the duvet. He only ever called her that when he wanted to wind her up. She'd already emptied the dishwasher, mopped the kitchen floor, written her grocery list for the coming days and got ready for another fun-filled shift at Espresso Yourself. Hattie had been working there for just over a year, serving up-market coffees, cakes and light snacks to its well-heeled clientele. A folded copy of *The Guardian* or *The Times* was almost de rigueur although rarely read as they glued themselves to their laptops and mobiles. The pay was decent, although not nearly enough to keep them afloat if Gary didn't get off his arse soon, and she got to bring home the odd mille-feuille or other sweet delight. These were inevitably demolished within seconds by either Gary or their twenty-year-old son, Johnny.

Driving back, with Gary snoring gently in the passenger seat, Hattie wondered if Johnny would be home. Since he'd quit university on the grounds that it was stifling his creativity and was only for the bourgeois elite (Hattie had been momentarily proud of his extensive vocabulary until the realisation of what he'd done kicked in) he'd demonstrated very little on the creative side. Unless you counted building a makeshift stool out of empty pizza boxes. The discarded business management degree had been replaced by the assertion that he was going to write a seminal novel on the topic of today's stressed-out and financially disadvantaged youth.

'You know, Mum, more and more people in their late twenties can't afford to leave the parental home or have to return because they can't get a foot on the property ladder,' he'd pronounced one morning over breakfast. Which was a miracle in itself as he seldom surfaced before midday. Hattie had bitten both her toast and her tongue, keeping her thoughts to herself. There'd been little evidence of the touted novel, aside from a few scribblings in an ancient jotter with *Johnny Hastings, Year 12* written on the cover. She loved her son to bits, of course she did, but she worried incessantly about what would become of him.

'It's only natural to worry, darling. Whether they're two or thirty, your child will always have the power to keep you awake at night. Trust me, I know!'

Those had been the words of wisdom from her mother. Rachel Anderson was an indomitable soul, still going strong at seventy-four. She'd raised Hattie and her younger brother, Jack, single-handedly from the age of twenty-eight when her husband had died after a brief battle with cancer. She'd never remarried but had what she called 'my gentlemen friends' who worshipped the ground she walked on. Rachel was never short of male company and frequently took off on walking holidays or cultural tours around Europe with one or other of her faithful fan club. Hattie was pretty sure there was nothing *physical* between them, not that it was something she wanted to visualise. Her mum and eighty-one-year old Nigel Higginsbottom getting jiggy with it.

Turning the key in the front door, Hattie reflected that her greatest worry about Johnny was his inability to follow anything through to its conclusion. From guitar lessons to rugby training, gym membership to the aforementioned uni course, he started out with great enthusiasm which rarely lasted longer than a few months. He had all the staying power of a three-day-old Elastoplast and the attention span of an amnesiac goldfish. His only real skill seemed to be the ability to drink his bodyweight in beer and still appear sober. Something he'd inherited from his dad as Hattie had low alcohol tolerance. Half a bottle of wine and she was giggling and tottering like a madwoman. Shame, as she often wished she could self-medicate herself into oblivion.

A merry but still compos mentis Gary followed her in, giving her bottom a cheeky tweak as she switched on the hallway light. Making her way towards the kitchen, she crinkled her nose up at the unpleasant stench emanating from within. Opening the door, her nostrils tried to seal themselves as 'eau de Johnny' became overpowering. Her delightful offspring had cooked himself a feast of instant noodles, something with eggs (judging by the plethora of shells decorating the worktop) and a chunk of blue cheese, the remnants of which lay oozing like the innards of a dead alien. He'd also managed to burn several slices of toast, their smoky haze still lingering in the air.

'Bloody hell! Is it too much to ask that he cleans up after

himself?' Hattie muttered to herself. She stomped over to the already full-to-the-brim bin and began cramming the debris inside.

'I'll do it, babe.' Gary scooped up the charred bread and expertly used it to wipe up the cesspool of Stilton. 'You head up to bed, and I'll get this tidied and outside for the bin men in the morning.'

She could cheerfully throttle him at times – probably on a daily basis – but she *did* love her Gary. As Hattie brushed her teeth and gazed at her tired reflection, she counted her blessings. The list wasn't long but it was more than a lot of people could hope for. She was healthy, her husband adored her and they were still (just about) solvent. Their son had a good heart and a sharp mind if only he could focus on finishing something (other than platefuls of food that starving wolves would turn their snouts up at). She had her mum, her brother and best friend Cat to rely on, and her colleagues at work were pleasant and sociable. Yes, life could be a lot worse …

A sudden *bang* outside saw Hattie drop her brush in the sink and rush to the bedroom window. She could just make out the outline of a car, its headlights dimmed, before the engine roared and it screeched down the street at high speed. For a moment, there was an eerie silence and then … The sound of someone screaming, a faint voice muffled by the double glazing shouting out, 'Ambulance! Call an ambulance!' At which point Hattie's life changed forever.

CHAPTER 2

ONE MONTH LATER

'Hats, you need to eat something! Here, I made this for you.' Hattie's best friend since primary school, Cat, thrust a plate of pasta in front of her. As cooking wasn't one of her strengths, it was ravioli straight out of a tin and liberally sprinkled with grated Cheddar. Still, it was the thought that counted.

Had it really been four weeks since that terrible evening? One minute she was getting ready to sleep, the next she was weeping next to a hospital bed as the doctors told her there was nothing more they could do. Almost twenty-one-years of marriage destroyed by a lunatic driver who'd mounted the pavement, smashed into Gary as he positioned the bin just outside their gate, then disappeared into the night. His injuries were so severe, he never regained consciousness. She'd never got to say goodbye, never had the chance to tell him she loved him. *You don't know what you've got 'til it's gone.*

The funeral had been a blur. Hattie had sat flanked by her mum on one side and Johnny on the other. Jack and his partner were next to Johnny, holding hands and fighting back the tears. Gary had always been clear that he wanted to be cremated, and his wishes were duly carried out. As the curtains closed and the coffin slid from view, she closed her eyes, aware of the quiet sobs of his elderly parents a few seats away. Gary had been Angus and Effie Hastings' only child, a late arrival as they'd both been in their forties when he was born. Both were increasingly frail and the tragic death of their son had only served to wither them further. She'd tried her best to comfort them, but what could she – or anyone – say or do to make right the worst of wrongs?

Johnny, bless him, had done his best to stifle his own grief and shoulder some of Hattie's. 'I'm the man of the house now, Mum,' he'd announced two days after Gary's death. Hattie had been slumped on the sofa, still in her pyjamas, the TV babbling away meaninglessly in the background. He'd gently placed another cup of tea in front of her, ignoring the others sitting cold and congealed on the table.

'Thanks, love.' Hattie had wanted to pull her son into her arms and cuddle him like she used to when he was little. All soft and warm and smelling of delightful toddler scents – well, maybe not *always* delightful – but she couldn't move. She couldn't feel, she couldn't think … no, she *could* think, but her thoughts steered her into dark places she didn't want to go. The sofa was safe. Perhaps she might never move from it. They would become one, squidgy and stained brown velour merged with ancient dressing gown and Primark nightwear.

'Eat!' Hattie was snapped back to the present by Cat proffering a forkful of ravioli that looked as appealing as a bowl of dog food. She recoiled, then wondered briefly if her friend was about to say, 'Open wide. Here comes the choo choo!' Just as Johnny had done so many times in his high chair, she kept her mouth clamped shut.

Half an hour later, and a very exasperated Cat had departed. 'You're nothing but skin and bone, Hats. I can't stand by and watch you do this to yourself. I'll be back tomorrow with your favourite Thai green curry and a bottle of Aldi's finest fizz. Take care, hon.'

Johnny was out and she'd declined an offer from her mother to drop by. The phone still kept ringing with condolences from well-meaning friends and acquaintances. 'Is there anything we can do?' they'd ask, their voices dripping with compassion and understanding. Except, they *didn't* understand, not really. *Is there anything we can do?* Sure, turn back time, make sure that stupid, stupid man decided smelly bins could wait until the morning. Persuade the moron responsible that driving after a bucketful of alcohol was a terrible idea. Not that he'd ever been caught – the stolen car was recovered just hours after the incident – but everything indicated that being under the influence was the most likely cause.

Hattie dragged herself upstairs. She needed a shower, otherwise she'd be reduced to spraying herself with Febreze. Her stomach growled, her head ached and it was still only five o'clock in the evening. When was it considered reasonable to go to bed? Would eight o'clock be too early? That was three long hours away. She could take a bath instead, but that involved far too much time and effort.

As she waited for the shower water to heat up, Hattie stripped off and tossed her clothes on the bedroom floor. Seated at the dressing table, she fiddled with the annoying clasp of her necklace. Unable to undo it, she clipped her hair up, and felt a peculiar warm sensation on the back of her neck. Almost as if someone was breathing inches behind her. What the … ? Hattie swivelled around but, of course, there was no one there. Get a grip, woman!

Ten minutes later, Hattie felt fresher and no longer likely

to be mistaken for a down-and-out. She dressed in her favourite pyjamas – or passion killers, as Gary had dubbed them – and headed downstairs. She still had little appetite, but a drop of liquor might help ease the path to sleep.

Back in the lounge, Hattie surveyed the drinks cabinet. There were half-bottles of strange liqueurs they'd picked up on their holidays. What was cachaça when it was at home? She squinted at the label. Brazil. They'd definitely never been there. Tanqueray gin. No idea where that originated from, but if it got you tanked … She poured herself a generous measure and topped it up with some tonic that was a year past its sell-by date. Flatter than Keira Knightley's chest but it did the job.

Taking a swig, Hattie wished again that she was more of a hardened drinker. A couple of these and she'd be lights out and nobody home. Admittedly, that was the effect she was going for, but the ability to chug a few more might help to numb the pain for longer.

As the gin sneaked its way around her bloodstream, Hattie swayed around the room. If Gary had been here – if Gary had been here during a party – there would be glasses everywhere. *His* glasses, to be precise. He'd been notorious for 'parking' his drink somewhere, forgetting where it was and pouring himself a new one. Hattie had tried everything, from dangly glass markers to indelible ink pens, to identify which drink belonged to whom, but Gary always left a trail of semi-supped glasses in his wake.

Suddenly, Hattie felt a peculiar sense of being watched. Had Johnny come home unexpectedly? No, she hadn't heard the front door opening and closing. In any case, he'd have at least spoken to her before heading to his room. Her sleep-deprived and grief-addled brain was playing tricks with her, that was all.

Reaching the CD player, Hattie considered putting on

some Fleetwood Mac. She could channel her inner Stevie Nicks and flap around a bit. All she needed was some dry shampoo to oomph her curls and a slightly gothic outfit. Nope, Pokémon pyjamas were *not* hitting the mark. She started rifling through the CD collection then ... hang on ... where had *that* glass come from? Hattie looked in disbelief at what appeared to be a shot of whisky topped up with water. Balanced slightly precariously on one of her precious Steps CDs, like it was a coaster. She nudged it nervously aside with her finger. A quick sniff confirmed her suspicions. It *was* whisky. One of Gary's favourites. Hattie would rather gargle bleach than touch the Scottish stuff. Eurgh! Who ever thought that a combination of smelly socks with a hint of plant compost would make a best-selling drink? Well, millions of people clearly did but ...

'Hey, babe. I'm home!' Hattie froze, pre-Stevie Nicks impression. 'Christ, that gin was bloody strong,' she thought, before realising that the voice she'd just heard was Gary's. Not, *I'm in heaven, be strong, flying with the angels now*, voice of Gary she'd conjured up since his death but his actual voice. Gruff, rough and impossible to misinterpret. Somehow, someway, Gary was back.

CHAPTER 3

HATTIE SQUEEZED her eyes tightly shut. This wasn't happening. This absolutely *wasn't* happening. She must have picked up the wrong bottle or something. What was that drink that caused hallucinations? Absinthe. No doubt Johnny had been mucking about with his mates one night and mixed up some brain-mangling concoction in the gin bottle. Yes, that would explain it … she'd been nobbled by the Green Fairy. No ghosts here, except the hairs on her arms were standing to attention and she was sure there was someone else in the room.

'Cheers, Hats.'

Hattie kept one eye firmly closed, and squinted through the other. Why she thought this would change anything she had no idea, but she wasn't ready for the reality of full-on vision. If she *was* hallucinating, then Johnny must have chucked some top-grade LSD into the cocktail. Standing before her, grinning from ear to ear, was Gary. A whisky tumbler in one hand and her glass of God knows what in the other. He looked exactly the same as the night he died, down to his drainpipe jeans and Bowie T-shirt he'd had since his twenties and refused to bin despite it having more holes than O J Simpson's defence plea.

'I don't understand … I don't know what to say. You *can't* be here, it's … it's not possible!' Hattie tried to form a coherent sentence but her brain was refusing to engage with her mouth. Both eyes were wide open now, still struggling to make sense of what – or who – was currently regarding her with a quizzical expression.

'I know, babe. It's totally weird, right? Don't ask me what's going on, 'cos I ain't got a bloody clue!' Even in his otherworldly form, Gary still spoke like a sixties stoner. Then again, did she expect him to sound like a toff from Downton Abbey? He'd died, not gone to RADA.

Hattie's legs were wobbling alarmingly. She sank down on the sofa, pausing only to grab her glass from Gary's outstretched hand. As her fingers made contact with his flesh, she felt the strangest sensation. He *looked* solid (Gary worked out regularly and was proud of his almost-six pack and enviable biceps), but touching him was like delving into a mound of candy-floss. She could feel *something* but it wasn't human. Hattie snatched back her hand and stared at it. She half-expected to see ectoplasm dripping from it. *Who you gonna call? Ghostbusters!* Damn, now all she needed was Dan Aykroyd and Bill Murray to burst through the door and suck her husband up into their vacuum doo-da. She could try it herself with her Dyson but it was already out of warranty and she couldn't afford a new one. Not that she *wanted* to use cyclone technology to dispose of Gary, or whatever he now was. A ghost, a spectre, a figment of her overwrought imagination, he was here and – judging by the way he'd just knocked back his whisky – he had no immediate plans to leave.

'Babe. Hattie. Look at me. I don't get this any more than

you do, but I'm here. It's a total mind fuck, but I've found my way back. And I don't know what to do next.'

Gary looked so lost and forlorn that Hattie forgave him for swearing. She hated the f-word and had a swear box on the kitchen window sill which had paid for some rather nice shoes as both Gary and Johnny were partial to its usage. Her mum had even contributed a pound one day when she'd spilt raspberry yoghurt down her new cashmere jumper.

'What do you remember? I mean … after the accident?' Hattie raised her glass to her lips, then set it back on the side table. She no longer believed that it was responsible for the events unfolding, but she needed to keep some sense of sobriety.

'Well …' Gary gazed at his own glass, saw it was empty and reached for a top-up. Hattie wondered how a being as insubstantial as a pile of carpet fluff could lift a bottle, never mind pour a drink. Wait, hang on, how could he even *have* a drink? Shouldn't that be against the laws of ghostliness, or whatever?

'I remember taking the bin out, then total darkness. Next thing I know, I'm in a hospital and I can smell all the stuff, you know, like antiseptic and poo and things you don't want to think about. And I could hear beeps and voices and – I could hear *you* – Hats, I could hear you crying.'

Hattie swallowed hard. So hard she felt the contents of her throat meet her stomach and attempt to bounce back in revenge. Vomiting now would not be a good move. A new carpet wasn't an option either.

'One minute I'm there, in a bed, then I'm floating above it. I always thought that was complete bollocks but, Hats, I swear it happened. I was up there, looking down on you.'

Neither she nor Gary were remotely religious. The afterlife wasn't something they'd ever discussed or given any thought to. Now, Gary was revealing his journey towards death in a way often catalogued but dismissed by them as complete hokum.

'Were you drawn towards a light? Were people calling you? What were you thinking?' Hattie felt like a question master on a quiz show. Fingers on the buzzer! Starter for ten! Oh, fuck! That was at least fifty pence in the jar. Still, you were allowed to swear when your dead husband put in an unexpected appearance.

Gary appeared to be pondering the questions. He had that look on his face that suggested deep thought but could also be construed as slightly wasted.

'Yeah, there was a light. It was a bit annoying, actually. Like, someone deliberately shoved an arc lamp in your face. Blinding, if you know what I mean. So, I moved away and towards the voices.'

Hattie pulled her legs up to her chin and wrapped her arms around them. If she made herself as small as possible, maybe she'd disappear. Or at least wake up suddenly in her bed to discover this had all been a bad dream. Except, was it bad? Gary was back and not in a shuffling, drooling *The Walking Dead* form. There were no signs of the terrible injuries he'd sustained when the car ploughed into him, which the hospital staff had done their best to mask for her benefit. He looked exactly the same, just a more ethereal version.

'When you were up there, looking down on yourself ... at me, what did you think? Did you realise you were dying? Oh, Gary, tell me what you were thinking!'

He hesitated before replying. His thoughts must be so painful to recall, thought Hattie, sliding her legs back to the floor as she now had pins and needles in her right foot.

'Well, babe, my main thought was, "Christ, you need your roots doing!" Sorry, but I was floating right above your head.

Come to think of it, you still look like you need a trip to the hairdresser. Is Jacqui on holiday, or what?'

What, indeed! Hattie shook her head incredulously. Her darling husband had departed his mortal body, hovered above her on his way to the afterlife (clearly not signposted well enough for him), and all he could recall was that her last date with hair dye was almost three months ago.

'Gary, forgive me for not devoting one hundred percent of my attention to my appearance, but I happen to be a grieving widow. Because you're dead! And you're not supposed to *be* here! Did you seriously think I'd be out primping and preening when you were barely cold in your grave?' OK, technically he'd been reduced to a pile of ashes which his mother had insisted should be scattered on his favourite playing field.

'He was never happier than when kicking a ball around here,' Effie had reminisced tearfully on a pilgrimage to the hallowed grounds where a young Gary had probably spent more time rolling spliffs than scoring goals. A few days after the funeral, they'd returned in a taxi, his mum insisting on carrying his urn in her capacious handbag. Unfortunately, the driver took a speed bump a little too fast and the contents of the urn upturned and mixed with the contents of the aforementioned bag. Thus, Gary's remains were scooped back into the receptacle along with ancient biscuit crumbs, loose change and a couple of mangled Werther's Originals.

Was he serious? She'd been a grieving widow for a month, tending to trivial matters like an inch of grey not really at the front of her mind.

'Sorry, babe. You still look gorgeous to me.' Gary shuffled closer – maybe he was a zombie after all – and Hattie retreated further into the sofa. He paused, then he raised his hand to his lips and blew her a kiss. As she had always done since their first dates, Hattie instinctively lifted her own hand as if to catch it.

'Love you, Hats. I want to hug you right now, but I think we both need time to adjust to this. I ain't got a clue what happens next but …' As Gary's words tailed off, his whole body seemed to shimmer as if it was made of a million fairy lights. Then – whoosh, he was gone.

Hattie snatched up her glass and drained it. For good measure, she knocked back Gary's half-finished whisky too. Yuck! Now what? One minute he was there, the next he'd vanished into thin air at the most inconvenient moment. Typical bloody Gary!

CHAPTER 4

'Nude's really in right now, Mrs Carter.' Cat pulled out her Perspex tray of nail polishes, suppressing a giggle as her client raised an overly pencilled-in eyebrow. 'I mean as a colour, not a lifestyle choice.'

Joy Carter – never had anyone been more inappropriately named – was a regular at Cat's tiny hair and beauty salon. Definitely at the back of the queue when senses of humour were handed out, she was so strait-laced it was a wonder oxygen found its way into her lungs. Only in her mid-fifties, she belonged in a different era. All twin-sets, faux pearls and stockings that could withstand nuclear attack. She was married to the long-suffering Ernest, a tiny man of indeterminate age who spent half his life sipping vodka and tonics at the Red Lion pub. Presumably to escape the reality of being married to a woman who made Mary Whitehouse look like a bra-burning liberal. Cat doubted he'd ever *seen* Joy naked. Heck, she wouldn't be surprised if Joy kept her undies on at all times, even in the shower.

'No, thank you. I'll stick to my usual.' Her usual being a

bright pink that was a great match for Ernest's glow-in-the-dark nose.

As Cat trimmed her client's cuticles and massaged in some oil, she wondered how Hattie was getting on. Four text messages had gone unanswered and she wasn't picking up her phone either. She'd pop round later, but for now she had back-to-back appointments and needed to pick up some food for dinner. Her boyfriend, Jamie, was coming round, and she didn't think having Domino's Pizza on speed dial would impress.

Ushering Joy Carter on her way, Cat glanced at the clock hanging in the waiting area. Five minutes until her next client. Time to give Hattie one last try.

'Hats! Thank God you picked up. I was about to send round a SWAT team to kick your door in. Why didn't you answer my messages? Did you forget to charge your phone again?'

Hattie was notorious for letting electrical appliances lose all battery power. Similarly, she never seemed to notice when her car was running on empty. The standing joke was that Gary carried a spare can of petrol strapped to his body like a superhero version of the AA. Oh, no. Gary. Every morning Cat woke and, for a split second, all was right with the world. Then she remembered, and it hit her like a punch to the gut. Party-loving, larger-than-life Gary, her best friend's husband and one of her favourite people in the world, was gone. Not a day had passed without Cat crying. Sometimes at home, occasionally in the back room of the salon and once – very embarrassingly – during a massage. She'd been kneading away at a client's knotted shoulder muscles when she recalled how Gary used to rub her neck when she complained of tension.

'Get your mitts off my mate, you old perv!' Hattie would remonstrate, but always in a joking way. She'd adored their bond, even going as far as to say that they had her permission to get together if she popped her clogs first. Not that *that* would ever have happened. Or could happen now.

'Hi, Cat. I've just been … it's too hard to explain … I need to talk to you face to face. I know you're seeing Jamie tonight, but is there any chance you could drop by in the morning? Please?'

Her next client, booked in for a rejuvenating facial, popped her crinkly face around the corner. Never mind rejuvenating, a good going-over with a steam iron might be a better solution.

'Be right with you!' Cat beamed in her best beauty therapist style, mentally counting down the minutes until she could escape and fill her trolley with tempting delights. As long as they only took a few minutes in the microwave and she could hide the packaging from prying eyes.

'Sure, Hats. I can be with you by nine o'clock but I can only stay an hour. I'd come this evening but …'

'No, it's fine. You're seeing Jamie, I get it. Have fun and try not to poison him, eh?'

Cat would never live down the disastrous date when she'd decided to cook something, as opposed to heating it up. Sadly, no one had ever explained to her that, while a steak was best served pink in the middle, a chicken breast was not. Hence a mad dash to A & E as her not-to-be future husband was doubled up with stomach cramps and wearing facial expressions befitting of a world gurning champion. She'd emerged unscathed, having only nibbled the cooked edges, but the relationship was doomed before it started.

'Don't worry, it's a meal deal for two. Can't go wrong there, unless I leave the cellophane on!' Which she had done – only once – when her dining partner had politely peeled the melted plastic from his plate and carried her off for some awesome sex. She never saw him again but still got a little frisson of excitement when she punctured holes in Tesco's Finest.

Promising on her heart to be there, (but omitting the *hope to die* bit), Cat ended the call. She felt horribly guilty for not rushing to Hattie's side, but she reasoned that whatever was troubling her friend could wait until the next day. They'd clung to each other, water-logged with grief, for the past four weeks or so; therefore a few more hours wouldn't make a difference, would it? Except … there'd been something in Hattie's voice, a hint of desperation that niggled at Cat. Her friend had been through the most awful nightmare but she'd come out the other side, damaged but still strong. Hadn't she? Cat made her way into the treatment room where her client was reclining on the towel-covered bench. She lined up the necessary lotions and potions, then pulled her phone out of her immaculate white tabard.

Hats, if you need me to drop by tonight, just say the word. Jamie can wait. C xx

Within seconds, a reply pinged back.

As if I'm going to get in the way of your pathetic excuse for a sex life. Lol. Haven't met Jamie yet but hope he lasts longer than the last one. Sleep tight, or not at all. H xx

Applying a layer of face masque to her eternally optimistic client, Cat found herself drifting back in time. It was 1989 and she and Hattie were channelling Madonna in her controversial, pseudo-religious phase. 'Like a Prayer' was everywhere and they were sixteen and untouchable.

They'd been inseparable from day one. Their English teacher, Mrs Harper, had dubbed them Cat and the Hat, something she had to explain to a bemused class who'd never heard of Dr. Seuss. Cat was Catherine and Hattie was Harriet, but they'd decided, quite separately, that they preferred the abbreviated versions. They'd snorted their way through maths classes; trigonometry and algebra as appealing as genital warts. French was OK, if you got to whisper 'Je t'aime' in the ear of the boy of the moment. That was the only time they fell out, when both lusted after Archie Andrews who looked like a movie star and was destined to study law at Oxford.

'He'll never go out with one of us!' Cat was busy hoisting up her skirt with the aid of several safety pins. Hattie was stuffing her bra with toilet paper and trying to smooth it down into a passable boob shape.

'Sure he will, but it won't be you! I've been swotting up on law stuff so he'll be blown away by my intellect.' Hattie had looked unbearably smug, as Cat was itching to gain the higher ground.

'So, what do you know about law? Apart from the fact your grannie was caught stealing carrots from the supermarket but got off on the grounds of being totally demented.'

'I think you mean she had *dementia* and it was actually a pound of leeks that she took. Which she made into the most *amazing* soup.'

They'd squabbled at times, fallen out on several occasions but their friendship remained strong throughout the years. When Gary came on the scene, Cat had worried that she'd be sidelined, but, very quickly, two became three. It was when three became four that things threatened to fall apart.

Stewart Hewitt may have had a name that was difficult to say, particularly after a few drinks, but his body was definitely made for sin (Cat adored the movie *Working Girl* and had taken to carrying her trainers everywhere and changing into them when her heels became unbearable). She'd met him at a bus stop one rainy evening as she was heading home from college. At just over five feet two, she'd wished she'd kept her stilettos on, her battered trainers reducing her to hobbit size. Stewart had towered above her, insisting on protecting her from the deluge with his umbrella. They'd chatted with ease, Cat about her beauty therapy course and Stewart on his favourite subject – himself. Not that she realised it at the time, so smitten was she with his good looks and effortless confidence, but there was only room for one ego in his world.

They'd dated for a few months, Cat reluctant to share him even with Hattie and Gary. The first time they all went out together, she'd been bursting with pride. *Look at me!* She'd wanted to climb up on to the bar and do a dance of sheer delight, because virtually every woman had checked him out, looked at their own boyfriends, and visibly sighed in disgust.

'Isn't he great?' Cat had nudged Hattie in the ribs, a little miffed that her best friend wasn't drooling over the man currently checking out his reflection in the mirror behind the optics.

'Yeah, he's good-looking, Cat, but doesn't he know it? I swear he'd shag himself if he could. And didn't you say he called you a porker the other evening?'

Damn! Cat knew she shouldn't have told Hattie about *that* comment. She'd greeted Stewart with an energetic kiss, aware that her dress was a bit on the tight side but she'd sacrificed undies in favour of a sleek silhouette. He'd held her at arm's length and looked her up and down, like a farmer appraising his prize heifer. OK, she was a generous size 14 on a good day, but previous boyfriends hadn't complained.

'Nice dress, Catherine, but you could do with losing a few pounds. I could help you with your diet, if you like. Low carb and high protein, that's the way to go. Unless you want to be Kermit's sidekick, that is!'

Cat had been stung by his words, casually tossed into the conversation but with all the destructive power of a hand grenade. Miss Piggy. Was that how he saw her? Stewart must have registered her stricken expression, as he'd pulled her back for another lip-blistering snog. Anyway, he was right, she'd reasoned. And it was really sweet of him to offer to help, although the comparison with a puppet porker was a bit brutal.

Becoming Mrs Hewitt was – she believed at the time – the happiest day of her life. Never had a bride been more elated, not only by the handsome groom by her side, but by the fact she'd slimmed down to a size 10 in six months. If only she'd listened to Hattie and Gary, instead of eating cabbage soup and doodling love hearts on the diet sheets Stewart had brought her every week …

CHAPTER 5

JOHNNY HASTINGS WAS OFFICIALLY BORED out of his cranium. He'd watched every episode of *Game of Thrones* twice (he couldn't believe his mum had never seen it) and half-heartedly attempted to write a few lines of his book. Twenty words in and he'd given up, the lure of the fridge greater than the desire to feature on the Amazon Top 100 best seller list.

Back in his room with a triple cheeseburger and a jumbo packet of salt and vinegar crisps, he popped open a can of lager. His mum was at work and the house was deathly quiet. Bugger, there was that word again. *Death*. He could think of little else these days, and the stabbings and skull-crushings in his favourite show hardly helped to lighten the mood.

Taking a large swig of beer and emitting a satisfying belch, Johnny thought for the millionth time: *I miss my dad. I really, really miss my dad.* He loved his mum, that was a given, but she could be a right old nag at times. His dad had been far more laid-back – to the point of being horizontal – and he'd always stood up for Johnny when Mum went on one of her rants.

'Give the boy a break, Hats. He's young and still finding his feet. Ain't that right, son?' He'd ruffle Johnny's hair, even when it hadn't been washed for a week because Johnny was on one of his 'shampoo is for the middle classes' phases.

The day Johnny had come home with a tattoo – YOLO, meaning 'you only live once' – across four knuckles of his right hand, his mum had gone ape. She'd given him money to buy some clothes, but he'd bumped into some friends who'd persuaded him that an inking was more important than new jeans.

'What were you *thinking?*' she'd screeched, reaching for a pot scourer. For a moment, Johnny had thought she was going to try and scrub away the offensive markings, then he'd realised she was venting her fury on the blackened chip pan.

'Calm down, darlin'. It's no big deal.' Gary had winked at Johnny before peeling back the sleeve of his jumper to reveal the 'H ♥ G' tattoo on his forearm. He'd had it done the day before their wedding, and Hattie had been singularly unimpressed. She loathed tattoos and never imagined that her son would get one. Although why it surprised her, when he already had an eyebrow and nose piercing, was anyone's guess.

'You know how I feel about body art,' she'd protested, but her words had fallen on deaf ears. Father and son were united – as always – in anything designed to wind Hattie up.

Mum had been really *weird* the past few days, come to think of it. She jumped every time he walked into the room, and he'd caught her saying, 'Gary, speak to me!' when he'd wandered in looking for clean underwear. Picking up a pair of boxers from his labelled box, he'd wondered if she was having a breakdown. Great, all he needed was for her to be carried off to some psychiatric unit, leaving him to fend for himself. Not that he couldn't look *after* himself; he just hadn't mastered the washing machine and Mum's Sunday roasts were the culinary highlight of the week. Conspicuous by their absence since Dad died. Still, Gran would look after him. Although she was always popping off on cruises or mini breaks with one of her men friends. And Dad's parents – Nan and Pops, as they liked to be called – kept a low profile, even more so now.

Johnny knew he really should be looking for a job. Mum didn't exactly earn a fortune and she was still wading through a mountain of paperwork and endless phone calls to access Dad's pension and life insurance pay-out. He'd worked in an indie vinyl store for a couple of weeks but got fired when the boss found him sleeping in the store room.

Licking the last of the ketchup from his fingers, Johnny picked up his mobile and called his best mate, Josh.

'Yo, man. What's up?' Josh sounded amazingly alert considering it was just after lunchtime and he rarely surfaced before two.

'Nothin' much. Just going stir crazy here. Fancy heading into town and shooting some pool at the pub?' Rummaging through his threadbare wallet, Johnny realised he was totally skint. He'd have to raid the biscuit tin in the kitchen where his mum kept loose change for charity callers and the window cleaner.

'Sorry, mate, but I've got a job interview at three.'

Johnny couldn't have been more shocked if Josh had said he'd signed up as a Scientologist. He'd left school with three GCSEs and barely worked a day since. His parents were loaded and gave him a weekly allowance that made Johnny's eyes water. He'd fully expected his friend to still be sponging off his folks into his thirties.

'What for? Are they a sloth short at the petting zoo?' Johnny sniggered, quite proud of his joke.

'Hilarious, loser. My dad pulled a few strings and got me a shot at his place as a runner.'

For a split second, Johnny pictured Josh in Lycra, knuckles to the ground and feet planted on the starting blocks. Then he remembered that his dad ran a very successful TV company that produced a couple of highly successful soaps and the odd one-off drama. His mum was the star of one of the soaps – *Road to Nowhere* – which gripped the nation every Tuesday evening. His dad had been a fan, his mum less so, sniping that, 'you only watch it, Gary, because Josh's mum makes sure her cleavage gets a close-up every episode.' Which wasn't far from the truth – she did have amazing breasts.

'Right, so, you're going to be making everyone coffees and doing the photocopying and generally wiping their arses? Sounds awesome, dude. Hope you're wearing your best suit.'

They'd exchanged childish jibes for a few minutes before Josh said he had to shower and shave. Johnny wished him luck, pushing away the feeling of envy that rose within him. Josh was getting his shit together, and what was *he* doing? Wallowing in a pit of feeling sorry for himself, grieving for his dad and wondering what the bloody point was.

IT HAD BEEN a long day at Espresso Yourself. Hattie had mixed up several orders, serving one old bitch a full-fat cappuccino when she'd asked for a skinny latte then giving a slice of almond cake to a customer with nut allergies. She'd snatched it back in the nick of time, before anaphylaxis kicked in, but she knew she was in a bad way. Who wouldn't be, when their deceased husband decided to pay a house call?

A week had passed since Gary first reappeared, then

disappeared abruptly. Hattie had tottered off to bed, half-convinced that she'd dreamed up the whole episode. Until the next morning ...

'Hats. Hattie! Wake up.'

She'd clamped the pillow to her ears, resolute in her belief that all was normal and today was just another day and ...

'You just farted! Silent but deadly. Christ, Hats, I might be on the *other side* but that could fell North Korea. Or serve as their nuclear deterrent. Go, girl!'

Hattie had squirmed, painfully aware that she *had* passed wind, but she'd not expected anyone to notice. Least of all, Gary.

'I *don't* fart, Gary. At least, not in front of anyone. In all the years we were together I never farted. It was something I vowed I'd never do. I forgave you the times you let rip but I didn't–'

Gary had chortled and pushed the duvet aside. As he slid in next to her, Hattie again had the sensation of him being *there* but not there. She reached out to hug him, gulping as flesh met something that wasn't human. Her hands didn't quite pass through him, but seemed to hover on the periphery. As if touching him would confirm everything she didn't want to know.

'Well, babe. Everyone does it. Even the Queen. Yep, HRH isn't averse to the odd bottom burp, trust me!'

Hattie sat upright in shock. Was Gary able to materialise anywhere he liked? Had he *actually* floated into the Queen's chambers in Buckingham Palace, or Balmoral or wherever she happened to be hanging her crown? Her expression must have been a picture, as Gary shook with laughter.

'No, darlin', I haven't witnessed the event. I'm just saying it don't matter who you are, a bit of gas is natural. Natural gas, get it!'

Speechless didn't come close. Not only was she

conversing with her dead husband, they were discussing their sovereign's alleged flatulence. Very disrespectful and more than she could cope with at seven-thirty in the morning.

'Gary, I'm really not up for this discussion. In fact, I'd like to go back to sleep, thank you.'

As if *that* was going to happen. Still, she burrowed down in the duvet and held her breath. Ten, nine, eight, seven, six … there was a sensation of icy cold air passing over her then–nothing. She poked her head up over the cover and saw she was alone. Gary had buggered off again. She'd upset him. Just as she'd upset Cat when she'd dropped round the other morning. That hadn't gone well. That hadn't gone well at all.

CHAPTER 6

HATTIE HAD OPENED the door to Cat, who was carrying an enormous bunch of flowers and a bottle of bubbly. She deposited both on the front step before flinging her arms around her friend. She smelt divine, she always did, a blend of aromatic oils she used at her salon and one of the many perfumes that graced her dressing table. Somehow, they never clashed. Her personal life might be a car crash – Hattie winced inwardly at the painful analogy – but Cat had personal grooming down to a T.

'Right, we're having a glass of this stuff. Got any orange juice? I can't be getting tipsy before work.'

Hattie rummaged in the fridge, locating a half-empty carton that Johnny may or may not have drunk directly from. Whatever. She topped up the glasses and smiled nervously at her dearest friend. They'd always shared everything, from period problems to pimple creams, providing shoulders to cry on when things went wrong. Hattie's shoulder had taken a serious soaking during the Stewart years, or Arsegate, as she dubbed it.

'How was last night? Was Jamie all he promised to be?'

If relationships were measured in baby terms, Cat and Jamie's had barely progressed beyond the embryo stage. She was naturally wary of men, having come out of a marriage that had well-nigh destroyed her self-esteem and seen her spend far too many nights alone watching drivel on the TV and channelling all her energies into her business. Hattie and Gary had done their best to drag her out, but she'd declined on most occasions.

'You guys are the best but I'm happier at home polishing my tootsies. Honest!' An outright lie, but they'd gone along with it. Gary – bless him – was the one who suggested they just turn up with a takeaway and a few drinks when they suspected Cat was sobbing into a cup of instant soup. She'd act surprised and reluctant to let them in, but half an hour later her tear-streaked face would reflect the mutual love they had for each other. The three Amigos, better off by far without that controlling and destructive fourth viper in the nest.

Hattie had no idea how to begin the conversation. She'd looked online but found little in the way of guidance as to how you explained your dead husband had decided his time on earth wasn't over. Yes, there were a few crackpot sites, but full of golden auras, fluttering angels and feelings of being closer to a higher being. No mention of whisky, bad hair days or flatulence.

'It was fine. Jamie's nice. *Really nice.* And, no – before you ask – we didn't sleep together. I'm taking it slowly this time. Once bitten. OK, more than once bitten, but you get what I mean.' Cat had looked crumpled, her beautiful face testament to all the men who'd done her wrong. Help! Hattie felt as if she was about to burst into a country and western song. She poured the rest of her drink down the sink and leaned against it, breathing heavily. If Gary could just put in an appearance, right now, she'd be off the hook. Cat might run screaming into the street but at least she'd know she wasn't alone in this mad place. A quick scan of the room and – nope – no sign of the bugger. Never around when you want him to be.

'Right. This is going to sound totally nuts but – he's back.'

Cat had looked at her, understandably bewildered. 'Who's back? What are you talking about? That old geezer at the club? He got barred for flashing his bits at a couple of seventeen-year-olds. Mind you, they said they'd have needed a microscope to detect anything worth reporting. No … that's not what you're on about. What is it, Hats?'

This was it. Speak now or forever hold her peace. Hattie stared back at the woman who knew her inside and out, and from every other available angle.

'Gary. He's back. I swear on my mother's grave – sorry, my *father*'s grave – my husband has found a way to return and now he's driving me up the wall.'

Cat eyed the bottle, lifted it to her lips and glugged. Hattie watched the progress of the liquid as it passed down her throat. She might have to drive Cat to the salon and hope the first customer wasn't booked in for a painful procedure.

'So, you see dead people? Like that kid in the Bruce Willis movie?' Cat took another swig, before thumping the bottle down on the table.

'No, I don't see dead people. As in, plural. I see Gary. He hasn't brought any mates round (which brought to mind another movie, but Hattie couldn't remember its name). 'I'm not kidding, Cat, it's true!' She stared pleadingly at her friend, completely aware how bonkers she sounded but desperate for someone to believe her. She hadn't confided in anyone else. Hattie didn't think Johnny would take it well. He'd adored his dad and – even if he accepted what she said – he'd be terribly hurt that Gary hadn't materialised for him too. Telling her mum was out of the question. Rachel was a no-nonsense lady with no time for anything that couldn't be explained in a rational, scientific way. She wasn't close enough to any of the staff at the café, and didn't fancy her chances of remaining employed if she talked about ghostly visits. Which left Cat. Who was twitchily gazing around the room, as if she expected Gary to pop out of the kettle like a latter-day genie.

'So, where is he now? Can't you, like, call him up, or something?' Cat poured herself a glass of water from the tap and rested against the sink, one immaculately threaded eyebrow raised in question.

Hattie felt the urge to bang her head repeatedly on the kitchen table. 'No, I *can't* call him up, Cat. He didn't provide me with a direct line to the great beyond, or wherever he is, and I don't think I can send him a WhatsApp message. He just appears randomly and then vanishes again.' She'd tried videoing him with her phone, but all that appeared was a grainy blob that could be put down to a smeared fingerprint on the lens. An attempt at a selfie of the two of them was a failure too. How come other people managed to snap alleged pictures of supernatural beings, but Gary remained resolutely camera shy? He'd never been one to duck a photo opportunity when he was alive.

Cat downed a second glass of water then started to unwrap the bouquet of flowers she'd brought. 'Where'd you keep your vases, hon'?' she asked, opening and closing cabinet doors.

Hattie almost combusted with frustration. Here she was, sharing the biggest and most terrifying thing she'd ever experienced in her life, and all Cat could do was show off her floral arranging skills? Struggling to keep her cool, she located her biggest vase – a wedding present – from the pine dresser Gary had picked up years ago in an antique shop. Well, more of a *junk* shop, to be honest. She'd always thought it a monstrosity, even when he'd lovingly sanded it down and painted it primrose yellow. 'Here.' She thrust the vase at Cat, who was now trimming stalks and discarding unwanted leaves.

'OK, I know it's been an awful time, Hats. Like, the worst. But don't you think maybe your mind's playing tricks on you? Grief can make people behave in strange ways. When my Uncle Ray died, my Aunt Peggy went a bit doolally. Started wearing hot pants and crop tops and going to raves. And she was sixty-three! How they ever let her through the door, I don't know. All that wrinkly belly flab hanging out everywhere ...'

Right. Hattie had heard enough. 'I am not, repeat not, doolally! I am one hundred percent sane and I really don't appreciate you suggesting otherwise. I thought you'd be on my side, but clearly you think your closest friend is one step away from being sectioned. So, I think you'd better leave.'

An open-mouthed Cat gawped at Hattie, one hand crushing a perfectly-formed pink rose. The petals floated to the floor and all was silent and fraught with tension for what seemed an eternity. Then Cat slammed the half-finished vase down on the worktop. 'Fine. I need to get to work anyway. Give me a call when you've simmered down a bit. I was only trying to help.'

Snatching up her bag and car keys, Cat stomped out of the kitchen, the front door crashing shut seconds later. Hattie felt wretched, knowing she had been out of order, but at the same time deeply miffed that Cat had implied she was losing her marbles. Was she? A sob snagged in her throat as she gathered up the rest of the flowers and rammed them into the vase.

'Oh dear. That wasn't pretty.'

Hattie whirled around, the vase slipping from her grasp and smashing onto the tiles. 'For fuck's sake, Gary, why couldn't you have bloody well shown up ten minutes ago? You really are a complete and utter arsehole!' She'd happily have deposited a week's wages in the swear box, so furious was she with Gary's belated appearance.

'Sweetheart, I don't make the rules. I could hear the conversation but I was stuck somewhere, like behind a glass wall. Sorry, Hats, but I don't even know if Cat would have *seen* me, anyway. Maybe only you can see me. I ain't been given an instruction manual, not that I'd probably read it anyhow.'

Despite her anger, Hattie moved forward – stepping over the debris on the floor – and wrapped her arms around Gary. He still felt wispy and unreal, but she felt comfort in his fragile embrace.

'What are we going to do, Gary?' she whispered, her voice choked with unshed tears. 'What happens next?'

Gary stroked her cheek, his touch as comforting as a mother's cuddle for a distressed baby. 'I wish I could tell you, babe, but for now … shouldn't you clean up that mess before you cut yourself? And I could murder a large whisky!'

CHAPTER 7

'Ouch! That really hurt!'

Cat tried not to pull a face as her client squealed in protest at the wax strip being ripped from her leg. Margie Benson was the mother of four children under the age of ten – surely she was used to a little pain? 'Sorry, nearly done,' she said in her brightest and most professional voice. Two more treatments to go – a facial and a manicure – and she could head for home. Jamie was picking her up to go for a pizza and see the latest Tom Cruise film. Cat was proud that she was, for once, dictating the pace of the relationship. Too many times in the past she'd leapt in with both feet and lived to regret it. Her marriage to Stewart being a prime example, but … she closed the lid firmly on those memories.

Almost a week had passed since Cat and Hattie's confrontation. Cat had picked up her phone countless times, ready to call or text, then put it down again. In truth, she didn't know what to say or write. Her best buddy claimed her husband was haunting her – was that the right terminology? – and she'd been less than supportive. Mainly because she'd been utterly gobsmacked at Hattie's revelation. Her friend was one of the most level-headed and grounded people she knew, so to say that Gary had returned from the dead was impossible to digest.

Locking up the salon an hour and a half later, Cat was still agonising over what to do for the best. Clearly Hattie was still mad at her, otherwise she'd have been in touch. At least she knew Johnny was still living at home, so Hattie wasn't on her own, but did that absolve her from any responsibility? No, this was her best friend and she needed to take action. She shot off a quick text.

Sorry, hon. Ranking highly on the crap-friendometer. Fancy a night out tomorrow? Promise I'll keep my gob shut and listen C xxxx. She pressed 'send', turned the key and made her way to her car.

* * *

A LOUD 'PING' signalled a new message on her phone. Hattie jumped, her nerves jangling like wind chimes in a strong breeze. She was always on edge now, never sure when or where Gary might pay a visit. Since her showdown with Cat, he'd graced her with an appearance three times. Once, when she was pairing Johnny's socks (as he always wore mismatched ones, it was a pointless task); the next, as she had her head in the oven – cleaning it, not trying to gas herself; – and yesterday, just as she dipped her toe into a bath foaming with fragrant bubbles.

'Nice ass,' he'd commented, prompting Hattie to almost dive headlong into the suds.

'Gary, is there any chance you could *flag* your arrival in some way? Before I do myself actual bodily harm.' She'd grabbed a towel and covered herself, not really sure why. He was her husband – OK, *dead* husband – and had seen her naked thousands of times. Except … this was the first time he'd seen her in the buff since his passing, and somehow Hattie felt it inappropriate.

'What d'you suggest, Hats? I blow a whistle or something? 'Cos I ain't got one on me, and the shopping choices are limited around these parts.' Gary had chortled as Hattie had tightened the towel closer around her body.

'Can you describe these parts? Is it heaven or … some other place? Do you recognise people around you? What's it like, Gary? I'm kind of coming to terms with you dropping by (jeez, she made him sound like an Avon lady), but I want to know where you are when you're not *here!*' Along with most of the planet, thought Hattie. Is there life after death? The big, unanswerable question. Different religions had their unshakeable views on the subject, but she and Gary had always agreed that death was the end of the road. No going back, no refunds, a one-way ticket to nothingness.

Gary had trailed a hand through the subsiding bath bubbles, winking suggestively at Hattie as he did so. Right, she was *so* not getting in the tub with him. Who knew what would happen if he got wet?

'Hats, I wish I could but everything's just a fog. The only clarity I have is when I'm here, babe … when I'm next to you. Sometimes I hear people talking but it's like white noise. I can't make out what they're saying. Then, suddenly, I'm back here and it's like I've never been away.'

Throwing caution – and her towel – to the wind, Hattie stepped into the rapidly-cooling bath and turned on the hot tap. As the water level rose, she gazed through the steam at Gary.

'I'm glad you're back.' As she said the words, Hattie realised she truly meant them. Much as it challenged her on every level to believe that he had returned, her heart told her she was happy to see him again. If only … 'Gary, remember that bell you bought in Austria years ago? The one we used to tell Johnny tea was ready? Not that he ever heard it, with his earphones superglued in place. Couldn't you take that and – you know – tinkle it when you're on your way?'

The corners of Gary's mouth quivered, before he erupted into laughter. 'Every time a bell rings, an angel gets his wings. Darlin', this ain't *It's a Wonderful Life* and I'm definitely no angel.'

He certainly wasn't an angel, but Gary's heart was big and he'd always been the kindest and most generous man she knew. Whether doing odd jobs for Cat or running a couple of old dears in the street to the supermarket or doctor's appointments, he'd endeared himself to everyone. Well, *nearly* everyone. Which brought her mind back to the message on her phone. From Cat, as she'd half-expected. She read it quickly, deciding there and then that a night out was just what she needed. She was confident that Gary wouldn't join them – so far, he seemed restricted to the house – and she could try again to explain the inexplicable. She fired back a reply.

Sounds like a plan. How about The Lemon Tree for dinner and drinks? 7.30? H xxxx She didn't add an apology, although she knew she owed Cat one. Better to say sorry face-to-face and pray for a more successful outcome this time.

'JOHNNY! JOHNNY!' Hattie yelled up the stairs. She hadn't seen him for twenty-four hours, unsure if he was still in bed or had sloped out somewhere. After a minute she heard foot-steps; then he appeared, yawning and scratching his bare chest.

'What's up, Mother?' He always called her that instead of

Mum when he was annoyed with her. Judging by his sleep-ridden face and saggy pyjama bottoms, she'd woken him from another epic slumber. Even before Gary's death, Hattie had battled with insomnia, and she still struggled to sleep more than five hours in a row. Johnny's ability to put in twelve hours or more was a source of bafflement and not a little envy.

'I'm off to work now, but I've left you the makings of a chicken sandwich for lunch and I'll rustle up some pasta this evening. Any plans for the day?' Apart from making tortoises look energetic, she thought to herself.

'Nah, not really. I've written a couple of pages of my book …' Hattie smiled hopefully, 'But it's shit. So I might head into town and see if any of the shops are hiring. Come to think of it, isn't Espresso Yourself looking for anyone? I mean, any idiot can make a cup of coffee and slice a cake. Oops, sorry, Mum.'

Great. Her son thought her job could be done by an untrained chimpanzee. OK, it wasn't too taxing on the brain cells, but it was physically demanding and required tact and good humour. Johnny could be good for a laugh, but diplomacy was another matter.

'Nope, we're fully staffed and I'm sure you can find yourself something much better. Why don't you brush up your CV and drop it off in a few places? Just play down the dropping out of uni bit, eh?'

In the car, Hattie knew she should talk to Gary about Johnny. She also knew that he'd tell her to lighten up, that Johnny would find his way eventually. She'd just prefer if he'd do it *now*, and not when she was collecting her pension. Perhaps she could ask her brother, Jack, to have a word. He was the golden boy, obtaining a first class honours degree in computer science at university and proceeding to build up his own software development company. She hadn't seen him since the funeral, and they'd only spoken briefly since. Yes, she'd call Jack later and arrange to meet up. And, if she couldn't convince Cat that Gary's ghostly visits were the real deal, maybe her beloved little brother might listen.

CHAPTER 8

Cat was getting ready for their night out. She'd booked a taxi to pick them both up, in little doubt that alcohol would be essential to smooth the waters. A small piece of her hoped that Hattie would put the whole 'he's back!' thing down to stress and exhaustion. Leaving them free to kick back, down a few cocktails and gorge on some yummy food. Unlikely, but she could live in hope.

Buckling up her favourite wedge-heeled sandals, Cat's mind drifted back to last night. It had been lovely. She and Jamie had shared a pizza diavolo, garlic bread and a carafe of Chianti. Their chat had been relaxed and filled with laughs, which was no surprise as Jamie was an aspiring stand-up comic with a breathtaking repertoire of one-liners.

'I have a fear of fat, balding, yellow men. It's called Homer-rphobia.'

'My girlfriend told me she needed more space. So I bought her an external hard drive.'

'What should you do if you find *Rainman* in your loft? Dust him off, man.'

Some she got, a few went over her head, but most of all

she enjoyed his company. What you saw was what you got with Jamie. Unlike her ex-husband, whose veneer of charm and eye-popping good looks concealed a deep core of malice and cruelty. They'd been divorced now for eight years but the mental scars hadn't completely healed. She wasn't sure they ever would.

She'd met Jamie – an English teacher by profession – at the local dump, of all places. He'd been disposing of a pile of paperbacks and Cat had pounced on a couple as he turned his back to close the car boot. She'd blushed scarlet when he saw her, and offered to do a swap. As she was binning moth-eaten bed linen and dead plants he politely declined, but they got talking, and before she knew it they'd arranged a date. As she'd driven away, Cat mused that it was probably the first time in her life she'd agreed to go out with someone not purely based on their looks. Jamie was average height, average build and had a slightly receding hairline. His face was pleasant if unremarkable, but he had the sparkliest blue eyes and a very attractive mouth. Which she *still* hadn't kissed, but he had put no pressure on her and – for that – she was truly thankful.

Right. The taxi had pulled up outside, and next stop was Hattie then on to the restaurant. She liked The Lemon Tree but it also reminded her of an evening long, long ago with Stewart. An evening that burned in her memory …

* * *

IT WAS a ten-minute ride to their destination. Neither of them had said much during the journey. They'd hugged each other, Cat complimenting Hattie on her dusky-pink maxi dress, then the words had dried up. It was a relief to tip the driver and clamber out of the car and into the restaurant.

The Lemon Tree had been a favourite haunt – unfortunate turn of phrase, thought Cat – for over a decade. With its limed oak flooring, reclaimed church pew seating and Art Deco bar, it was an eclectic hotchpotch of styles that just *worked*. The menu was small but always perfectly presented, and the cocktail list drew in the punters searching for something different (and usually very potent).

'Two Fountains of Youth, please,' said Cat, as Hattie was clearly dithering over her choice. They both watched as the bartender deftly mixed the vodka, pomegranate juice and slivers of ginger in a shaker, along with a generous measure of ice. Their table was already prepared, the chalkboard menu propped up on a miniature easel next to the condiments.

'Whenever you're ready, ladies.' The waiter gestured to the table so, picking up their drinks, they followed him over.

Hattie was fidgety, running her finger around the rim of her glass, then smearing the condensation on the chalkboard. The dishes of the day became illegible, the writing blurring as she continued her unconscious destruction. Cat stilled her hand and signalled to the waiter to bring a new board.

'OK. I'm sorry I wasn't very sympathetic or empathetic or whatever you call it the last time, but you have my full attention now. Just tell me what the hell is going on, Hats.' She lowered her voice to a whisper, although the buzz of the restaurant meant it was unlikely they'd be overheard.

Hattie looked at her sadly, pushed her drink to one side and seized both of Cat's hands in a fierce grip. 'What I said ... everything I told you ... it's all true. I know I sound like a complete fruitcake but Gary is *back*. I don't know how, nor does he, but that's how it is. Plain and simple. He hasn't shown himself to Johnny or anyone else, but he is *back*, Cat. And I'm torn between disbelief and joy that I haven't lost him.'

Cat ignored the pressure of Hattie's vice-like hold and focused on what she'd just heard. Her friend was no liar and not prone to exaggeration or flights of fantasy. In fact, she *loathed* anything mystical or magical and had fallen asleep during the first *Lord of the Rings* movie. She and Gary had always pooh-poohed any notion of a hereafter, whereas Cat liked to think – but only privately – that there might be something more. They'd joked about the film *Ghost* and how being haunted by Patrick Swayze would be a good thing, but otherwise …

'I know it's beyond insane, but I'm not cracking up, I swear. If you could come home with me after dinner, I could try … I could try and get Gary to appear. Because I know he loved you too, Cat, and then … you'd have to believe me!'

The waiter was now waiting, pencil poised over pad for their order. Cat had little appetite, but asked for the satay chicken salad. Hattie chose maple syrup-roasted duck with bok choi. They each took a swig of their barely-touched drinks; then Hattie raised her glass.

'To us. That is, the *three* of us. It's going to be all right, Cat. Wait and see. It's going to be fine.'

Cat robotically raised her glass and clinked it against Hattie's. The sooner they got this over with, the better. Hadn't Hattie already said she had no control over Gary's comings and goings? So how, precisely, was she going to lure him into showing up for her benefit? By promising him a threesome? (They'd joked about it in the past, Gary teasing that he'd be a rose between two thorns. It would never have happened. He loved Hattie and Hattie alone; Cat was the amiable sidekick, but so glad to have the pair of them covering her back). It wasn't *going* to happen, but she had to play along with the charade, for fear of what *might* happen if she didn't.

The food was in front of them, looking amazing, but neither of them had any appetite. Cat eventually caved in, scooping up a morsel of chicken. It was undoubtedly delicious but she could have been chewing the insole of her trainer for all the impact it was having on her taste buds. Hattie cut a sliver of duck and looked at it with zero enthusiasm. They simultaneously dropped their cutlery on the plates with a clatter, prompting the waiter to rush over with a concerned look on his face.

'Is everything OK? Something wrong with the food? He hopped anxiously from foot to foot, awaiting their response. Which was to knock back their cocktails in unison and ask for the same again.

The food totally abandoned, Cat knew she didn't have a choice. If she refused to go back with Hattie, she risked shattering their friendship for good. She had to play along, even if she was certain the outcome would be humiliation for Hattie and embarrassment for herself. Because she couldn't bear to see her best friend clutching at straws, clearly unable to let Gary go. She was disgusted with herself too, for not seeing the signs sooner. It had suited her to think that Hattie was coming to terms with her loss, when the truth was she was drowning in it. She needed help – professional help – and Cat would persuade her to seek it. But first …

* * *

THEY BUNDLED into the taxi the young waiter had ordered for them, still looking distressed about their barely-touched meals. Hattie was silent again but visibly quivering with pent-up emotion. In a few minutes they'd be at her place. Then all would – or would not – be revealed.

'Gary. Psst, Gary! Are you there? There's someone here

who'd love to see you. Please, Gary. Just for once, can you do as you're told?' Hattie raised her palms up in a gesture of 'what's a girl to do?' Cat wrapped her coat tightly around her, although the central heating was turned up to the max, and looked helplessly at her friend. She'd give it five, maybe ten minutes; then she'd call another taxi and look up psychiatrists or bereavement clinics. Should she offer to hold Hattie's hands like in a séance? Nope, little chance of that happening. Hattie was flapping dementedly around the room, her voice growing louder and louder as she implored Gary to 'get his bloody arse in gear'.

* * *

ALONE AGAIN, Hattie appreciated Cat's efforts at humouring her but knew she didn't believe for one second that Gary had found his way back. There seemed little hope of convincing her without concrete evidence, which only left Jack. She looked at the clock on the mantelpiece. It wasn't yet 11pm and her brother was a notorious night owl. She fished her phone out of her bag and scrolled through to find his number … then paused as she heard a strange sound. A sound suspiciously like a bell ringing. It couldn't be … he'd laughed out loud when she suggested it, but there was definitely a jingly noise coming from the hallway. She edged closer to the door, just as Gary stepped into view. He held the hand-painted Tyrolean cow bell aloft, his grin befitting the Joker.

'Hey, Hats. Thought I'd give it a go after all. What d'ya think?' He jangled it again with enthusiasm. Hattie folded her arms, willing herself not to grab the bell and whack him over the head with it.

'What do I think? I'll tell you exactly what I think, Gary.

Yet again I've made myself look like a madwoman in front of Cat. She's probably on the internet right now checking out affordable homes for the seriously deranged. I could … ooh, I could murder you right now!'

Gary put down the bell and ruffled Hattie's hair affectionately. 'Bit late for that, babes!'

CHAPTER 9

'Checkmate. You lose, sucker.'

Jack Anderson gazed in disgust at the chess board. Thrashed yet again. He couldn't remember the last time he'd won. All the more galling as he'd been the undisputed chess champion at secondary school for three consecutive years. Admittedly, that was a quarter of a century ago, but still …

'Fine. Bask in your pathetic glory while I go and put dinner on. Cheese on toast OK for you?'

His partner of two years, Ben Williams, pulled a face as he started packing away the chess pieces. He knew that Jack was a whizz in the kitchen and had been marinating strips of beef in a mouth-watering mix of herbs and spices for several hours. Sliced vegetables and pre-soaked rice noodles would combine to make one of his legendary stir fries.

Pulling on an apron to protect his pristine white shirt from spatters, Jack whistled along to the radio as he finely chopped a clove of garlic. Life was good right now. Well, aside from the chess thing. His business was thriving, he was the proud owner of a spanking new apartment with views over the Thames in the Georgian market town of Marlow and he had Ben. Lovely, funny and entirely adorable Ben. Through his twenties and thirties he'd despaired of ever meeting The One, until one fateful evening his car had broken down during a thunderstorm and Ben had pulled over to help. They'd been together ever since.

Putting on the wok to heat up, he reflected on how lucky he was. He had a good circle of friends, his mother, Rachel, was a constant source of support (although never in an 'in your face' way) and his big sister, Hattie, still looked out for him as she'd always done since their childhood. When he first 'came out', at the age of seventeen, he'd been apprehensive. No, wrong word, he'd been absolutely terrified. Not because of his family's reaction but more how he would be seen by his peers. A couple of boys had already picked up on his lack of interest in the opposite sex, at least from a dating point of view. Girls gravitated towards him because he was kind-hearted, witty and – although he was never one to brag – not beaten with the ugly stick. One or two had hinted at him taking them out, but he managed to dodge their advances by pleading pressure of school work and his devotion to chess. The only girl he'd ever kissed in his life was eighteen-year-old Jennifer Rogers. It came about during a boozy barbecue at her parents' house a week before Jack was due to start university. Emboldened by half a litre of cider, she'd sidled up to him, eyelashes fluttering and off-the-shoulder top threatening to fall off completely. 'You look a bit lonely, Jack,' she'd murmured in his ear. As she swayed alarmingly like a sunflower in a strong wind, he put a gentlemanly arm around her waist to prevent an embarrassing tumble. Needing no further encouragement, she'd clamped her mouth over his, engulfing him in a kiss that tasted of bitter apples and a hint of mint. For a few seconds he'd responded. He'd often wondered what it would be like to kiss a girl (and spent many frustrated nights agonising over what it would be like to kiss a *boy*). Any lingering doubts over which scenario was the preferred one was eliminated in the time it took to extricate himself from Jennifer's lips. Luckily, she hadn't taken offence, simply tottered off in search of more cider.

His next kiss came almost six months later. By then he'd been 'out' for half that time, his encounter with Jennifer giving him the courage to tell his mum and sister. The former had simply smiled, pulled him in for a hug and announced, 'Well done, darling. I wondered when you were going to get around to it!'

A little flabbergasted, Jack had asked her how long she'd known, or at least, suspected.

'Ah, let me see. Since you were about ten, I'd say.'

Jack wracked his brains, trying to remember what he might have done at the tender age of ten to signal his true sexual orientation. Had he dressed up in Hattie's clothes? Played with her dolls? (Nope, he'd always preferred his Action Men – had been a bit fixated with their peculiar anatomy – which might, in itself, have been a clue).

As it turned out, it was no one thing in particular, just a general sense that he was drawn to boys rather than girls.

'I know a lot of parents say they'll love their children no matter what, then fail to cope when faced with something that goes against their beliefs. All I know is that you and Hattie are my world, and I know it's a world that's a better place for you being in it.' He'd blubbed his eyes out at her words, only pulling himself together when she cooked his favourite dinner.

Hattie's reaction was similar, if a bit cruder. He'd taken her out for supper and they'd sat, sheltered from a light drizzle, chomping on vinegar-drenched chips and battered saveloys.

'Jeez, bro. You took your time getting *that* off your chest! I had you down as a bottom bandit for – ooh! – at least three years.' She'd waggled her giant sausage provocatively in his face, Jack slapping it away in mild but amused irritation.

'You *do* know that phrases like that are highly offensive to sensitive homosexuals like me,' he'd retorted. Hattie's response was to pinch his last chip and proceed to chant more politically incorrect terms for people of his sexual proclivity.

Jack grinned as he added the final touches to the stir fry. Hattie had continued to wind him up for days, teasing him that she'd keep future boyfriends hidden lest he try and snare them for himself. Shortly after, Gary came on the scene, and – much as Jack liked him and could see their immediate rapport – he knew his type was a far cry from Gary's loud, boisterous and in-your-face personality.

Leaving Ben to do the washing-up after every last noodle had been slurped up, Jack sprawled on the sofa and grabbed the remote control. At which point his phone began to chirrup, the familiar ringtone of 'Tarzan Boy' by Baltimora prompting a predictable squeal of horror from Ben. He'd only been eight when the song came out but recalled dancing around his bedroom, beating his chest and imagining gleaming manly torsos and swinging vines. His mum had clearly been a couple of years adrift when it came to figuring out which team he batted for.

'Hi. Jack? It's Hattie. I hope I didn't disturb you. How are you? How's Ben? I know it's been too long, it's just …'

Guilt prodded at Jack's conscience. He'd found it hard to deal with the funeral, particularly as Hattie had remained stiff-upper-lipped throughout, her focus solely on getting through the proceedings. He didn't know how to react in the face of her stony acceptance, so he chose to slink away. Ben had been furious with him. 'She needs you right now, more than ever! Just because she isn't bawling her eyes out doesn't mean she isn't breaking apart inside.'

'Hattie, of course you're not disturbing me. I'm good, Ben's fine – he winced as his partner flicked him across the face with a soggy tea towel – and … I'm sorry. It *has* been too long, and the fault is mine.' He moved the phone away from his mouth and hissed at Ben who was nodding in fervent agreement. 'Anyway, more to the point, how are you?'

He listened as Hattie expressed her concerns about Johnny, and promised he'd have an uncle-to-nephew chat. He was a good kid (OK, technically a young adult now), but he seemed rudderless and adrift whereas at the same age Jack knew exactly where he was going and how to get there. Still, he'd try his best.

'Is there something else bothering you, Hats?' Stupid question, of course there was something bothering her, like the untimely death of her husband. Ben was now rolling his eyes in an 'I can't bloody believe what a dickhead you are' fashion. Jack made a rude gesture back then signalled a cup of coffee would go down a treat.

'I can't talk about it over the phone. It's better if I could see you. Are you free in the next couple of evenings to drop by? With Ben, of course, although it might be easier if …' The words 'you came alone' hung in the air, not that Jack took offence. Ben and Hattie got along well, so it was clear whatever she wanted to say she preferred to keep it between them.

'Sure. Let me think.' Jack rifled mentally through his calendar, recalling a five o'clock meeting the next day that was likely to drag on for hours. He'd tentatively booked a game of squash with Ben the following evening, but that could be changed. 'Tomorrow's tricky – sorry – but I could make it on Thursday? Is that OK, Sis?'

Hattie agreed, and they arranged for him to come to the house around 7.30.

'I'll make us a bite to eat and then … I'll try to explain. See you soon, Jack.'

He lowered the phone from his ear, puzzled and a bit concerned. Hattie didn't sound her usual self, but again, that was no doubt due to the burden of grief she still carried. Even so, he sensed that whatever she wanted to tell him wasn't going to be easy to hear.

'What was that all about? Poor Hats, I hope you're going to be a supportive sibling and not the useless waste of space you've been since the funeral.' Ben positioned a cappuccino with chocolate sprinkles on the coaster next to Jack's chair. He was right, of course, and had been nagging Jack constantly to get in touch with Hattie.

'To be honest, I'm not quite sure, Ben. But I'm going to see her and try and help any way I can.' He took a sip of the piping-hot coffee, unable to shake an icy feeling of dread that crept up his spine.

CHAPTER 10

RACHEL ANDERSON WAS PLAYING with her new toy, an iPad Pro she'd bought on a whim the day before. Her old PC was cranky and prone to crashing (a bit like dear old Nigel, she'd chuckled to herself), and she considered herself a bit of a whizz when it came to modern-day gadgetry. Many of her friends couldn't get to grips with mobile phones and computers, muttering grumpily that things were better *in the old days.* Yes, wouldn't it be wonderful to go back to three channels on the TV and ancient phones that almost garrotted you with their twirly cords when you tried to move anywhere?

She loved online shopping, particularly books and a once-a-week grocery order. How liberating it was to have the friendly Ocado driver pull up and unload all the boring and cumbersome stuff she'd previously had to cart home in her Ford Fiesta! Now she just needed to stock up with some fresh meat and fish, some fruit and veg, and she could skip out with a mere basketful.

Jack had mentioned something about Siri, a kind of personal assistant available on Mac devices. Apparently, you could tap in questions and it would come up with suitable responses. You could even *talk* to it, for heaven's sake!

Rachel held down the Home button – ridiculously pleased that she even knew what that was – and Siri sprang into action. As she debated what to ask, a few suggestions popped up.

How long do beagles live? Hmm, not sure she actually gave a hoot.

Find coffee near me? Right above the kettle in an earthenware jar. Next!

How do I show my selfies? More likely to streak down the high street than take photos of myself and share them on social media.

After a pleasant half-hour of browsing new releases and ordering a couple of promising-looking thrillers, Rachel closed down her iPad. Getting to her feet, she grimaced as a sharp pain in her lower back momentarily winded her. Gripping the desk top, she eased herself warily into an upright position. The pain gradually abated, but her fear of what it meant did not. Rachel had been doggedly ignoring these pains for several months, putting them down to nothing more than the inevitable signs of ageing, but their increasing frequency coupled with the unexplained loss of almost half a stone made her weep inside. It wasn't good, deep down she realised that, but resilience in the face of adversity was her default setting. When her husband had died at a tragically young age, she'd refused to buckle under the reality of being an impoverished young widow with two small mouths to feed. When Jack had announced his homosexuality, she'd thanked her lucky stars for such a loving and caring son, knowing too well that others had to deal with selfish and distant offspring who conformed to the 'norm' but gave little in return. Hattie had given her sleepless nights during her teenage years but subsequently found stability and happiness with Gary. In a line-up of prospective husbands, Rachel wasn't sure she'd have picked him out as the perfect match, but he'd proven her wrong again and again. What he lacked in finesse, he more than made up for in bountiful charm and sheer adoration of her daughter. During the funeral Rachel had prayed to a god she had little faith in that Hattie would find inner strength and a means to move on. She was still praying, as Hattie appeared increasingly distant and distracted, especially in the past couple of weeks.

Rachel was aware that she viewed herself as indestructible and, therefore, she never allowed anyone else to see the slightest chink in her hard-won armour. Hattie and Jack teased her about her 'gentlemen callers' – very Tennessee Williams – but equally she kept them all at arm's length. With the possible exception of Ralph (pronounced Rafe like the actor) Lyall. They'd met a mere six months ago, at a dinner organised by her dear friend of half a century, Alice. In spite of her protestations that she didn't need any more men in her life, Alice had insisted that she come along.

'Ralph is that rare beast, my darling. Single all his life but definitely not gay.' No offence taken or meant, Alice was totally au fait with Jack's situation and was always well-meaning in her attempts to find a suitable match for Rachel. She'd never quite grasped how her friend glided from one man to another, keeping them in her thrall. There was no question that Rachel was still a very attractive woman. She acknowledged it herself, but not in a vain, 'look at me!' way. No, more in a quiet, reflective way, accepting that there were lines, creases in her neck, crepey skin where she'd neglected the sun cream. To her, they were badges of a life well-lived. She'd smoked (and still had the odd puff when she felt the need), drank and partied hard in her younger years. Being a single mother to two toddlers at an early age had taught her to disregard other people's views and focus on being the best

she could be. It had been a struggle but she had got there.
Wherever *there* was. At what point in your life did you pat
yourself on the head and say, *Well done! Nice job!* As far as
Rachel was concerned, you kept on trying and probably failing, but you never, ever, gave up. She'd scrimped and saved
to provide the best possible life for her children, taking night
classes in art which had led to a nice career as a book cover
designer. The market was now awash with people offering
the same service at cut-price rates, but Rachel's carefully
built reputation pre-internet meant she still retained a
handful of devoted clients. Children's books were her
speciality, although she'd never cause Quentin Blake sleepless nights. She'd recently completed the illustrations for a
series about poltergeists who were trying to mend their
ways, as well as the furniture they hurled against walls. It had
taken her several months, but she'd captured the author's
vision and the books were riding high in the charts.

Washing down a couple of painkillers with a glass of tap
water, Rachel contemplated cancelling tonight's dinner with
Ralph. Hattie was coming over tomorrow and she had
promised Alice a shopping trip the day after to choose a new
outfit for an upcoming wedding. All she really wanted to do
was crawl back into bed with a hot-water bottle, but she
knew that wasn't an option. She also knew she should make
an appointment with her GP, instead of taking an ostrich
approach to whatever was wrong with her. Soon, she told
herself. Another few days wouldn't make a difference, and
Rachel hated letting people down. Ralph was witty and
entertaining, so a night out would boost her flagging spirits.
Seeing Hattie wasn't something she could possibly postpone,
considering her concerns about her daughter's wellbeing.
And trying on expensive dresses and over-the-top hats with
Alice would be great fun, particularly as such outings always

earned them a glass or two of bubbly and some delicious cake.

Her mind made up, Rachel made her way slowly upstairs to pick out something to wear that evening. The pain was almost gone, and she pushed any lingering worries deep into the recesses of her mind.

CHAPTER 11

'HEY, Mum! It's me. I know I'm a bit early but I needed to get out of the house.' Hattie slipped her shoes off as she entered the pristine hallway with its cream carpets and magnolia walls, adorned with framed prints of Rachel's favourite book covers. Clustered together on the small side table which housed the landline phone was a collection of family portraits. Hattie paused, as she always did, to look at the photo of the four of them – Mum, Dad, herself and Jack – taken just a month before their father had died. There they were, all sand-covered and beaming at the camera, Hattie with a smudge of raspberry ripple ice-cream on her nose. She couldn't remember him, not really, but Rachel had always kept his memory alive.

'He was a good man, the best. His heart was always bursting with pride when he looked at you two. I know if he's looking down right now, he'll be thinking, "I did a good job." Although I like to take a *little* credit!'

How many times had Hattie listened to that line and rolled her eyes in that way only teenagers could? Yeah, right, whatever. Dad was gone and was never coming back. Mum was brilliant (how she loved to brag to her friends that her mum was a *famous* book-cover person) but Dad was no more looking down on her than Ryan Gosling was checking her out on Tinder and deciding to swipe right.

OK, things had changed in the past couple of weeks. Hattie now knew that death wasn't the end. At least, not for Gary, who'd never been renowned for toeing the party line. Perhaps he'd broken through the barricades, screaming abuse at the archangels who tried to block his escape with harps and flailing wings. That would be *so* like him. Belligerent and bolshy to the max.

Still no reply from Rachel. Hattie tiptoed up the stairs, aware of the squeaky ones and trying her best to manoeuvre around them. As she sidestepped her way to the upper landing, she wondered why her dad had never paid a visit. Perhaps he had. She vaguely remembered nights when her mum had tucked her up in bed, a tender kiss placed on her forehead, before she drifted off to sleep. Just a fleeting moment of clarity, the feeling that he was *there* – a mere breath away – willing her to fulfil her dreams and ambitions. *Reach for the stars, my angel. If you can't quite grasp them, make the most of what you have. And never settle for second best.*

Outside her mum's bedroom, Hattie inhaled and exhaled rapidly. Get a grip, she urged herself. She was going to pour her heart out to Jack tomorrow night; for now, she just wanted to assure Rachel that she was functioning and coping and all that stuff mums wanted to hear. Her main concern was how her mum was. She'd seen her attempts to conceal something, a barely-there hunch of the shoulder, a gone-before-you-know-it expression that hinted at troubles that would not be shared. Losing Rachel was not a road Hattie could imagine travelling. Her mother was a constant in a life that had been – up until recently – unremarkable but contented and satisfyingly safe.

'Mum? Are you OK? I know I'm a bit early but I just ...'

Hattie let out a sigh of relief as she saw her mum sitting at the small desk she had positioned at the bedroom window. She was surrounded by pieces of paper and crayons, preferring to draft out her book designs by hand before using computer software to create the finished product. She looked a little pale and, as she rose to her feet, Hattie detected a stiffness in her movement.

'Hello, darling. Sorry, I meant to be done and dusted with this before you arrived. Just working on a few new ideas for an author who's written about warring gerbils and hamsters. Don't ask! I'll give it my best shot, but ...'

Making their way down to the kitchen, Hattie watched Rachel carefully. She *seemed* OK, the colour returning to her cheeks as she prepared tea and produced a batch of homemade scones. Thinner, perhaps, although she'd always maintained a slender figure despite having a wicked sweet tooth. If there was something wrong, Hattie would have to prise it out of her with a crowbar. Rachel Anderson played her cards close to her chest, particularly with anything health-related. She'd nursed Hattie and Jack through the usual childhood illnesses with patience, love and limitless supplies of colouring books, favourite treats and cuddles. The handful of times she'd been poorly herself – a severe kidney infection, bout of pneumonia and shingles – she'd only agreed to medical help and friends' support when she could barely drag herself into an upright position. No, if something was troubling her, Hattie would have to bide her time and hope that her mum confided in her – or someone else – when she felt ready.

As they both slathered their scones with clotted cream and strawberry jam, Hattie asked how things were going with Ralph. She'd only met him once – he'd visited the house with Rachel just days after Gary's funeral when she was still a crumpled, sodden mess – but he'd struck her as a good sort. Again, her mum gave little away with regard to her love life, but there was a distinct lightness in her demeanour when his name was mentioned.

'We had supper together last night. A new place he discovered down a small side street, you'd honestly never know it was there! The food was excellent, as was the service. I already posted a review on Trip Advisor.'

'And … did you go back to his for a nightcap?' Hattie knew she was pushing it, but compared to the geriatric crew who swarmed around Rachel like decrepit drones desperately trying to impress the queen bee, Ralph was a bit of a catch. A retired anaesthetist, he was good-looking in a Nigel Havers way, well-spoken and very gentlemanly. From her huddled position on the couch in the aftermath, Hattie had observed his attentiveness to her mum, taking her coat and hanging it up. Squeezing her hand as she'd looked at a loss what to do with her heartbroken daughter. Even fetching a fresh box of tissues and gently leaning over to touch Hattie's trembling shoulder, and not recoiling at the smell of her unwashed body.

'No, I didn't, and that's all you need to know. Ralph is a dear friend in a circle of lovely friends, and at my age that's all you need.' Rachel looked stern, clearly signalling that this conversation was at an end. Hattie, on the other hand, had the mad urge to start singing 'All You Need Is Love' and sway back and forth with a lighter held aloft. God, she was losing it, wasn't she?

Her mum had started on a second scone, her frown lines melting away as she bit into a mouthful of crumbly sinfulness. For the briefest moment Hattie debated telling her about Gary, but she dismissed the idea as rapidly as it had popped into her mind. She couldn't shake the sense of foreboding that rested on her shoulders like a scratchy shawl.

She'd talk to Jack first, see if he too had picked up any bad vibes concerning Rachel's health. Then she'd drop the ghost bomb and wait for the shock waves to subside.

'Have you heard anything from Barry recently?' her mum inquired, dabbing up the remaining crumbs with a dampened finger. 'I know he couldn't make the funeral as he was working in Japan, but it seems odd he hasn't been in touch. Has he? He *was* Gary's closest friend, after all.'

Hattie had been puzzled and rather hurt that Barry – or Baz – had been incommunicado since hearing of Gary's death. Unlike Hattie and Cat, they'd been friends only six years or so, but they'd gelled quickly over a shared passion for music and craft beers. Baz and Gaz (was there no end to the name shortening?) had met up when they could for a game of pool or a quiz night at the local pub. With Barry frequently overseas as a TEFL teacher and no partner or children to tie him down, there were often long gaps in their acquaintance but, aside from a short text expressing his shock and sadness, there'd been nothing. Total radio silence.

'I'll message him, Mum,' Hattie replied. 'There's been so much to deal with I guess he slipped my mind. Perhaps he's working abroad again?' Although Hattie was sure she'd heard on the grapevine that he was back. And he only lived a short drive away.

Back home, Hattie changed into her black skirt and white blouse for an afternoon shift at Espresso Yourself. She was only working until five, then planned a chilled evening with a soppy movie and lots of hot chocolate. She contemplated ringing Barry, but decided she couldn't cope with any more angst today. If Gary materialised tonight – hopefully not when she was sniffling her way through *The Notebook* – she'd ask him what he thought.

CHAPTER 12

'I TRIED DRAG RACING the other day. It's murder trying to run in heels.' Jamie looked expectantly at Cat, who gave a good-natured eye roll. His painful puns and rapid-fire gags might have driven some women up the wall, but Cat appreciated his humour, which she suspected concealed an inner shyness. She'd read that a lot of big-name comedians were fundamentally reserved and insecure, using comedy as a barrier to hide behind.

Jamie was sitting patiently at the kitchen table as Cat put together a pasta salad. Miraculously, the pasta was cooked 'al dente', rather than 'call the dentist', as she usually misjudged the timing and drained it far too early. The pesto was straight from a jar and the chicken pre-cooked and ready sliced. With Jamie, Cat felt no need to pretend she was anything other than a hopeless cook, and he seemed more than happy at her entry-level efforts.

'Did I tell you about the time I performed at the Edinburgh Fringe?' Jamie poured an ice-cold beer into a glass and took a satisfying sip. 'Well, technically it was on the *fringe* of the Fringe, in the tiniest room you can imagine. I think it sat about twenty people at a pinch.'

'That's exciting!' Cat energetically grated a chunk of Parmesan, managing to avoid adding the skin of her knuckles to the pile of cheese. 'Lots of famous people launched their careers there, so twenty people is a pretty good start, right?'

Jamie snorted. 'The audience comprised of four people, three of whom were my mates and the other a down-and-out who'd snuck in from the rain and snored his way through my entire performance. I don't think I'll be challenging Michael McIntyre for the comedy crown anytime soon.'

Cat squeezed in behind his chair and gave him a hug. 'I still think it's amazing that you did that. Don't give up; even Michael struggled in the early days.'

Jamie swivelled around and regarded her with those twinkling eyes. Cat felt her stomach do a little flip, which had nothing to do with hunger. Or, at least, not of the food kind. As Jamie leaned in closer, she chanted in her head: *Take it slowly. Take it slowly. Take it ... Oh, bugger it!* Their lips met, just the lightest brushing together but enough to awaken feelings Cat had shoved into a metaphorical box marked 'only open in case of emergency'. Did this count as one? It had been so long since she'd slept with a man – *kissed* a man – she wondered if her libido was fighting for freedom. As Jamie's tongue tentatively probed her mouth, she found herself responding and it was nice. Very, *very* nice. Drawing apart for a second, she straddled Jamie and allowed herself to get lost in the moment. A moment that seemed to go on forever, until—

'Should we continue this upstairs?' The words were out before she'd even thought them through. Not that she wanted to take them back, with every atom of her being screaming 'Yes, please.'

'That would be lovely, Cat, as long as you're sure. I don't want to pressure you. We could eat first …'

Cat cut him off with another kiss, before taking both his hands and guiding him to his feet. 'It's salad. It can wait. Just promise me one thing.'

Jamie looked confused, until Cat added: 'No one-liners about sex in the bedroom!'

Laughing, they made slow progress into the hallway, each step punctuated by a lingering smooch. As they climbed the stairs, Cat thought she heard a peculiar sound; like a faint bell tinkling. She listened again but … no, she must have imagined it. Her heart was beating so fast it was probably making her ears ring. They slipped into the bedroom, Jamie nudging the door closed with his knee as they attempted to undress each other with indecent haste. Neither of them noticed a vague shadow passing them, nor did they hear a low chuckle as they tumbled onto the duvet …

* * *

'THAT WAS INCREDIBLE. You are one amazing lady, Cat Cooper.'

Cat stretched her limbs, arms above her head, legs akimbo. All the time so wonderfully aware of Jamie's closeness, his right hand stroking her neck and his left grazing her thigh with butterfly touches. The sex *had* been incredible, as if they'd skipped the preliminary fumbling and self-consciousness and gone straight to 'hello, you know *exactly* what I want and vice versa.' Cat had always been an 'eyes closed' girl, but she'd opened them a few times to see Jamie's piercing blue ones watching her. Not in a weird, creepy way, but more like he was connecting with her and truly seeing her. The *real* Cat, not the desperate-to-please, am-I-good-enough, am-I-too-fat Cat who'd taken all the withering remarks and snide asides from Stewart and allowed them to dismantle her self-worth piece by piece.

'Why, thank you, kind sir. I must admit it was rather pleasing.' Cat wondered why she was speaking like a medi-aeval wench, then she realised she was actually enjoying herself. Playing along with a man who dreamed of making a living cracking jokes, and would no sooner put her down than indulge in a bout of self flagellation. OK, she didn't know him *that* well, but somehow she doubted he was into that stuff.

Showered, dressed and ready to eat, they made their way back to the kitchen where the pasta salad was slightly wilted but still appetising enough. Cat ladled it into two bowls and they dug in with enthusiasm. She was wearing his shirt – a cute, pink-striped number – and he was bare-chested and clearly trying to suck in his stomach. Cat wondered – not for the first time – why men and women needed to put on a show, behave in ways that went against their core instincts. If one human being couldn't accept another, flaws and all, why bother? Were we all striving to better the person by our side, yet choosing to ignore our own failings? God knows, she'd tried to be the person Stewart wanted her to be but always missed the mark. Now she knew it wasn't her fault, that his benchmark was set too high – quite deliberately – so she was always doomed to fail. That's how he liked it. Stewart liked to dislike people. It gave him the upper hand and allowed him to sit in high judgement. She'd accepted it for years until …

'Great pasta. All those carbs have given me renewed energy. How's about a rematch?' Jamie scraped their plates into the bin, stacked them in the dishwasher and gave Cat a smouldering look that would have melted ice caps. She shrugged off the memories that threatened to tarnish her new-found happiness and allowed herself to be bodily scooped up and carried off to a place she never believed existed.

As Jamie carefully placed her back on the bed, she rolled on to her stomach and waited breathlessly for his next move. He shimmied alongside her, reaching for the buttons of the purloined shirt, necessitating another wiggle as she flipped over to allow him access.

'Cat?' She grinned and wished she could actually do a feline purr. OK, she'd give it a shot …

'Erm, I don't know quite what noise you're going for, but it's definitely turning me on. Could you keep it going and … turn over again? Perfect.' Cat dutifully did as she was told, not sure where this was going but completely cool with it. Yes, out with the old, in with the new. That was her motto. Jamie might not be a *forever* man, but he was here and he was *now* and that was …

'You know, I just saw a woman with the perfect bum.' Cat grabbed a pillow, awaiting the punchline. 'Hind sight is a wonderful thing.' The pillow was whacked over Jamie's head and they continued what they'd started, again and again.

CHAPTER 13

'You did what! Tell me you're kidding me, Gary, before I kick your otherworldly butt into the neighbours' garden. And you know how well that'll go down. We nearly had the police on our doorstep when Johnny thought it'd be hilarious to spray-paint their front door with a peace sign.'

Not Johnny's finest hour, thought Hattie. Admittedly, their neighbours were not the friendliest or most liberal minded of people, but each to their own. She'd had a few conversations with them, mainly along the lines of 'too many immigrants, need more nuclear deterrents, what's the world coming to?'

'Soz, Hats, but I swear I didn't mean to. I was just thinking about Cat and suddenly – boom! – I'm in her house. In the lounge, but I could hear her talking to someone in the kitchen. So … I kind of crept around the corner just as they were heading up the stairs. And you didn't need to be Einstein to figure out what was on the cards.'

Gary had the grace to look contrite, giving his bell a little jingle by way of apology. Hattie couldn't get her head around this latest development. So, Gary wasn't restricted to the confines of their own home, but did that mean he was free to roam wherever he liked? And did that mean that other people could see him? Before she could open her mouth, Gary shook his head. He'd always been able to guess what Hattie was thinking, particularly when the thoughts were angry ones.

'No, they didn't see me. I've no idea if they could 'cos I certainly wasn't going to interrupt them just before some serious rumpy pumpy. Although I *might* have made a bit of a noise. With this.' Gary jingled the bell again, his expression one of pure mischief. Hattie didn't know whether to hug him or clout him over the head with something. Preferably larger and heavier than the bloody bell.

'Did she hear it? Do you know? If she *heard* it, that means I have proof that I'm not away with the fairies, or rather, the ghosts.' Hattie felt a rush of excitement at the thought of finally persuading her friend that Gary really had returned. The only problem was ...

'Hats, if you mention the bell and Cat *did* hear it, she's gonna completely freak to think I was there just as she and – whatshisname – got down and dirty. And, no, before you ask, I did not sneak a peek at them in action. Jeez, I'm a ghost not a bleedin' pervert.'

Hattie knew he was right, damn him, but she was sorely tempted to call Cat and casually ask if she'd heard anything strange recently. Like a ringing in her ears. Yeah, that would sound like a *completely* normal question. Nope, she'd have to think of another way of finding out if Cat had experienced anything strange when she was with Jamie. Ooh! That reminded her ...

'What's he like, then? Jamie, her new bloke. She's been keeping shtum about him, I guess because of all the duds in the past. Is he good-looking? Does he seem a good sort?'

Gary shrugged his shoulders. 'Hats, I barely caught a

glimpse of him, and I didn't get the chance to give him the third degree. He looked OK, although he was pretty wrapped up in unwrapping Cat, if you catch my drift. All I know is that their relationship looks like it's going well.'

Hattie unconsciously twirled her wedding and engagement rings around her finger. She'd talk to Cat soon and see what she could coax out of her. For now, she had other issues to deal with, including asking Gary about Barry.

'I'm assuming you haven't paid him a visit,' – a nod of assent from Gary – 'so I'm just wondering if he's OK. You two were so close, yet I haven't heard a peep from him since the funeral. D'you think I should give him a ring?'

Gary nodded again, his face clouding over as he wallowed in a moment of matey nostalgia. 'That'd be great, babes. Some people just ain't good with death, let's face it. Lucky I'm not one of them!'

* * *

'BARRY? Hi, it's me. Hattie. Listen, I don't mean to bother you, it's just I hadn't heard from you in a while, and …' Oh, help. The unmistakable sound of sobbing came down the line, followed by a prolonged bout of nose-blowing. She held the phone away from her ear until the racket subsided. 'Barry, are you still there? I'm sorry, I just wanted to check you were OK.'

There was another snort then he finally spoke. 'Hattie, I'm the one who should be apologising. I feel like an absolute bastard not being there to support you and Johnny. No excuses, except I couldn't believe it when I heard the news, and in a stupid, selfish way I thought I could pretend it wasn't real if I didn't face up to it. We might not have been lifelong friends like you and Cat, but Gaz was like a brother to me. You know my parents are long dead and I never had any siblings. In truth, I didn't have many friends – not ones I could really talk to – until I met your man. He was the best, Hattie, absolutely the best. And knowing I'll never see him again …'

As Hattie allowed Baz/Barry a few moments to compose himself again, she flicked on the kettle and grabbed a tea bag from the caddy. Poor man, she thought as she sniffed the milk and ignored its faintly sour odour. He'd been suffocating with sorrow and guilt, while she'd been having regular catch-ups with the man he so clearly adored. Not that she could *tell* him that – for the time being at least – or he'd be ganging up with Cat to have her locked up.

'Barry, I do understand, and obviously I miss him like crazy too, but … please don't be a stranger. We'd love to see you. It'd probably help to chat about Gary, the good times, that kind of thing.'

With more effusive apologies from Barry, they concluded by arranging to meet up for a drink the following week. Hattie said she'd bring Johnny along too, as the promise of free booze was a sure-fire way of luring him out of his pit.

The more she churned it over in her head, the more Hattie was sure there *had* to be a way to connect the people who loved Gary as much as she did with the man himself. Sure, she'd almost gone into mental meltdown when he first showed up, but now she was used to his visits. Looked forward to them, in fact, aside from the ones when he caught her plucking out a few chin hairs or had an adverse reaction to a particularly spicy curry Johnny had cooked. Yes, having your deceased other half hand you wodges of toilet paper while your bowels evacuated in explosive style wasn't a romantic moment to cherish.

Jack was coming over later. She'd decided against a full-blown meal, opting instead for a tapas-style spread of nibbles and plenty of Rioja. He was a public transport fan so would be taking the train to her place. It was a five-minute walk from the station, and the journey itself was under twenty minutes.

Gary had done the shimmery, whooshy thing again seconds after she'd hung up on Barry. He appeared to have no control over when he arrived and departed. It was as if some cosmic being teleported him back and forth, a bit like someone randomly changing channels on the TV. Gary used to do that all the time, just as Hattie was settling down to watch *The Great British Bake Off.* Instead of cakes with soggy bottoms, she'd find herself faced with men built like outhouses grunting around a rugby pitch. Or a dreary documentary about life on some remote Scottish island, where the sheep outnumbered the humans. At least nowadays she could watch what she wanted, which struck her as a terrible thought. *Hey, my husband's dead, I have absolute power over the remote!*

Ding dong. The doorbell chimed, signalling Jack's arrival. OK, deep breaths and stay calm. Time for another go at describing the indescribable.

CHAPTER 14

'HEY, Johnny boy! How's it hanging? Still milking the Bank of Mum and Dad … I mean, sorry, Sis. Size ten brogue in mouth disease.' Jack looked apologetically at Hattie. She smiled back, not in the least offended by what he'd said. She adored her younger brother and had long been accustomed to his habit of saying the first thing that came into his head. Jack was witty, erudite and wore his heart on his sleeve. Hattie had liked Ben from the moment she met him. They were a good match. She'd witnessed their good-natured one-upmanship, whether it be over a squash match result or a game of Scrabble. They inhabited a different world from the one she and Gary had shared, but Hattie felt no resentment or envy. Their paths might have taken them in very different directions, but she knew Jack would always be there for her.

'S'fine,' grunted Johnny, never comfortable when pulled into a man's embrace. That had nothing to do with Uncle Jack's sexual preferences, more that he preferred fist bumps or – if forced – a shared back slap that could dislodge molars.

Settled in the lounge, plates piled with food and drinks

served (Rioja for Hattie and Jack, Carlsberg for Johnny), they chatted about this and that. Jack tried his best to engage Johnny in a *where do you think your future lies?* conversation but was met with blank looks and monosyllabic responses. Hattie wanted to shake her son like a snow globe, praying that when the flakes settled, he would have a moment of clarity. 'Yes! Right! I will apply myself to something and make a success of myself and not worry my poor mother into an early grave.' Instead, he crushed his beer can, fetched another from the fridge and announced he was off to murder innocent pedestrians with a few of his online gaming buddies.

'Hattie, don't stress about him. He's a twenty-year-old sea of hormones and post-teen apathy, which is a dangerous mix. He'll find his niche, but nagging him will only make him shut you out even more.' Jack snagged an olive with a cocktail stick, his handsome face creased with concern.

Here she was again. Teetering on the precipice of sounding like a complete basket case in front of someone she loved dearly. Cat might have *heard* something but she had yet to formulate a way to broach that subject. She'd asked – begged – Gary to show himself tonight but, as always, he'd been unable to commit. Her ears were out on stalks, desperate for the tiniest bell tinkle. Anything to indicate he was in the building.

'Just nipping out the back door for a ciggie. Back in five.' Jack maintained he wasn't a serious smoker, but after a glass or two he often snuck off for a sly puff. Hattie was sorely tempted to join him, but she'd given up five years ago and knew once she had one she'd be on the rocky road to ruin.

'No probs. I'll just top up the glasses and put the kettle on in case you fancy a coffee.' Hattie gathered up their plates and headed to the kitchen. Thankfully, tapas-style dining meant no washing up. She did a quick tidy-up, noting that Johnny had taken a four-pack of her favourite yoghurts with him. Their remains would fester in his room, breeding their own sub-cultures until she ventured in to remove them.

Tinkle, tinkle. Hattie froze, her whole being unable to accept what her ears were conveying. He was here. Gary – for once in his life (or death) – had stepped up to the mark and met his obligations. He was going to show himself to Jack and Hattie would do a little dance of *I'm not nuts, no one believed me, I'm not nuts* ... OK, Jack was strolling back and the kitchen door was slightly ajar and ... 'I don't believe it! I do not fucking believe it!'

Hattie watched as the next-door-neighbours' cat, Goebbels, strutted across the kitchen tiles, tail held aloft. As repulsive as its namesake, its fur was a manky grey with splodges of brown, its face one that would induce nightmares. The only time Hattie had tried to stroke it, it had sunk its teeth into the back of her hand. Now it was parading around like a bit-part player in a Stephen King movie, the bell on its scarlet collar jangling away.

'Nice cat,' said Jack, his voice oozing sarcasm. 'Not yours, I hope?' At that point, Goebbels leapt on to the kitchen table and lunged for the leftover Serrano ham.

'Shoo, you vile creature!' screeched Hattie, whacking it with a tea towel. With a parting hiss, it jumped down and made its exit, pausing to spray Hattie's beloved cane chair in the corner that she'd restored and repainted herself.

As Hattie wiped away cat pee with a liberal dose of disinfectant, Jack picked up his refilled glass and gestured to the lounge. Tossing the soiled cloth in the bin, Hattie grabbed her own glass and followed him through.

'Right, Sis. We've had the food, the wine's slipping down a treat, so how about telling me what's causing the extra frown lines on that ugly mug of yours?' Jack reclined on the sofa, the ball placed firmly in Hattie's court.

'Well, the thing is ...' Hattie could feel her nerve wavering.

Maybe she could convince Jack that her main worry was what to do about Johnny, on top of still dealing with the loss of Gary. Those two things alone were enough to age anyone overnight. No. She wasn't going to wimp out now. 'You see, Jack, I've been having …'

'Oh, Hats, it's about money, isn't it? It must be a bloody nightmare keeping on top of the mortgage and everything else. Hasn't the insurance paid out yet? Look, tell me what you need and I'll help.' Jack reached across and squeezed Hattie's hand. She, in turn, wanted to scream like a banshee and tear her hair out in frustration.

'No, it's not about money, Jack. I'm not rolling in it but I'm managing and the pay-out is due soon. It's something else. Something I know you're going to struggle to under-stand but I really, *really* need you to hear me out.' *Now would be good, Gary. Enter stage left or stage right. Float down from the ceiling (but don't mention my roots again or I'll knee your ghostly nuts), I don't care, just be here for me!* Hattie waited. And waited. Jack watched in silence, sipping his wine and looking bewildered.

'Right. I'm just going to spit it out. Now. This very instant. And you say nothing, *absolutely* nothing until I'm finished. Got it?' Hattie glared at Jack, who visibly shrank back into the sofa. Then she began to speak …

* * *

JACK'S normally olive complexion had visibly paled as Hattie related her story. To give him his due, he hadn't interrupted her once, although he had finished off the Rioja and looked in need of a second bottle. Hattie darted back to the kitchen, grabbed another from the wine rack along with the corkscrew, and was back within seconds.

'I know I sound like a total loony tune but I need you to

believe me. I need *someone* to believe me! Please, Jack, tell me you believe me ...' Hattie was trembling all over, unexpected tears dripping down her cheeks.

Before she could say another word, Jack gently eased the bottle from her vice-like grip and expertly de-corked it. He refilled the glasses, handed one to Hattie and clinked his against hers.

'My darling Hats, you've annoyed me, teased me and wound me up endlessly over the years, but the one thing you've never done is lie to me. So, how could I *not* believe you? Now come here and give me a hug.'

Hattie did as she was told, the trickle of tears turning into a flood as she nestled in her brother's comforting embrace.

CHAPTER 15

GARY WAS SINGING AWAY to himself about being lonely. He couldn't remember all the lyrics but he improvised with a few of his own. And it was friggin' depressing. Not like the nights when he was rocking the rafters at The Nobody Inn (although Hattie always joked that the only way he'd bring the house down was with a pile of Semtex). Mind you, she was the best wife a man could have, even if she'd never appreciated his vocal talents.

Being dead wasn't exactly a bundle of laughs, but it was certainly a whole lot different to how he'd imagined it. For starters, he could talk, and feel, and *drink whisky!* Which was far less important, he quickly reminded himself, than being able to be with his gorgeous Hattie. It had taken them both some time to get used to it, but Gary saw the way she smiled when he dropped by. Well, not *every* time. She'd had a face like thunder when he appeared minutes after her brother, Jack, had headed home. Still, at least he *believed* her, or maybe he'd just been playing along. Jack was a good sort and Gary wished he could have provided the concrete – or rather, spectral – proof Hattie so desperately needed. Sadly, he was still clueless as to how this haunting thing worked. He felt like a yo-yo being manipulated by an invisible hand. *Boing!* Down to earth he plummets. *Bedoing!* Back he goes. And to *where*, exactly? He'd tried to describe it to Hattie, but the best he could come up with was likening it to being shrouded in a thick mist. A real pea-souper, as his old dad would have said to describe heavy fog. He had no perception of time passing, and it was only through Hattie that he learned it was just over a month since his demise. And where was everyone else? He hadn't encountered another soul – nice turn of phrase, Gazzy boy – and was feeling more than a little isolated.

Just as Gary was sifting through his mental repertoire of songs about being Billy No Mates, he sensed a subtle movement in the mist. Like a curtain slowly parting, it revealed a shadowy figure that gradually came into focus. Christ, was that Alan Rickman? Gary blinked hard and looked again. No, this guy *did* look a bit like the Sheriff of Nottingham in the film starring Kevin Costner but it wasn't him. Anyway, why would Alan Rickman show up, as opposed to … who? His dear granddad, or Auntie Margaret with her never-ending supply of liquorice allsorts? Gary had attended a few funerals in the past decade, so it would surely be more rational if someone close to him in life approached him after death.

'Greetings, Gary.' The shadowy figure was now a substantial presence/ person/ spooky thing standing right next to him. He was dressed head-to-toe in black, hands clasped together as if in prayer. He glided closer, causing Gary to step back and look down to see if he was using a hover board. Nope, this dude was gliding of his own accord.

'You are wondering who I am and why I have appeared before you.' The figure unclasped his hands and spread his arms apart. *What now? Do I bow or something? Compliment him on his outfit?* Gary settled for a non-committal nod of the head. Whoever spookface was, he'd better start talking, and soon.

'Gary, I am your companion, your guide, as you complete the journey from earthbound to empyrean.'

Empyrean? Gary had a few school qualifications to his name and prided himself on being pretty shit-hot at *Pointless* but what the *fuck* did that mean?

'Gary, I would appreciate it if you didn't use profanities. Here, we prefer to express ourselves in simple terms. Swearing is unnecessary and a poor substitute for eloquence and profound thinking.'

OK, scary dude could read his thoughts but Gary took issue with the cursing thing. Hadn't Hattie just read him an article the other day, saying that people who swore a lot were smarter than your average punter? So, he could go and …

'My name, the one I have chosen, is Clarence.' Gary contemplated taking off a sock and stuffing it in his mouth, then decided just to go with the flow and see where it took him.

'Clarence? As in … the angel from the film? With James Stewart and other dudes I can't remember?' Gary groped in his pocket, found his bell and dangled it in his guide's face. *Tinkle, tinkle.* His guide looked unamused and moved the bell to one side without even touching it. Fecking freaky, thought Gary, mentally censoring his language.

'I do not know of whom or what you speak. I have been here for many centuries, and my role is to ensure a path between the earthly and the plane on which we now move. You may call it heaven but I prefer to name it The Present. It is somewhere between what mortals perceive as the afterlife and what those who have passed view as a gift. You see, we have a sense of humour after all!'

OK, clutching my sides with laughter – not – thought Gary. Clarence might consider himself a laugh-a-millennium kind of guy, but he wasn't going to sell out the O2 in a hurry. Time to cut to the chase.

'The thing is – Clarence – I don't know why I'm here. Or what I'm supposed to be doing. I *love* that I can see Hattie again and I almost got to see our mate, Cat. She might have heard me but ...'

Clarence did the hand thing again. Gary figured it was a symbolic gesture, to show he was at one with the cosmos. Or he had really sweaty palms and was trying to dry them off. No rapid, moisture-removal Dyson gizmos here.

'You have a mission, Gary. I cannot tell you what it is. Only you can follow your true path and make right what is wrong. I am merely the conduit between the two worlds. When you find the answer, and make peace with your heart, all will be revealed.'

Mission friggin' impossible, thought Gary. No point in sharing that one with Clarence, who clearly had no knowledge of anything later than a little live Shakespeare in the round.

'Stop speaking in riddles, will ya, and tell me what I'm supposed to do! My wife is going ape trying to convince people I'm back from the dead and I ain't too thrilled myself at this bollocks. Pardon my language, but could you please, *please* spell out what I have to do?'

Clarence was already retreating, his Alan Rickman-ish form devoured by a shroud of black, if-this-was-a-horror-movie-I'd-be-wetting-myself spookiness. So much humble and empathetic angels, thought Gary. His *guide* had given him nothing more than a headache and a realisation that he was in this on his own. Whatever *that* meant.

CHAPTER 16

ANOTHER DAY, another treatment. Cat applied a soothing face masque to her client, having already cleansed, exfoliated and extracted a few blackheads. Calming music played quietly in the background, the sound of waves lapping on a shore combined with bird tweets and harp strings. Cat bloody loathed it and was often tempted to blast out a bit of AC/DC. Somehow, she didn't think 'Highway to Hell' would achieve the necessary air of tranquillity.

Two days had passed since she'd gone to bed with Jamie. Cat was desperate to see him again, but he was snowed under marking essays. He'd promised to ring her this evening and fix up another date. She couldn't wait. Jamie had put a spring in her step and a lightness in her heart. She hadn't realised how low she'd felt recently, what with Gary's death and her worries about Hattie. She'd looked up bereavement organisations and found Cruse, who had a team of trained volunteers to support people struggling with grief. The contact number was saved in her phone but she didn't want to just send it to Hattie. She'd probably delete it or ignore it. No, the best thing was to meet up and gently coax her to contact them.

'All done! Just give yourself a few minutes before you get up.' Cat's client murmured her assent, clearly lulled into a semi-conscious state after forty-five minutes of pampering.

* * *

THE REST of the day had sped by. Not only was her love life on the up, Cat's business had hit a purple patch. She'd invested some money in a website and leaflets that Johnny had distributed in local shops and boutiques (for a small fee, of course). The next couple of weeks were almost fully booked; then Cat was planning on taking a short break. Maybe she could suggest it to Jamie, see if he could get some time off and join her. Or was that too pushy at this early stage?

Her feet and legs were throbbing after standing for hours. Delving into her well-stocked bathroom cabinet, she located a tube of gloopy mint-scented goo that promised to alleviate all manner of aches and pains. She also grabbed a pair of super-comfy socks and headed downstairs for some pampering of her own.

Ah, that was better! Sprawled on the sofa with her feet and legs tingling pleasantly, Cat searched through the TV channels until she found one of her favourite home improvement shows. She also loved cookery programmes, even though she could barely boil an egg. Right, the title credits were just starting to roll and …

The strident sound of the doorbell made Cat jump. Damn and bugger! It was probably a double-glazing salesman or someone collecting for charity. Either way, she'd just ignore it and … no, whoever it was had no intention of going quietly.

Cat hitched up her socks to cover the layer of lurid green goo and shuffled to the door. The bell chimed again, this time for several seconds. 'All right, all right! I'm coming,' she hollered, fiddling with the obstinate handle that always took a few attempts to turn. The door opened and Cat gaped in disbelief at her unexpected caller.

'Hi, Catherine. Goodness me, you look as if you've seen a ghost!' Stewart gave one of his dazzling – and well-rehearsed – mega-smiles that had women falling at his feet. Cat had been one of them, and she still carried the bruises.

'Stewart. What a surprise.' And absolutely not a pleasant one, thought Cat. A doorstep discussion on the merits of cavity wall insulation would be preferable to this encounter.

'Well, aren't you going to invite me in? I've been driving for hours and a nice cold drink and a catch-up would be just the ticket.' Now he was giving her his wounded look, which involved sticking out his bottom lip like a petulant toddler.

A huge part of Cat wanted to slam the door in his immaculately tanned face. But a teeny, tiny part was wondering just what the hell he was doing here, and what his motives were. Because Stewart Hewitt always had a motive. Curiosity won the day, and she moved aside to let him in. *Curiosity killed the cat.* Not that he was planning to murder her, of that she was sure, but she doubted his visit would inject sunshine into her life.

Stewart followed her into the kitchen of the house they'd once shared as husband and wife. One of the few decent things he'd done was allow her to keep it, although the mortgage payments swallowed a hefty chunk of her income. The last she'd heard – they hadn't seen each other for more than five years – he'd moved to Switzerland where he was something big in private banking. Levering a bottle of white from the top shelf of the fridge, Cat allowed herself a small grin as she recalled Hattie insisting that a 'w' was more appropriate than a 'b'.

'So, what brings you here, Stewart? If you're after a stroll down memory lane, then you've picked the wrong walking buddy.' Ooh, that was a good line! Cat mentally high-fived herself, before turning to face Stewart. Who was staring at her legs, and not in an *I'd forgotten what great pins she had* way, more as one would regard a giant, hairy spider in the bath tub. Dammit, she'd momentarily forgotten the green goo. Anyway, she didn't give a flying fuck what Stewart thought of her now. Those days of endlessly fretting about her appearance and waiting for the next carefully executed jibe were long gone.

'Catherine, I know things didn't end well between us.' *Understatement of the century.* 'But time is a great healer and I've changed. I know you'll find that hard to accept, but I've had a long time to reflect on my behaviour, and I know I treated you a little badly.' OK, he was building up a bullet-point list of understatements. 'The thing is, I've been in a few relationships since we broke up, but no one has ever matched up to you. Now I'm back working in England and I wondered … I hoped … I could take you out some time. We could get to know each other again, and I promise you'll like the new me!'

Cat was speechless. The sheer arrogance of the man! For all he knew, she could be married again with several children. Although a cursory glance around the toy-and high-chair-free house and at her ringless finger was probably a giveaway. Stewart obviously interpreted her stunned silence as a positive sign, his body language shouting *Victory! The pushover succumbs again!*

Rescuing her voice from where it had retreated in disbelief, Cat opened her mouth to tell Stewart exactly what she thought of discovering the new him. But before she could say a word, a completely different voice rendered her mute again.

'Well, bugger me sideways! Look what the cat dragged in!'

Cat turned around slowly, her brain desperately trying to make sense of what she'd just heard. It wasn't … it *couldn't* be … she was just in shock at seeing Stewart. Except … Oh My God!

Stewart just managed to support her as Cat's legs buckled beneath her …

THE HAUNTING OF HATTIE HASTINGS

PART TWO

Cat came to slowly. For a brief moment, she wondered where she was, before realising she was tucked up in bed. Tentatively, she lifted the covers, relieved to note that she was still fully dressed. Her brain felt foggy, her thoughts jumbled as she fought to recall why she was here and what had happened. There'd been someone at the door, a bloody annoying somebody. It hadn't been a salesman or a Mormon that much she could remember. So, who had it been? And why was she pleased to discover that she was wearing clothes? Cat never went to bed without stripping off and leaving make-up on was a cardinal sin according to the beauty therapist bible. She ran a finger through her eyelashes – yup, still rigid with mascara.

A faint ringing interrupted her scrambled thoughts. It wasn't the doorbell this time; no, it was her mobile chirruping away downstairs. Jamie! He'd said he'd call, and she knew he was a man of his word. Swinging her legs out, Cat's brow creased as she surveyed their Shrek-like hue. That would be a nightmare to get out of the pristine-white sheets.

Later, she thought, her mind focused on reaching the phone before Jamie hung up. Ring, ring. Ring, ring. Why couldn't she move any faster? And why was her memory screeching to a halt, refusing to move on, like a bungee jumper teetering on the brink and cursing friends for saying, 'this will be so cool!'

And then it all came flooding back. The doorbell, Stewart smirking in the way only Stewart could. Her horror at his return, her attempts to gain the upper hand, that other voice. Oh God. That other voice! Cat steadied herself on the handrail as she replayed what she'd heard. It had been Gary. He'd been there, spoken to her and she'd swooned like a feeble heroine in an amateur dramatic playlet. He'd been there, just as Hattie said, but Cat had dismissed her as over-wrought and borderline bonkers. But … she'd heard him. Clear as day, and unmistakably Gary. Had Stewart heard him too? Cat willed her little grey cells to form some semblance of order, but they were too busy break dancing and busting some moves. No, she didn't think he'd been aware of anything else other than Cat plummeting to the floor. Stewart had scooped her up, deposited her on the bed and swanned off, no doubt patting himself on the head for having had such a major impact on his still-so-easy-to-manipulate ex-wife.

The phone stopped ringing. Cat debated whether to hop in the shower first to remove the green stuff or call Jamie back. Assuming it had been Jamie, of course. Only one way to find out …

Edging her way cautiously downstairs, Cat heard ringing again. But it wasn't her phone this time. It sounded like a bell, an old-fashioned one the upper classes used to summon their servants. No, that wasn't right; the sound took Cat back to a long-ago school trip to Switzerland where she and her classmates had witnessed the spectacle of cows being brought down from the mountains to spend winter under shelter. They'd been decorated with flowers and enormous, clanking bells and the event had attracted huge crowds, intent on making merry. Cat had found it all a bit surreal and as far removed from suburban UK life as possible. A stray Swiss cow clearly hadn't crossed the Channel and strayed into her living room, so what was making the noise? Seconds later, she had the answer.

'Cat, darlin', looking the bomb as always. Well, apart from the Incredible Hulk leg thing. Sorry about before, but I couldn't help myself. What was that sleazy piece of shit doing here?'

There he stood, in all his undead glory, looking exactly as she remembered him. Apart from the fact he was clutching a cow bell and Cat could see the outline of the fireplace through his semi-transparent body. Hattie had been telling the truth and Cat had chosen not to believe her. She felt the burn of hot shame creep up her chest, which was marginally better than collapsing in a heap of stunned denial.

'Cat got your tongue?' chuckled Gary, totally at ease with the situation. He'd always prided himself on his wit, even when both she and Hattie groaned and pelted him with peanuts or any other objects they had to hand. She decided against chucking anything at him now, sure it would pass through him and add to the weirdness of the situation. As if it could get any weirder.

'Gary, you're right. And don't look so bloody smug about it. I'm lost for words, which you don't need to tell me is a rare thing.' Cat slumped into an armchair, mindful of her green legs which she propped up on the side table. Gary took the seat opposite her, his smirk reduced to a look of concern and sadness.

'Cat, I know you've found it hard to hear what Hattie was telling you. It ain't been a picnic for me either, coming to terms with the fact that I'm dead but still hanging around like a ghostly gooseberry. Not that Hats is seeing anyone else yet, but I know at some point in the future she will. Maybe in six months, or a year, but I don't expect – or want – her to be the grieving widow until her dying day. It's just doing my head in that I'm here but I can't pick who I see or when. I just seem to float around and land without warning. Well, not exactly without warning.' He did his impression of an Alpine cow again, and Cat felt a sudden rush of déjà vu. She'd heard it before. Climbing the stairs with Jamie, en route for some serious steaminess in the sack. Oh, no. Gary had been there. She hadn't experienced the onset of tinnitus, just her best friend's husband sneaking around. She felt sick inside, wondering what he'd seen. Or heard. Her impression of a contented kitty, for one. Please, please say that he hadn't … 'When I was with Jamie, you didn't happen to float into the bedroom and …'

'Cat, it's cool. I was there, but I didn't spy on you. Scout's honour.' Gary did the finger thing, which looked more like an 'up yours' than the three-fingered salute synonymous with the organisation. Cat doubted he'd ever been a Boy Scout. More like a street gang member, all swagger and lager.

'Fine. If you say so. But it's a bit creepy, knowing you were prowling around while Jamie and I were … getting acquainted. I really like him, Gary, and the last thing I need is you hovering around like Banquo scaring the pants off him.' Cat picked a bit of gunge off her left leg, not sure if Gary would get her Shakespeare reference. She'd loved Macbeth at school, thrilled to bits when she got to play one of the three witches. Even when Hattie had remarked that she'd only got the part because of the wart on her chin. Which wasn't a wart, just a pimple that outstayed its welcome.

Gary looked contrite as well he should. If he'd popped up a bit sooner, she wouldn't have had to treat Hattie like a straitjacket contender. As it was, a question forced its way out of the chaos of Cat's muddled mind.

'Did he see you? Stewart, I mean? I guess he put me to bed after I fainted but … it's all a bit hazy.'

Gary shook his head. Solemnly and with absolute certainty. 'No, darlin'. He thought your swooning was all about him. I was lookin' straight at him but he didn't react at all. Not a flinch, nothing. Yeah, he carted you off upstairs, and I went back to Clarence. Don't ask, I'll fill you in another time.'

'Did you hear what he said? About never having met anyone who matched up to me? Gary, I don't know what's going on, but Stewart was wooing me! After all the misery and pain I've tried to bury, he's back and thinking we can start all over again.' Cat rewound her sentence and compared the situation with Gary and Stewart. Both resurrected from the dead – well, kind of – and both trying to make amends. Gary she could forgive, because she loved him to bits, but Stewart? Was it possible that he'd turned over a whole new leaf and wanted her back?

Gary appeared to gain access to her thoughts. 'Sweetheart, I listened to what he said to you. Which seemed like a farm load of excrement to me, but who am I to judge? I'm just a dead guy, hoping that the living get a few kicks before they end up doing the earth-to-fuck-knows-where shuffle I'm doing right now. Maybe he's telling the truth? How do you know he's lying?'

Cat was itching for a shower. And a sleep. Followed by an awakening that told her none of the above had happened, and she could go back to her simple life of beauty treatments and Jamie. It wasn't to be.

'I know he's lying because his lips were moving. Can I

clean up now, and we'll continue this conversation at a later date?'

Gary shrugged his shoulders, gave Cat a salute and – just as suddenly as he'd appeared – he was gone.

CHAPTER 18

HATTIE KNEW she was mouthing like a marooned goldfish, but no sounds would come out. She'd answered the door to an unexpected Cat, who'd grabbed her by the arm and manhandled her into the kitchen. Twenty breathless minutes later, she'd delivered the double-whammy of Stewart's return and – even more shocking – Gary's grand entrance.

'So, I wanted to say how horribly sorry I am for not believing you. I'm a poor apology for a friend and if you want to replace me with a better one, then I'll completely understand.'

Cat looked like a toddler caught crayoning on the walls and made to sit on the naughty step. Hattie decided to put her out of her misery, pulling her into a 'nothing to forgive' hug.

'Don't be so daft. You know nothing would stop us being friends. Unless you got a hot date with Paul Rudd, then I'd seriously never speak to you again!' Both had a major crush on the actor and even Gary had confessed when they were catching up with old episodes of Friends that he found him strangely attractive. Speaking of whom …

'Did you talk much? Oh, God, it's such a relief to not be the only person who can see him. What I don't get, though, is why Stewart couldn't see him. You said you heard Gary first, then you turned and saw him. Isn't that right?'

Cat nodded before pulling up a kitchen chair. Hattie sat down across from her, wondering if a glass of something would be in order. For a woman who didn't really drink, she'd been making up for it in recent weeks. Still, she'd had a tough few hours at work when her colleague, Beth, called in sick. Friday afternoons were one of their busiest times and she was rushed off her feet. Bugger it, she'd poured enough lattes and cappuccinos today, alcohol it was.

With a bottle of supermarket plonk on the table, Hattie listened again as Cat told her what Gary had said. She swallowed hard at the bit when her husband said he didn't expect her to remain single. The thought of dating again hadn't even crossed her mind. Nor should it, so soon after losing Gary. Hattie wasn't sure if there was an acceptable time frame within which someone could see other people. Was it six months, a year or maybe even longer? Anyway, it was all well Gary *saying* that, but how would he react if she brought home another man? Most widows probably had to contend with some criticism from well-meaning friends or family, but she doubted many of them had a disapproving ghost huffing and puffing down their neck. She took a sip of the wine – fruity with an undernote of anti-freeze – and switched the subject back to Cat's ex-husband from hell.

'I can't imagine what was the bigger shock; Gary appearing or Stewart turning up like that. He's really got some nerve, after the way he treated you, Cat. I hope you slam the door in his self-satisfied mug if he dares to show up again.'

Cat wiped away a drop of wine from the base of her glass. She had a faraway look in her eyes, which Hattie hoped wasn't due to misplaced nostalgia for a man who'd crushed her confidence as casually as an empty Coke can.

'I'm not sure he'll come back, to be honest. I didn't exactly welcome him with open arms. Whatever his game is, I'm not playing. I've got Jamie now and we're good together. Oh, Hats, in some ways he reminds me of Gary. With his jokes, I mean, although he's much funnier. No offence!'

'None taken. Gary knows his attempts at one-liners are as funny as an enema. So, what's the latest on Jamie? You guys getting serious, or what?' Hattie didn't know much about him, but she sensed that Cat was letting down her defences for the first time in years. Nothing would make her happier than seeing her friend settle down with someone who adored her and treated her with respect.

'It's still early days, Hats. He left me a message last night, but I haven't replied yet. I will because I want to keep seeing him. He's sweet, and kind, and makes me feel special. Unlike …'

Hattie completed the sentence. 'Stewart, who was mean, spiteful and did his level best to control every aspect of your life. Heck, why am I using the past tense? Leopards don't change their spots and the fact he's trying to wheedle his way back into your life makes me feel sick! Please, Cat, if he comes back, don't give him an inch. I know he can put on a charm offensive but that man is toxic. You gave him your heart and he wiped his feet on it. You are not a doormat! Jamie sounds fantastic, and if you don't introduce us soon, I'll get a serious case of the sulks.'

Cat gave a watery smile. Stewart had kept the power to affect her, which wasn't surprising. He'd been the ultimate puppet master, pulling her strings, controlling her thoughts and shrinking her ego to amoeba size. It was a shame he hadn't seen Gary, as that might have sent him shrieking down the road, never to return.

'I'd love for you to meet Jamie, honestly, but I'm scared too. What if you don't like him? It's unlikely – he's lovely – but it seems a big step at this stage. Although not as big as introducing him to my parents!'

Cat wasn't close to her parents, Reg and Ann Cooper. They lived two hours' drive away but might as well be in darkest Africa for all the time they gave to their only child. They'd never made a secret of the fact they'd wanted a boy, and one who excelled academically. Cat was a disappointment on both counts, and when she announced she wanted to be a beautician, their reaction had been predictable.

'Goodness, girl, you might not be the brightest bulb on the Christmas tree, but couldn't you apply for something a little less … mundane?' Her father was a master of withering remarks, while her mother had perfected the art of sighing and looking harassed. Ann Cooper had devoted her entire adult life to pandering to her husband's every whim. A difficult man to please, it was little wonder she also devoted herself to gin. Something Cat had discovered in her teens when she was searching for a scarf in her mother's wardrobe and uncovered a secret stash of Gordon's bottles.

The only thing she'd ever done right in their eyes was marrying Stewart. Her father, never known for showing any emotion apart from displeasure or disdain, had blown his nose repeatedly during the ceremony. He'd attributed it to a touch of hay fever, whereas her mother had maintained a look of glazed bewilderment, sloping off to the ladies' several times 'to powder my nose'. Both Reg and Ann looked on Stewart as the son they never had, even when Cat told them of his bullying and domineering ways. Their separation and divorce underlined their belief that their daughter was doomed to a life of failure.

Hattie had often wondered if Cat was drawn to Stewart because of his intimidating nature. She was no psychologist, but didn't Jung say women liked men with similarities to their fathers? If Reg Cooper had been a kind-hearted, jovial soul instead of a mean-spirited pig, she could have understood, but ...

'Listen, let's organise something. Why don't we go out somewhere together for a drink, just the four of us ... 'Hattie stopped talking, aware of what she'd just said. Cat gazed at her open-mouthed, and all was silent for an instant until ... 'tinkle, tinkle.'

'You'll catch flies if you don't close that gob of yours.' And there Gary was, making his debut in front of them both.

'Your new man seems a decent sort, Cat, but I'm not sure going for a pint with him is the best of ideas. But good to know I'm still part of the fab foursome, darlin'!' He winked at Hattie, who rolled her eyes at Cat; then the three of them collapsed in a fit of uncontrolled and unhinged laughter.

CHAPTER 19

HIS SOCIAL CIRCLE might be improving marginally on earth, but Gary could still count his unearthly acquaintances on the fingers of one hand. Correction – on one finger. Two months had passed since his passing, and the only conversations he had were either with himself or Clarence. And he was a man of few words, to put it mildly. Plus, he always spoke in riddles, at least as far as Gary was concerned. Their last chat had involved Gary pressing him again on what his 'mission' was.

'Ah, Gary, I realise you are discombobulated by the situation, but it would be indecorous of me to declaim the journey before you.' Clarence had smiled in an inscrutable fashion, and Gary made a mental note to swipe Johnny's school dictionary the next time he dropped by. Dammit, he still hadn't been able to show himself to Johnny, despite his very best efforts. Which chiefly involved him screwing his face up tightly and chanting his son's name a hundred times. He so wanted to speak to his son, and not only because Hattie had been bending his ear again about Johnny's lack of purpose. Gary knew he hadn't exactly left a lasting legacy behind him. Certainly, nothing that had warranted more than a few column inches in the local rag about the accident, and a brief obituary referring to him as 'a devoted husband and father'. And he had been. His proudest achievement was his boy, although he gave all due credit to Hattie for enduring swollen ankles, morning sickness that lasted for weeks and haemorrhoids. Gary could have happily lived without knowing about that unfortunate side effect.

His thoughts of piles (why the heck were they named that?) were interrupted by a tugging at his trouser leg. What the … ? He looked down and found himself staring into the chocolate-brown eyes of a young boy. He couldn't be any older than ten, with a mop of auburn hair and a smattering of freckles across his nose. He was wearing shorts and a well-worn T-shirt. *A boy after my own heart*, thought Gary, still proudly attired in his own ancient top. Then his heart did a flip-flop as he took in what their encounter meant. This little lad was dead like him. He'd never grow up like Johnny, go to big school, drink beer, meet girls and eventually marry someone as amazing as Hattie. This was all wrong.

'Do you know where we are, cos I'm scared and I want to go home.' The boy's eyes filled with tears, prompting Gary to kneel down until they were face-to-face. He saw that the boy was clutching something tightly to his chest, but all he could make out was a tuft of ginger and a pair of tartan-clad legs.

'Well, I ain't sure, but I think we might be in heaven. Sorry, do you know what that means? Look, why don't we start by introducing ourselves. My name's Gary, and you are … ?' Gary extended his hand and his young companion eyed it warily. After a few seconds, he moved his plush toy to one side and accepted the greeting.

'I'm Marty and I'm eight. Well, eight and a half, but Mummy says you have to wait a whole year before you can have a proper birthday. When I was eight, I got a party with a bouncy castle and a big chocolate cake. My mummy said I shouldn't eat it before I bounced but I did. And I was really, really sick!'

Gary grinned. Marty was the first real person he'd met, even if it tore him apart to accept that this little mite was in the same sad boat as himself. He ruffled Marty's hair then gave him a tickle which prompted an infectious giggle. The tears vanished as quickly as they appeared, replaced by a gap-toothed grin.

'Well, Marty, it's really nice to meet you. I've been pretty lonely here, so it's good to make a new friend. Speaking of which, who's that you've got tucked under your arm?' Gary nodded at Marty's toy companion and waited as it was slowly brought to the fore.

'He's Grump,' said Marty. 'Mummy and Daddy gave him to me when I went into hospital. The first time, cos I was in hospital lots and lots of times. He isn't *really* grumpy, not like my teacher Mrs Wicks. She was always grumpy, specially when we were doing sums and didn't get them right.' He thrust the toy into Gary's hands. It was some kind of troll, with an orange face and an exaggerated frown.

'So why did you call him that? He doesn't look too happy, I have to say.' Gary couldn't quite place it, but Grump reminded him of someone …

'It was Daddy who gave him that name. He said he looked like some important person from the TV, but I can't remember who. Just that his name sounded a bit the same.'

Ah, the penny dropped. Grump was none other than the Donald himself. Come to think of it, he was about the same colour and the hair just needed a comb-over.

'You said you were in hospital, Marty. Do you know what was wrong with you? Here, have Grump back.' Gary handed over the Trump effigy and Marty hugged it close to his skinny body.

'I was really, really ill. It was a big word, it made Mummy and Daddy cry when the doctor first said it. Look … look … leukaemia!' His joy at finding the right word made Gary want to cry himself. Life was so cruel, snatching away the innocents while the depraved and evil were left to roam the world.

'What do you last remember? I mean, about being with your mummy and daddy. Do you have any brothers or sisters?' Gary hated asking these questions, but he wanted to know if Marty's experiences in any way matched his own. Although it sounded as if his new little friend hadn't been able to make his way back to his family.

Marty bottom lip quivered. He closed his eyes tightly as if trying to delve into painful memories. Then he shook his head, almost angrily.

'I can't remember anything, cept Mummy and Daddy crying more than ever. I wanted to cuddle them and say it was OK, but then I fell asleep. I think I was asleep a long, long time and when I woke up I was here and I couldn't find them. And I don't have a brother or sister, but now I wish I had. Please, Gary, can you help me find them?'

Rarely lost for words, Gary was struck dumb by Marty's heart-wrenching request. His own vision clouded over with tears as Marty slipped his tiny hand into Gary's and gazed at him pleadingly. What could he do? He doubted if the rules – whatever they were – would allow him to take Marty with him on his next foray into the land of the living. Even if it *were* possible, introducing Marty to Hattie and Cat wasn't going to achieve much. Apart from reducing the pair of them to sobbing heaps at the sight of a ghost destined never to pass puberty.

'Mate, I dunno if that's something I can do. I could ask the boss …' Gary saw Marty's eyes widen in awe, clearly thinking that he had a hotline to God himself. The wee lad would be bitterly disappointed if he knew that 'the boss' was called Clarence and specialised in talking gibberish rather than serving as the figurehead for believers worldwide. Gary's dismissal of a *higher being* had taken a serious knock since he'd died and 'risen again', but he was pretty sure that welcomes from the upper echelons were reserved for those higher up the pecking order.

'But I *need* to talk to them! If I'm … if I'm … in heaven, then they're going to be so sad. And I need to tell them something. Something that'll make them happy. Please, it's really important.' Marty was now squeezing Gary's hand with all the force an eight-year-old could muster.

'Listen, Marty. I just don't think I can help you in that way. I'm so, so sorry. The thing is, I *can* go back, but I ain't got any say in when or how it happens. And the only people I've been able to talk to are my wife, Hattie, and her best friend, Cat.' The pressure on his hand increased as Marty squeezed it even harder. Gary looked at him, expecting to see an expression of bitter disappointment and probably more tears. He was taken aback when he saw Marty's face radiate hope and not a little excitement.

'That's brilliant! You can tell your wife – Hattie – and she can go and see Mummy and Daddy and tell them what I need to tell them. That'd be OK, wouldn't it?' His last few words were more hesitant, but his whole demeanour shouted eager expectation. Gary had no desire to turn down Marty's heartfelt plea, but he couldn't see any way of fulfilling his wish.

'Marty, I really don't think that'd work. Your parents would think Hattie was a crazy lady if she turned up claiming that she had a message from you.' Gary also thought it unlikely that Hattie would agree to such a harebrained scheme. He could just imagine the doorstep conversation …

'Hi, my name's Hattie Hastings, and I've been getting visits from my dead husband who happens to have made friends with

your dead son, Marty. He wanted me to tell you something ...' Best-case scenario, the door slammed in face. Worst-case scenario, police called and Hattie arrested on the grounds of insanity. Nope, it was a non-runner. Now he just had to break it gently to Marty that he couldn't help with telling them – what exactly?

'Mate, you haven't said what it was you wanted to pass on to your mum and dad. Maybe if we talked about it, it might ease your mind a bit. A problem shared is a problem halved as my old mum used to say.' Not that she'd felt *quite* that way when he'd been suspended from school for cling-filming the girls' toilets as a bit of a lark.

Marty shifted from foot to foot, Grump clasped even closer to his body. Gary waited patiently, aware of a familiar itchy sensation that generally preceded one of his trips to terra firma. It reminded him of the prickly heat he used to suffer on long-haul lorry journeys in hot weather. He'd only recently clocked the connection between the feeling and his return visits. It wasn't always immediate, and Gary prayed that he wasn't about to vanish before he discovered what was troubling his young companion.

'Well ... you know I said I didn't have a brother or sister? One night, before I got sick, I snuck downstairs when I was supposed to be asleep cos I wanted a biscuit. And I heard Mummy and Daddy talking, and they said they wanted to have a new baby. I got angry and went in the room and said I didn't want a smelly, noisy baby in the house, and why couldn't we get a dog instead? Daddy was cross and said I shouldn't sneak around, but Mummy hugged me and said I'd always be her best boy. And I tried to be, but now I'm not there, and I don't want them to be sad. So ...'

Gary knew what was coming next, both in terms of what Marty was going to say, and the fact that the itch growing stronger. *Not yet, please, not yet.*

'I want to tell them that they should have a baby. Gary, I need Mummy and Daddy to be happy. If I can't ever see them again, they have to know that! Please!'

Marty's imploring face faded from Gary's view as he was transported from one plane to another. Except, this time his vision was blurred with scalding tears ...

CHAPTER 20

'I CAN DO COIN STUFF, and the whipping things out from behind people's ears, and a few nice card tricks.' Johnny stuttered to a halt, unable to conjure up – ha, ha – the other dazzling sleights of hand he'd mastered in his youth. His mum and dad had bought him a magic set for Christmas when he was seven, and he'd spent many a happy hour teaching himself simple tricks in the privacy of his bedroom. Over the next few years he amassed a growing collection of material obtained from the internet or the occasional visit to a specialist shop. Cups and balls, silk scarves, metal hoops and a stuffed rabbit. Johnny had tried to persuade his mum to buy him a real one but – following the early demise of hamsters Daisy and Duke – she was having none of it. Encouraged by his parents, he built up an hour-long show and performed at younger children's birthday parties. Getting paid for it was brilliant, but the real buzz had been watching his audience – mums and dads included – gasp at his tricks.

However, when puberty kicked in with a vengeance, Johnny's passion for magic did its own disappearing act. He was around thirteen, his voice on the verge of breaking, whereas many of his friends already sounded manly. They also did more 'manly' things, like play rugby or football, neither of which interested him. When word got out that he was a magician (he'd been proud of the title), Johnny took a serious ribbing in the playground.

'Do you wear, like, a dress and sparkly tights?' sneered one spotty lad who Johnny had loathed ever since the day he'd deliberately tripped him up on the way to maths class. Just as he was about to retort that it was magicians' assistants who dressed that way, another voice piped up: 'Magic's for poofs! Or weirdos. Which one are you, eh?'

Looking back, Johnny regretted letting their juvenile jibes get to him. He remembered sloping home, cheeks burning, and shoving all his magic equipment into the special metal case his dad had bought for him. The look of dismay on their faces when he pulled down the loft ladder and hoisted the case up, tossing it among the cobweb-shrouded ancient boxes, the contents of which remained unknown to this day.

Johnny had learned of the job through his best mate, Josh, who'd heard about it at work. A friend of Josh's dad ran a magic shop in town and was looking for a part-time assistant.

'He's a bit of a nut job, but harmless enough,' said Josh. 'Apparently, he could have been the next Paul Daniels, but he chopped the top off someone's finger when he did a TV audition. Anyway, with your background I thought it might be worth checking out.'

Outside the deep purple and star-emblazoned shop front of Spellbound, Johnny had experienced a flutter of nerves. Both at the prospect of holding down a proper job and dusting down his long-neglected magic skills. The owner, Richard Ravenscroft, was adamant when Johnny called to enquire about the position that he needed someone who could demonstrate tricks to customers.

'What I don't need is an assistant who lolls around all day looking bored and treating potential buyers like annoying mosquitos. The last lad I hired assured me he had a few things up his sleeve; what I didn't realise was he was stuffing fivers from the till up his jumper on a regular basis.'

To his amazement, Johnny was offered the job after he'd fumbled his way through some of his old repertoire. With a promise to practise hard, they agreed he would start in a week's time, hours to be decided after an initial probation period.

'That's brilliant, love! I am proud of you, and your dad would be too.' Hattie looked on the brink of tears at Johnny's news. He wasn't sure working a few hours a week in a magic shop warranted such emotion, but he figured it was more to do with his dad not being around to witness him gaining employment.

'Thanks, Mum. Fingers crossed he keeps me on. The pay's not much but at least I can help a bit with bills and stuff.' It was unlikely he'd be able to contribute much, but every little helped. Mr Ravenscroft had also mentioned the possibility of Johnny performing at parties – he'd enjoyed them when he was younger, despite being given a hard time at school – and that would mean extra money. He'd treat Josh to a good old piss up next time he saw him.

* * *

'THAT'S MY BOY!' Gary was pleased about Johnny's job. All the time Hattie had stressed about him dropping out of uni and lacking purpose, Gary had maintained that, 'life's too short to do shit. Happiness, that's what it's all about, Hats.'

Squeezing past him to find bags of nuts and crisps, Hattie

realised her attitude had changed. Life had been too short for Gary and she was desperately worried about her mum's health. She'd seen her a few days ago and thought Rachel had a yellowy tinge to her complexion. Her mum had typically brushed it off, saying she'd made a mistake with a new foundation, but Hattie wasn't convinced. Johnny might not be destined for a high-flying career, but health and happiness were what mattered.

'You are going to hang around now? Jack and Ben'll be here soon and I really need for them to see you.' Dumping the snacks in earthenware bowls, a bubble of panic rose from Hattie's stomach. This could all go horribly wrong. Gary seemed to have a bit more control of how and when he appeared although he was adamant it was more a question of luck than skill. Since pouring her heart out to her brother, she'd hesitated to engineer a meeting. Having Cat on side had helped, yet still she debated the wisdom of others learning of Gary's ghostly presence.

'Sweetheart, I'm here and I ain't got that tingling feeling that means I'm on the verge of vanishing. The last time I really felt it, well, it wasn't good. Thing is, Hats, I've met someone ...'

Hattie's grip on a packet of salt and vinegar tightened. The contents crumbled, along with her confidence. Gary had said he'd always love her; now he was indicating that some celestial crumpet had caught his eye? It was all too much: Johnny, Rachel, Jack and Ben. Plus, she still hadn't hooked up with Barry, who'd sent several texts asking when they could meet.

'No, you daft woman, I haven't met someone else. Not of the female variety, anyway. It's a boy, a wee thing, his name's Marty, and he's only eight. I don't know why we've bumped into each other – and that annoying bugger Clarence is as much use as a chocolate fire guard – but he's asked me to help with something. Or rather, he's asked *me* to ask *you* to help.'

Before Hattie could say a word, the doorbell signalled the arrival of Jack and Ben. She shot Gary a look that conveyed several things. Tread carefully. Do not freak them out. And what the hell am I supposed to do to help Marty?

'Hey, sis. Brought you some flowers. Lovingly hand-picked from the finest florist in town.' Jack handed over said bouquet, which looked suspiciously like …

'He's a lying bastard, Hattie. Picked up at the local petrol station, when he realised we were running on empty, and he'd forgotten to buy you something. Luckily, Saint Ben had a trip to Belgium last week and got you these.' Ben produced a gold and pink-ribbon wrapped box of something sweet and delicious from behind his back. Jack cuffed him on the head, albeit in an affectionate manner.

'Total suck-up. You know it's the thought that counts.' Jack kissed Hattie, play-pretended to shut the door in Ben's face and swaggered through the hallway. She sensed his air of nonchalance was masking a deep-rooted terror of what might be about to happen. Jack was a man of the world, comfortable in his skin and not afraid to speak his mind. He'd nudged her for weeks about Gary, always insistent that he believed her. She'd been too afraid to try, to hope that Gary would show himself. Even after Cat discovered her friend wasn't delusional, Hattie had deliberately postponed any face-to-face. Until now. Somehow knowing that she was stepping out of her widow's shadow and dealing with the issue head on, she felt emboldened and able to deal with whatever the evening had in store.

'Have you missed me?' Gary blew over-the-top kisses at Jack and Ben. Both looked on blankly. Oh crap, thought Hattie, they can't see him. She moved forward and wrapped her arms around Gary. He was still more cushion stuffing than an actual person, but she'd grown used to that. She no longer leapt out of her skin when he appeared, had become accustomed to him dropping in and out of her life. She just wanted to widen the circle of people who were in on the whole weird story. Right now, it wasn't even a circle, just a triangle comprising herself, Gary and Cat.

'What are you doing, sis?' Jack looked perplexed. Understandably, as Hattie must look as if she were embracing thin air. Damn, blast and bugger! More money in the swear box and her brief sense of bravery melting away like the first flakes of snow on a winter's day.

'Erm, nothing! Just a bit chilly. Brrr! I should have cranked up the radiators earlier. Right, what can I get you two?'

Popping the caps off a couple of beers in the kitchen, Hattie glowered at Gary, who'd followed her in and was tossing peanuts in the air and attempting to catch them in his mouth. A habit he shared with Johnny. 'Why can't they see you? There must be something you can do! Please, Gary. Otherwise they'll both think I'm stark raving mad.'

Back in the lounge, Hattie had a sudden burst of inspiration. She thrust the beers at Jack and Ben, deftly swiped the tablecloth off the dining table and tossed it over Gary. For a split second, she thought it would flutter to the floor – leaving her looking crazier than ever – but it shrouded his form perfectly. Pure Halloween, reminiscent of the time she'd cut eyeholes in one of her mum's favourite sheets, and crept up behind her. No after-school treats for a week as punishment.

'What the ... ?' Jack's untouched beer clattered to the floor, its contents oozing and fizzing across the carpet. Ben knocked his back in one breathless gulp. Hattie pushed aside thoughts of stain removal and grabbed a corner of the tablecloth. Like mother, like son she thought as – with a magician's flourish – she whipped it away. 'Ta-da!'

'Evenin' lads. Pleased to see me?'

For a heart-pumping moment, Hattie feared Gary had vanished again. Until she took in the expressions on Jack and Ben's faces.

Jack recovered first. With Ben still sucking on his empty bottle, looking wide-eyed and ready to run screaming from the room, he took a step forward. And then another.

'Evening, Gary. Yes, we're very pleased to see you, aren't we, Ben?' He nodded at his partner, who nodded back mutely.

'Oh, this is wonderful!' Hattie clapped her hands together with glee. 'We're all together again, just as I dreamed of. This calls for a celebration, doesn't it, Gary?' Hattie beamed at him, then turned back to see Jack standing on his own. With the unmistakable noise of retching coming from the downstairs toilet.

CHAPTER 21

CAT WAS HAVING A GOOD DAY. Two new clients in the morning, both delighted with their treatments and already booked in for follow-ups. Jamie had sent her several texts. The first few had been sweet and loving, peppered with ♥ ♥ and smiling emojis. The last one made her snort with laughter: *My auntie went to Boots and asked for a vajazzle. She meant Vagisil xxxx*

Knowing that Hattie approved of Jamie was the icing on an already delicious cake. For the first time in years, Cat felt her life was on an upward trajectory. Business was great, Gary was back on the scene – although she still had to pinch herself from time to time – and she'd ignored messages from Stewart asking to see her again. There had been radio silence for a few weeks now, and Cat was quietly confident he'd taken the hint.

With an hour to go until her next client, Cat decided to test out her latest beauty purchase. A chin mask that promised to eliminate saggy jowls and tighten the jawline in a matter of thirty minutes. She slathered on the special serum, then carefully strapped the fabric band around her head and chin. A quick check in the mirror confirmed that she wouldn't look out of place in a horror movie, but no one was going to see her. And if it shaved a few years off her appearance, Cat would happily wear it down the shops.

Hopping up on to the treatment bench, she lay down and closed her eyes. Bliss! She could have a little power nap, and awake refreshed and energised for the rest of the day.

Cat was just drifting off when the electronic *ding dong* of the salon's doorbell shook her out of her reverie. Dammit! She'd forgotten to lock the door. It was probably a passer-by who'd seen this week's promo offer in the window: Book a pedicure and get a manicure at half-price.

Not wanting to ruin the mask's effect, Cat decided she'd keep it on and hope the would-be customer didn't freak at her Hannibal Lecter appearance. Striding out to the main reception area, she forced her lips upwards into a smile. Which shrivelled up when she saw who was leaning against the desk.

'Catherine, you don't seem very pleased to see me. Mind you, it's hard to tell with that contraption on your face. Is it for medical reasons?' Stewart, as always, looked effortlessly chic. Artfully crumpled linen shirt tucked into chinos, a lambswool sweater draped over his shoulders. Cat knew achieving that look would have taken him at least an hour, factoring in the amount of time he spent primping and preening in the bathroom.

'No, it's not.' Cat could hardly speak with the mask tightened to the max. She ripped it off, tossed it on a chair, and glowered at Stewart. 'What are you doing here? I thought I made it quite clear that you and I are ancient history.' Well, she'd *tried* to relay that message, but Gary showing up had silenced her prematurely.

Stewart passed her a tissue from the box on the desk. 'There's gooey stuff dripping down your neck, Catherine.

OK, pass the sick bag. Wiping away the excess serum, Cat cursed the fact that the two times he'd seen her, gooey stuff had been involved. Then she reminded herself that how she looked in his eyes was no longer important.

'I tried to message you, to see how you were after you fainted, but you didn't reply,' Stewart continued. 'It's not every day I have a woman swooning over me – well, it's been a while. Joke, Cat, joke! You're OK, I hope?'

Cat's earlier feeling of all being right with the world sank to her feet and dribbled into the Italian slate tiles. Why, oh why, had he turned up again?

'I'm fine. I … erm … hadn't eaten much that day, probably low blood sugar.' She certainly wasn't about to reveal the real reason for passing out. All she wanted was for Stewart to leave her alone to get on with her shiny new life.

'Speaking of food, I hoped I could take you out for dinner some time. No, wait please, and hear me out.' Stewart raised a palm in her face, cutting Cat off before she could speak. 'No strings, I promise, just a chance to catch up. Come on, Cat, we *did* have some good times, didn't we?' If she didn't know him better, she'd think he was sincere. Had he really forgotten all the put-downs, the subtle digs, the way he ensured she had so little self-esteem left that staying with him was the only option? To this day, Cat still wasn't sure how she'd found the courage to tell him it was over. All she knew was it had been the best decision of her life even if her battered ego had begged to differ. She'd sobbed herself stupid for days afterwards, torn between relief and fear. Fear that she'd never meet anyone else, that she was too fat, too dumb, too unworthy of being loved. If it hadn't been for Hattie and Gary …

'I know you have doubts, but let's put the past behind us, just for one night. Come on, Cat. What harm can it do?' Stewart went for the full-on Hewitt charm offensive, eyes slightly lowered and a little half-smile that hinted his heart would be broken if 'no' was the answer.

Cat's resistance wavered. Would it really be so terrible? She could draw a definitive line through their relationship. Let him know there was no way back, that she now had the upper hand.

'OK. But just dinner. Nothing else. I'm seeing someone …' Stewart's half-smile drooped marginally, 'and I'm very happy. My next client will be here soon, so …' Cat gestured towards the door.

Stewart whipped out his phone and fiddled with it for a few seconds. 'I'm out of town for a couple of weeks but I'll buzz you when I get back.'

The door opened, and Cat's three-thirty for an eyebrow wax and tint walked in. Stewart treated her to his full-voltage smile, which had the usual effect. All aquiver, she made her way through to the back.

'Be right with you!' Cat turned to say goodbye, but Stewart had already gone. She debated chasing after him – already she was doubting her sanity – but her client was waiting.

Two minutes later, as she was warming up the wax strips, Cat's phone pinged.

Whoops! Forgot to say, I thought The Lemon Tree? Will be great to see the old place again. I'll be in touch.

Oh, God. Cat felt hot and cold as if she were coming down with flu. It was a miracle Mrs Boyce had escaped with any eyebrows at all. Cat's hands had trembled as she'd applied the strips, her mind ricocheting back through the years to that fateful night. The Lemon Tree. Her last ever meal out with Stewart. The one that had brought the whole thing crashing down. How could he have forgotten? Then again, Stewart had always had selective amnesia. Editing everything that didn't fit his carefully calculated blueprint. Whenever Cat had hit back at one of his snide comments (which wasn't often, she rarely had the courage), he would find a way to twist it around. Make it seem that Cat was overly sensitive or downright paranoid. 'I really don't know what you're talking about,' he'd say. 'You always take things the wrong way, Catherine, when all I try to do is help you.'

* * *

IT HAD BEEN HER BIRTHDAY. The day had started well, with Stewart bringing her warm croissants and freshly brewed coffee in bed. He'd even suppressed his usual irritation when a dollop of strawberry jam landed on the duvet cover.

Cat was excited about the evening. It was their first visit to The Lemon Tree, which had recently opened but already created a buzz in town. She took over an hour to get ready, putting on a new fitted dress that emphasised her slimmed-down waist and amped up her bosom. The chunky, Mexican silver bangle Stewart had given her as a present adorned her right wrist, and she'd put her hair in an up-do. Boxes ticked to keep him happy.

Seated in the restaurant Cat scanned the menu, mentally eliminating anything that was too rich, too creamy, too fattening. She opted for a mixed salad to start and grilled pork chop with Mediterranean vegetables to follow. Stewart's smile of approval helped offset the tinge of envy when he ordered wild mushroom risotto and chicken Kiev with a side of home-made potato wedges and sour cream dip.

'You look lovely, Catherine,' he pronounced, topping up their glasses with Veuve Clicquot. 'That colour suits you, although you may have been a little heavy-handed with the make-up. Sometimes less is more, don't you think?'

The bubbles from the champagne caught in her throat at Stewart's comment. Cat spluttered helplessly, prompting a waiter to dash over and enquire if everything was all right. Gulping down some water, Cat struggled to regain her composure, aware of Stewart's deepening frown. He liked to be the centre of attention, but only if the situation painted him in a flattering light. Having his wife choking and turning bright red was attracting curious looks from other diners, which would only add to his displeasure.

'For goodness' sake, go to the ladies' and sort yourself out!' Stewart hissed under his breath. 'People are staring, and you need to sort out your face. There's mascara all down your cheeks.'

Grabbing her clutch bag, Cat blindly pushed back her chair and collided with the man seated behind her. His forkful of food went flying across the table and landed on the lap of his dining companion. With exclamations of annoyance ringing in her ears, she fled to the sanctuary of the wash room.

Staring at her distraught and streaky face in the mirror, Cat tried to control the trembling in her hands. Yet again, Stewart had derailed her with words, dressed up in the guise of well-meaning guidance. *Sticks and stones may break my bones* …He'd never lifted a finger to her, but his verbal attacks always hit the mark. Wiping away the damage with a damp tissue, Cat reflected that at least her make-up was toned down. Practically non-existent, in fact.

Returning to the table, she smiled apologetically at the couple behind them. Stewart was dunking wedges into the dip and Cat's barely touched salad had been replaced by the main meal. He looked up, shuddered and returned his attention to the chicken Kiev.

The evening was careering towards disaster, but Cat had some news she hoped – prayed – might turn it around. Since gaining her beauty therapist diploma, she'd worked in various salons. A week ago, she'd learned that an outdated hairdressers' in the centre of town had closed down, and the premises were up for lease. Cat had made tentative enquiries and paid a visit. It needed a total make-over, but the rent was reasonable and it would be perfect for launching her own business. Something she had long dreamed of but been too nervous to pursue. She hadn't said anything to Stewart, but Hattie and Gary were one hundred percent behind her.

'Stewart. There's something I wanted to run by you. If that's OK.' *Why did she need to question if it was all right to discuss something so important to her with her husband?* The answer was simple. Nine times out of ten, anything she suggested was given the thumbs down by Stewart. He booked their holidays, dictated their diets, told her what to wear (or return, if she'd bought something on her own) and generally ran their relationship like a designer-clad dictator. How had she let it come to this? Something buried deep inside Cat was clawing its way to the surface. It wasn't anger or hatred. She didn't hate Stewart, but she loathed what he'd turned her into. No, it was the last vestiges of her self-worth readying themselves for battle.

'Eat your food. It's getting cold.' Stewart sliced the last piece of chicken. Cat picked up her cutlery, then dropped it heavily on the plate. She pushed back her chair – gently this time – and got to her feet.

'Actually, I don't feel hungry any more. What I *do* feel is sick and tired of you telling me what to do and how to behave. I was an idiot to think tonight would be any differ- ent. You are a bully, Stewart, with a mean streak a mile wide. No, don't you dare say a bloody word!' Cat placed her hands on the table and leaned towards him. 'As of now, consider yourself my soon-to-be ex-husband. I'll be consulting a lawyer and I suggest you find yourself somewhere to stay because I won't be moving. I plan to start my own business and a whole new life where I can be myself. The *real* me, not the pathetic imitation moulded by you!'

Pausing only to consider tipping her pork chops in his lap (but deciding against it), Cat marched for the door. Her cheeks were flaming, her heart was pounding, but she held her head high. And felt the tiniest of smiles creep across her face as a smattering of applause rang out around the restaurant.

CHAPTER 22

'I'M SO SORRY, Rachel. I wish I could give you better news, but ...'

Rachel had sat quietly, her hands pleating the fabric of her favourite skirt. The softness of the silky fabric acted as a comforter, like a small child snuggling up to a well-worn but adored toy. She'd taken in the doctor's words but didn't process them immediately. Instead, she'd shook his hand, thanked him and headed to the supermarket to pick up a bottle of rhubarb and ginger gin.

Now, she sat in semi-darkness, nursing a glass of the gin, topped up with Prosecco. It was a celebratory drink, meant for parties and celebrations. She wasn't celebrating. She was gradually allowing the full meaning of what he'd told her to seep through her mind, the sharp sweetness of each sip fighting against the bitter taste of shock.

Pancreatic cancer. The second word was bad enough; the first had made her gasp inwardly. Rachel knew the statistics. She'd looked them up long before she'd been diagnosed. Had she known all along? No, she'd had her suspicions, but didn't want them confirmed. Eight out of ten patients don't discover they have the condition until it is at an advanced stage. Surgery by then is not an option. It wasn't an option for her. At least, not straight away.

After two visits to the GP, an ultrasound scan and a CT scan, Rachel had received a call to see the gastroenterologist. It had all happened so fast, one benefit of having private health insurance.

'So, the results are in,' he'd said, his face a mask of professional calm. Rachel had almost laughed out loud, his phrasing bringing to mind the popular TV ballroom dancing show. The judges were holding up their paddles, but the scores were in the minuses.

A potent cocktail of chemotherapy drugs was what the doctor ordered. Which might shrink the tumour enough to enable them to operate. Ifs, buts, maybes. Rachel was familiar with the old adage: nothing can be said to be certain, except death and taxes. The latter she'd paid diligently, the former was a given. She'd always fancied just passing away in her sleep, no fuss, no drama. Did she want to go through endless rounds of chemo with all manner of hideous side effects, and no guarantee of a positive outcome?

Rachel had told no one of her diagnosis. Not Hattie, who would be distraught and prepared to drag her screaming and kicking into hospital. Alice would take the same stance as would her posse of male companions. The only one she felt she could trust to understand her predicament was Ralph. He had a medical background and was used to dealing with death. Their relationship was still new, but for Rachel it was an eye-opener. Popular wisdom had it that women over seventy – Helen Mirren, Susan Sarandon and a few others aside – were meant to disappear into the background. Invest their meagre energy into bouncing grandchildren on their creaking knees or crocheting things. Rachel had happily bounced Johnny on her knee when he was little, but he was unlikely to be a father in the immediate future. Jack and Ben seemed content as a couple and had never mentioned wanting a child. Until the onset of her illness, Rachel considered herself one of the lucky ones. She still worked, her mental faculties remained intact and she knew Ralph found her attractive. Unlike her other male friends, he looked at her as a woman, not just someone to have by their side at social functions or trips abroad. Or was that more to do with Rachel finding him attractive too?

Her sketch pad lay on the side table, the open page blank. She had a new commission, a book about spiders who decide their image needs an overhaul. From creepy crawly to cute and cuddly. She couldn't see it flying off the shelves, but that wasn't her problem. No, her problem was she couldn't think straight, creative juices drained away by the brutal reality of what lay ahead.

She could call Ralph. He would be round in a flash, of that she was sure. Could she tell him? Would it be fair to burden him with her problem when she should be sharing it with family? Rachel's head throbbed, thoughts bouncing back and forth like a Newton's cradle. *Yes, I'll tell him. No, I can't. Yes, I'll call Hattie. No, I can't.*

She'd barely touched her drink. It had done nothing to ease her inner turmoil. Nothing would. The only person who might empathise was the one she'd grown close to. Closer than she'd imagined was possible. You knew people for years, decades, and kept things hidden. Then you met someone who connected, saw you and liked what they saw. So many years in the wilderness, barriers put up to protect not only yourself but your child. Hattie was far from a child now, but Rachel would give her life to ensure a happy one for her daughter. Death had dealt a hefty blow to Hattie; now it was taunting her too. She would give her life. But not without a fight. Rachel knew what she had to do.

* * *

'RALPH. Thank you for coming by at such short notice. Can I get you a drink?' Rachel took his coat, slung it on a hook and led the way into the kitchen.

'You know I'm happy to see you any time. And you saved me from the tedious task of filing paperwork. Never put off till tomorrow what you can do next week.' Ralph grinned, and Rachel felt better.

'Would you like something to eat?' She realised it was after seven, and – even if her appetite had disappeared – Ralph was probably hungry. She opened the fridge and surveyed its contents, wondering what she could rustle up. Her hand alighted on the opened bottle of Prosecco and she removed it, just as Ralph touched her on the arm.

'You look exhausted. Why don't you fix us a drink and I'll deal with the food? I'm no Galloping Gourmet but I make decent scrambled eggs. Then we can chat about what's on your mind. Deal?'

Minutes later they were seated at the table, glasses fizzing and creamy eggs with a sprinkling of chives and wholemeal toast before them. Rachel took a mouthful – it was delicious but her stomach was knotted with apprehension. They clinked glasses, Rachel grateful that Ralph suggested drinking 'to good company' rather than 'good health'. She wanted to talk but didn't know how to begin. Was it fair to burden Ralph in this way? Maybe she'd misread the situation. Perhaps he only saw her as someone to pass time with, a pleasant distraction from the mundanities of life?

'Rachel.' His deeply refined voice cut through her thoughts. 'You're a million miles away. And you've barely touched my eggs. I won't take it personally, but please – whatever's troubling you, I'd like to know.' She raised her eyes from the plate and his look of gentle concern opened the verbal floodgates. Out the words tumbled, punctuated by sobs and shudders. As Rachel related the details of her diagnosis and the proposed treatment, Ralph drew his chair closer, wrapping an arm around her quivering shoulders. Finally, she juddered to a halt. Emotionally and physically spent, but also lighter having shared the news. Ralph was now holding her hand, and he brushed her cheek which she realised was stained with tears.

'My darling girl. It's a complete bugger, but I am so glad you called me. No one should go through this alone, and you won't. I understand why you don't want to tell Hattie, but you must. If it helps, we can tell her together. And I'll be with you every step of the way. Every chemo session, every appointment, I'll be there. If you want me to.'

Rachel knew then that Ralph was much more than a casual companion. His face and words conveyed the clear message he regarded them as a couple. Two people in their twilight years who had a chance of happiness together. For how long? Impossible to say, but wasn't that true for everyone? Death came knocking regardless of age. Her late husband, Hattie's Gary, too many friends had passed away over the years. She'd 'stand up to cancer' – wasn't that the campaign phrase? – and let fate decide the outcome.

'Thank you. Truly, thank you. Yes to all the above. You are a wonderful man, Ralph. A great friend and …' Rachel hesitated. Should she say what she really felt? Or did actions speak louder than words? As she went to top up their drinks, Ralph put a hand over his glass.

'I'd love some more, but I have to drive home. A cup of coffee would be nice, but I'll make it.' He went to stand, but Rachel pulled him back. Filled both glasses to the rim and the liquid frothed over and pooled on the table.

'Stay. Please, I'd like you to stay.' She dabbed at the drips with her napkin, conscious of her heart beat accelerating. *Thump, thump. Thump, thump. I need you tonight.*

Ralph gazed at her steadily. Rachel looked into his pale blue eyes and willed him to read her mind. *I need you with me. Properly with me.*

'Of course. I'll be perfectly happy in the guest bedroom, although I didn't bring my toothbrush. Or my pyjamas.' Ralph waited for Rachel to speak, or perhaps show him where he would be spending the night. Instead, she pushed the damp napkin aside and took his hand.

'I have a spare toothbrush and the bedroom is warm enough. My bedroom, that is.' Her hand tightened on his, willing him to accept the tacit invitation. If he politely declined and headed into the night, Rachel would feel like a fool. An old fool, but at least she'd know where they stood.

It was only seconds but seemed like an eternity before Ralph replied. Not with words but with a gentle caress of her cheek. Heat rose to the surface, Rachel sure he would feel it beneath the coolness of his fingers.

'There's nothing I'd like more than to stay with you. As long as it's what you really want, Rachel.' Ralph looked at her steadily, his eyes seeking the response that would change everything between them. She was balanced on the brink – both of battling illness and embracing a physical relationship for the first time in decades – and it was terrifying. Terrifying and exhilarating at the same time. There could only be one answer.

'It's what I want, Ralph. It's been a very long time …' Rachel giggled as Ralph pursed his lips and nodded in agreement, 'but they say it's like riding a bike. Although we might have to go through a few gears to hit our stride.'

With a final sip of their drinks, Rachel and Ralph rose to their feet. There was no awkwardness when Ralph pulled her close and kissed her with such exquisite tenderness she felt a long-forgotten ache below.

'Lead the way, my wanton woman. The night is young. We may not be, but just being with you is enough to make me feel like a twenty-year-old.'

As they climbed the stairs, hand in hand, Rachel felt the years slip away. Tomorrow was another day; tonight was theirs alone.

CHAPTER 23

ONE MONTH LATER

HATTIE WAS FILLING up cocoa shakers when she felt a sharp nudge in her ribs.

'He's watching you again!' whispered Beth, who was dolloping cream on a slice of apple and cinnamon pie.

'Who is?' Hattie replied in a less-than-hushed tone. She scanned the café, packed with the usual punters getting their caffeine and sugar fix. Her eyes alighted on a man she reckoned was in his late forties, with cropped greying hair and a smart navy suit. He was tearing an almond croissant apart, but for a moment they looked at one another. Hattie flushed as he raised his teacup in her direction, and quickly she turned away.

'He definitely fancies you,' said Beth, with all the confidence and self-awareness of someone not yet staring down the barrel of her third decade. 'He's been in here three times this week and it's like everyone else is invisible. Come on, Hattie, you must have noticed?'

No, she hadn't, although now that Beth had pointed him out, she realised he wasn't a regular. Hattie had a good memory for faces, and his was a new one. Although, not an unpleasant one.

'Please! You're imagining things. He's probably eyeing you up, Beth.' Her workmate was all willowy curves and flawless skin, and very popular with the male clientele. Hattie thought herself attractive, but it had been so long since she'd considered being the focus of a man's attention it seemed a ludicrous notion.

'Fine. I'm just popping out the back for more cream,' said Beth. 'By the way, your ardent admirer is heading this way.'

Sure enough, mystery man was weaving through the tables towards the serving counter. Perhaps he fancied another croissant, or …

'This is a great place. I can't believe I've only just discovered it, although I only moved to the area a few weeks ago so everything's a bit strange and new. Are you the owner?' He smiled at Hattie, who let out a loud laugh. I wish!

'No, I just work here, but it is very popular. How are you settling in, erm …' Hattie was unsure how to continue the conversation. Normally, she had no problem bantering with the customers, but Beth's comments had unsettled her.

'The name's Richard – Rich to my friends – and I'm pleased to meet you …' He stuck out his right hand, which Hattie accepted. It was a nice hand, she noted, and the handshake was brief but firm.

'Hattie. I'm Hattie. Well, Harriet, but no one calls me that. My husband sometimes did to wind me up, but not for a long time.'

Rich released her hand and looked at her quizzically. 'I don't mean to be nosy, but does that mean you're … no longer together? Tell me to mind my own business if you like. My ex-wife always said I asked too many questions. Not always the right ones, though, otherwise I might have found out sooner she was having an affair with an old flame she'd hooked up with again on Facebook.'

A queue was forming behind Rich, and Beth had clearly popped off to Devon for the cream. Hattie debated what to say, then decided honesty was the best policy. 'He died. My husband. It's OK, I'm getting on with things, but you must excuse me now, people to serve and all that stuff.' She expected him to move away, but instead he reached into his jacket pocket and produced a business card.

'Look, Hattie, I might be bang out of order here, but I wondered if I could take you out for a drink sometime? I haven't met many people yet and I'm getting cabin fever cooped up in my bachelor pad. No pressure, just text or call me if you fancy it.' He placed the card on the counter, smiled and headed for the door.

'See, told you so!' pronounced Beth, who had finally reappeared with a large tub of cream and a vindicated smirk on her face. Before Hattie could stop her, she'd snatched up the card. 'Ooh, Richard Evans, Financial Adviser, Evans & Harty. Very posh! I hope you'll take him up on it.'

Hattie grabbed the card and shoved it in her apron. 'Beth, you do realise my husband only died three months ago? Don't you think it's a bit soon to be going on dates?' She'd been with Gary so long, she doubted she could remember how to behave on one. In any case, it was far too soon, wasn't it? Somehow, Hattie couldn't imagine Gary doing a ghostly jig of glee if she said she was going out with another man, and as for Johnny …

Her shift over, Hattie got in her car and set off for Cat's. She was meeting Jamie, as Cat had decided it would be nice for them to get together for a takeaway curry and a few drinks. She recalled her remark about the four of them meeting up and felt the familiar prickle of tears that always struck when she pictured what life would be like now if Gary were still around. Well, technically he was around, but Hattie didn't think him materialising in front of Cat's new man would advance their relationship. More like scupper it completely.

'I AM COMPLETELY AND UTTERLY STUFFED.' Hattie pushed her plate to one side and groaned. Cat had ordered enough food to feed a small Indian village, and there were still left-overs. Jamie was spooning korma sauce on to half a naan bread, Cat dolloping pickle on the last poppadum. Hattie knew she already approved of Jamie, not just because of his laid-back demeanour, but also because of how he doted on Cat. When she'd dribbled sauce down her T-shirt, he'd dashed off to the kitchen to fetch a damp cloth. Much hilarity had ensued as Jamie tried to clean up the mess without touching her chest. He'd been the one to bring the food, set the table and cater to their every need.

'Right, that's me done!' Jamie announced, wiping his mouth with a piece of kitchen roll before planting a kiss on Cat's cheek. 'I love a good Indian, but I never say no to a nice chicken chow mein either. In fact ...'

'Here we go,' whispered Cat in Hattie's left ear. 'It's pun time!' Hattie had heard all about Jamie's penchant for puns and promised to laugh accordingly.

'My local Chinese takeaway has started serving wildfowl ... so I thought I'd have a gander.' Jamie looked hopefully at Hattie and Cat, who responded with a raucous round of applause. With an exaggerated bow, Jamie stacked up the plates and empty cartons and took them into the kitchen.

'What do you think? Do you like him? Oh God, Hats, please say you like Jamie!' Cat gazed at Hattie, as if her answer would unravel the mysteries of the universe. Having a dead husband still ever-present was a big enough enigma, and not one she could solve in a hurry. If ever. At least she could put her best friend's mind at rest.

'He's adorable. Sorry, sorry, that makes him sound like a Labrador puppy, but – hand on heart – I really like him. And I suspect he more than likes you.' Hattie was almost flattened when Cat lunged at her, gratitude and delight etched on her face.

'OK, before Mr Wonderful comes back, there's something I have to tell you. And (*please, please let Gary not hear this*), I need you to be honest with me. Do you think it'd be crazy for me to go on a date? Not that I'm probably going to, but it's just that this guy in the café said he'd like to take me for a drink, and I wondered …'

Before Cat could reply, Jamie reappeared with a tray of coffees. As he passed them around, Hattie saw he'd placed little chocolates at the side of each cup. A teddy bear for her, a triangle for himself, and a love heart for Cat.

'Not my place to interfere, but I couldn't help overhearing and – Hattie – I really don't see anything wrong with going for a drink with a guy. Don't you agree, Cat?'

Hattie bit the head off her chocolate teddy and waited for Cat's response. Since it had taken Cat a long time to get back on the dating scene after Stewart, she couldn't imagine it would be a positive one.

'Actually, I do. Agree, that is. It's only a drink, for heaven's sake. It'd do you good, Hats, getting out more instead of spending your time either working or hanging out with me. Although maybe you should run it by …' Cat spluttered to a halt. Gary, she was about to say Gary.

'Johnny. You might ask him first. Not that I think you need permission from him to spend a couple of hours in another man's company. Come on, Hats. What's the harm in it?' Good recovery, thought Hattie. Rich seemed like a decent person, and it wasn't like they were going to run off to Gretna Green and tie the knot. He was lonely, she made hermits look like party animals, and at some point, she needed to take a step into the unknown that was her future.

'OK, OK. I'll speak to Johnny and I'll text Richard. That's his name, although his friends call him Rich ... stop sniggering, Cat, I have no idea how big his bank balance is, or anything else for that matter. And I'm unlikely to find out, seeing as it's just a quick drink, nothing more.'

Hattie rubbed the side of her nose where an unwanted blemish had appeared that morning. It felt the size of a small hillock, and she bemoaned the fact that she still suffered from the blighters when Johnny was a zit-free zone. Perhaps she'd wait a couple of days before seeing Rich.

Cat touched her shoulder in a gesture of comfort. She popped the chocolate heart into her mouth whole and snuggled up to Jamie who'd wiggled close to her on the couch. 'Stop fiddling with it; you'll only make it worse. I've got cream you can try, organic and guaranteed to work.'

Jamie looked like he was about to explode. Either from curry overload or the need to hit them with another from his repertoire. The latter won the day. 'I went for an interview at Clearasil yesterday. They offered me a job on the spot.'

Hattie gave her pimple another disgruntled rub. To date or not to date. That was the question. But was it such a big deal?

CHAPTER 24

SHE SHOULD HAVE TOLD GARY. She really, *really* should have told him. Hattie had wrestled with her dilemma for several nights, thrashing around in bed until she was a duvet-devoured mound of sweat and straggly hair. Her rational voice said, *What's the big deal? It's only a drink or two with a nice man.* Her bloody conscience kept prodding her with a hot poker, screaming *Shame on you, woman! Where's your sense of decency?* It didn't help that Gary had appeared on a couple of occasions, expressing concern that she was 'coming down with something' and offering to make her a hot toddy.

'You don't look so great, babes,' he'd said, perched on the side of the bed. Whereas Gary had looked ridiculously hale and hearty for someone who was dead. Hattie feared that he might be able to read her mind even though she was deliberately thinking of anything but her upcoming date. Must pay car insurance. The boiler needs a service. Toilet rolls. Did Johnny really need to use half of one every time he took a dump? His wording, not hers.

'It's a man thing,' Gary had said, jolting her out of her mental avoidance tactic. 'We sit there for longer, get bored and grab handfuls of the stuff. None of that dainty swipe and wipe you ladies go in for.'

Gary's intimate knowledge of how women cleaned up in the loo – and the fact he'd tapped into her thoughts again – kept her date with Rich buried deep. At least, she *hoped* it did.

Hattie had texted him, nerves causing her fingers to press all the wrong buttons. After ten minutes of fumbling and cursing, she managed to type: *Hi, it's Hattie. If you're still free, a drink would be nice.* She'd toyed with adding a smiley emoji but decided against it. Minutes later his reply lit up the screen. *That's great! How about Bar Belle on Friday at 7? I hear the cocktails are dynamite.* She wasn't sure explosive liquor was a great idea, but some Dutch courage would be needed.

Johnny hadn't batted an eyelid when she mentioned she was going out with another man. His new job was proving a success, and he loved the kids' parties sideline, despite having to wear a crushed velvet suit and rotating bow tie. 'No probs, Mum,' he'd said over dinner when she told him. A dinner that *he'd* cooked, much to Hattie's amazement and delight. OK, the potatoes were rock hard and the meat of indeterminate origin, but Hattie gamely chewed and swallowed every mouthful. Johnny was often up before her these days, Mr Ravenscroft being happy to let him open the shop at 9 am. His hours had increased, and at the end of the week he handed Hattie a crumpled handful of notes towards the housekeeping. Johnny was finding his feet; now it was time for her to step into the unknown.

* * *

'I'M SO glad you agreed to meet, Hattie.' Rich was dressed casually, in faded jeans and a cream shirt with the sleeves rolled up. He smelled nice, his aftershave musky and manly. Hattie had opted for a simple woollen dress with a chunky belt and her favourite brown suede boots. She'd experienced another pang of guilt zipping them up. They'd been a Christmas gift from Gary, after she'd spotted them in an upmarket boutique but decided they were far too expensive.

'Me too. I don't get out much apart from going to work.' Great, she sounded like an inmate on day release. Hattie stared into her glass of soda water with a dash of lime. And vodka. She'd been flustered when Rich asked her what she wanted to drink, and that was the first thing that came into her head. He was making steady progress with a pint of lager, his second since they arrived. Perhaps he was nervous? Hattie certainly was. What should they talk about? Brexit? Gun laws in the US? How many squares of toilet roll was acceptable for a regular bowel movement? So far, they'd skirted around the big issues. Rich hadn't mentioned his ex-wife or how long they'd been divorced. Hattie didn't feel it was the time or place to talk about Gary. Partly because she was still feeling guilty for not mentioning her date, and also in case he somehow picked up on it and berated her later for being secretive.

'So, tell me more about yourself,' said Rich, wiping a frothy moustache from his upper lip. 'I know where you work but that's it. Do you have children? What do you like doing in your spare time?'

Before Hattie could reply Rich's phone beeped to signal an incoming text. He glanced at the screen, pulled a face, and put down his empty glass. 'Sorry, a problem at work. I'll just pop outside and deal with it. I won't be long, and I'll get some more drinks on the way back. Same again?'

Hattie nodded, although the vodka made her feel a bit queasy. 'Maybe you could pick up some crisps too? Cheese and onion if they have them.' She hadn't eaten any dinner, but didn't want Rich to feel obliged to take her for a meal. Another drink and she could make her excuses and go home.

She wasn't clicking with Rich. Perhaps she'd never click with anyone else.

Almost ten minutes passed before Rich returned with drinks and crisps. 'Sorry again. Took longer to sort than I hoped. All good now. So, where were we?'

Hattie explained that she had one son and that he'd recently started work in a magic shop. Rich's face conveyed interest, but his body language told a different story. He was clearly on edge, his fingers drumming a tattoo on the table. Whatever the call had been about, it had rattled him.

'I don't really have many hobbies. I do a bit of DIY, refurbishing old furniture, that kind of thing. Oh, and I'm a sucker for romantic movies, anything that makes me blub at the end.' Hattie's stomach grumbled like an ancient radiator creaking to life. She snatched up a packet of crisps, ripped the top apart and – in a scene befitting a slapstick comedy – the contents flew up in the air and cascaded over Rich's head. His look of surprise quickly turned to one of shock as Hattie lunged forward, the remains of her drink catching him full in the face.

'What the … ?' Rich coughed and spluttered, reaching for a napkin to wipe himself. As he did so, his chair slipped from beneath him, and he slid to the floor in a graceless heap. Hattie looked on in horror as did most of the bar. There were a couple of cries of 'take it easy, mate!' and 'you're supposed to eat them, not wear them!'

Hauling himself to his feet, Rich gave Hattie a look that suggested a second date would not be on the cards. Which was fine by her. All she wanted to do was apologise – although she still wasn't sure how it had happened – and exit as quickly as possible. But before she could do so, Rich's phone buzzed again. It had fallen out of his pocket when he hit the deck and was now inches from Hattie's chair. She picked it up, meaning to hand it straight over, until …

Darling, I've kept some dinner for you. Hope the meeting doesn't go on much longer. Especially if your client is as dull as you say! Xx

Hattie looked at the message again, then slowly passed the phone to Rich. Her earlier inclination to pick the crisps out of his hair was replaced with a burning desire to club him over the head with something. She eyed the poker in the fireplace stand, then decided he wasn't worth an assault charge.

'Ex-wife, you said. It must have been a very cordial breakup if she's still making you dinner … **darling**.' Hattie spat out the final word, part of her wanting to laugh at Rich's face. Guilt was etched across it, even as he fumbled for a plausible explanation.

'It's not what you think.' *It never was, thought Hattie.* 'We've been having a rough time since we moved here. She didn't want to come and was threatening to leave me. Honestly, Hattie. I just thought—'

'That poor old widowed Hattie would be a pushover? That I'd fall for your crap and into your bed after a few vodkas? Or rather, *my* bed, unless you were proposing a threesome.'

Before he could say another word, Hattie seized the remaining packet of crisps, squeezed it open, and popped one in her mouth. 'Hmm, at least you got the flavour right. Now, excuse me, but I have better things to do than waste an evening with a lying, cheating tosser.'

* * *

Slamming the front door so hard the windows rattled, Hattie waited. No response from Johnny. Then she remembered he'd gone to a pub quiz night with Josh. Right, deep breath, and: 'Gary! Get your ghostly arse here right now before I call a priest and have you exorcised!'

Seconds later, she was face-to-face with her husband, who was trying for sheepish but instead looked unbearably smug.

'It was *you*, wasn't it? The whole crisp and drink and chair thing. You were there, in Bar Belle! How did you know I was there, and how did you manage to pull off that stunt?'

Gary tut-tutted. 'Hats, I can read you like a book. You've been twitchier than a caffeine addict with an empty Thermos for days. I was worried so … I followed you. I know, I know, I ain't figured out all the ins and outs of this thing, but it seems like … if something is important, I can do it.'

Gary had followed her, heard revolting Rich's conversation with his wife and taken action. Now his ghostly activity wasn't restricted to showing up; he could make things happen. Unseen, and with pretty impressive comic timing.

'He's a bad un, babes. Even his aftershave was rank.' Hattie begged to differ, but now wasn't the time to discuss cologne preferences.

'OK, I appreciate you looking out for me. Really, I do. But I need to make my own mistakes, Gary. I'd have sussed him out sooner or later.' Although later might have been a lot harder to deal with.

Hattie yawned. It was only eight-thirty but the events of the evening had left her feeling wrung out. An early night would suit her down to the ground. She just needed Gary to take his leave, which made her feel ungrateful. He was just looking out for her, wasn't he?

'By the way, Hats, you had me worried when you mentioned exercise. Thought I'd be down on the floor doing fifty bungees as a punishment for sticking my nose in!' Gary crouched and did a fine impression of an arthritic frog.

'The word is "burpees" and I was talking about … oh,

never mind. Please, just let me go to bed.' Hattie gave him a hug, so used to his barely there form it now seemed normal.

'Night, babes. Sleep tight. There's just one thing. Before you go.'

Hattie pulled back and looked him straight in the eye. *No more dates? Only ones pre-approved by her dead husband?*

Gary shook his head. 'No, darlin'. Something much more important. We need to talk about Marty.'

CHAPTER 25

DESPITE HIS BEST EFFORTS, Gary still couldn't get Clarence to elaborate on why he had been chosen to return to earth. The enigmatic one (or knob head as Gary privately dubbed him) swooped around like a character from The Matrix, one minute there, the next gone. Gary had pressed him on the subject of Marty, to no avail.

'It is indeed a terrible vicissitude, Gary, but here we must accept that death cannot be prognosticated. The little one is with us for reasons that are difficult to fathom by mortals. As companions, we are constrained to act in accordance with the ancient ways. As I explained before, my role is not to command but to guide.' Clarence did his wavy-hand thing again. Whatever was meant to be on the cards for Marty, he wasn't giving anything away.

Since his first meeting with Marty, they'd bumped into each other a few times. Or rather, Marty had materialised next to Gary, Grump always safely by his side. He'd asked if Marty also had a 'companion', but the wee fella had looked blankly at him.

'There is an old lady who speaks to me sometimes. She

says her name is Anna, and she fell off a ladder when she was fixing a lightbulb. She's OK, nicer than Bob. But I don't think they're my companion. Maybe you are, Gary?'

Gary wasn't sure what to say. Deep down he was a little miffed that an eight-year-old was amassing more friends than him. And who the heck was Bob? Before he could ask, Marty had fixed him with those beseeching eyes.

'Did you talk to Hattie? Will she go and see my mummy and daddy? You're a nice man, Gary, and I know your wife must be a nice lady. My mummy always said that nice people do good things and this would be a really good thing.'

At a loss what to say, Gary had sat down cross-legged and pulled Marty on to his lap. Tears threatened again as he remembered doing the same years ago with Johnny, reading him bedtime stories or watching silly movies together. 'OK, mate. First of all, I can't make any promises but if you tell me a bit more about yourself and where you come from, well … let's just see, eh?'

Marty had beamed at him. 'That's easy. I know my phone number and my address off by heart. Even the post code!'

* * *

'EDINBURGH? AS IN SCOTLAND?' Hattie looked at Gary as if he'd suggested climbing Mount Kilimanjaro to hand-deliver a letter.

'Yes, Hats, the city with the castle and the festival. We went there once, remember?'

Hattie did remember. It had been when they were first married, and they'd decided to visit all the UK's capital cities. Money was tight, and two days' in London and two in Edinburgh had wiped out their savings. They'd never made it to Cardiff and Belfast in the end.

'So, you're seriously suggesting that I hop on a train or whatever to the frozen North …'

Gary shook his head in amused irritation. 'Babes, it's Scotland, not friggin' Iceland and it won't be that cold.'

Hattie was less sure. She recalled being propelled along the Royal Mile by a forceful and freezing wind, then nearly throwing up when Gary told her how haggis was traditionally made. She'd forgotten that he'd mentioned Marty before, events with Jack and Ben having wiped it completely from her thoughts. Thankfully, Ben had recovered quickly from the shock of seeing Gary, and she had sworn them both to secrecy for the time being.

'Look, I know you want to do the right thing for Marty, but I don't see how I can help. His parents aren't exactly going to welcome me with open arms, are they? A total stranger, claiming to have a message from beyond. I mean, how long ago did he die? Six months? Gary, they'll still be consumed with grief; the last thing they need is some nutter turning up to tell them they should have another baby. That's insane!' Hattie stomped off to the kitchen where she'd been in the middle of chopping vegetables for soup when Gary had whooshed his way into the lounge. She picked up her sharpest knife and began attacking a carrot with indecent fervour. Gary followed her and stirred the onions she'd left sautéing in oil on the hob.

'Darlin', I know it's a huge ask, and I wouldn't be asking, but he's the sweetest wee guy and he's got me right here.' Gary patted his chest with his free hand. 'I dunno, but maybe this is my mission. You know, like creepy Clarence keeps banging on about? Look, just *think* about it, Hats. That's all.'

Twenty minutes later, with Gary gone and the delicious smell of lentil and ham soup wafting around the house, Hattie slumped in a chair. She was supposed to be meeting up with Barry later, but first she had another shift at

Espresso Yourself to get through. Beth had texted her to say they were short-handed as the new boy Colin had called in sick. He'd only worked there for a week, and Hattie doubted he'd be back. He'd already managed to bugger up the coffee machine twice and been slapped in the face by Beth when he'd mentioned her 'nice baps'. To be fair, Colin *might* have been referring to the tray of bread rolls she'd been arranging on the display counter, but Hattie doubted it.

Arriving at the café, she grabbed her apron from the back room. Beth was there, touching up her lipstick in front of the cracked old mirror above the wash-hand basin. Holding the fort out front was the owner, Miriam, who was usually more elusive than the Scarlet Pimpernel. A tiny woman, always clad in the highest heels imaginable, she commanded a mini empire in the town. As well as Espresso Yourself, Miriam owned an upmarket hair salon, a boutique and a small art gallery. She dropped in every week at the café to meet with the staff and make any changes to the menu or general running of the place. Seeing her teetering around gathering up dirty plates and cups was like watching the Queen tackling the hoovering.

'Beth, you'd better get out there pronto, before Miriam hands you your P45,' hissed Hattie. Beth gave an indifferent shrug and adjusted her 'baps' for maximum effect.

'Keep your hair on, Hattie,' she replied. 'There's only been a couple of customers since she arrived, and she'll be off the minute you get out there. Before you go, though, *how was it?*'

Hattie couldn't think what Beth was talking about. Then it dawned on her. The date, with Rich, which she now regretted telling Beth about.

'A total disaster. Turns out he's married and just looking for a bit of leg-over action on the side. Guess that's me finished with men.'

Hattie exchanged a few words with Miriam, who she

knew regarded her as a stable and reliable team member. Miriam mentioned increasing Hattie's hours, and Hattie mumbled that she'd give it some thought. Beth finally appeared, just as a group of pushchair-wrangling mums fought their way to the furthest corner and the largest table. Miriam wafted off in a cloud of expensive perfume, and Hattie took the orders for coffees, herbal teas and slices of cake.

With no new customers, and the mummy brigade slurping, chomping and bitching merrily among themselves, Hattie and Beth fixed themselves cappuccinos and perched on stools within sight of the door.

'Shame about your date. Not to worry, plenty more fish in the sea,' said Beth consolingly, licking froth from her upper lip. 'Speaking of which, my Uncle Roger is staying with us at the moment, and he's definitely single. We used to think he was gay, but Dad – his brother – says he's just never been good with the ladies. He's quite good-looking, and he's old like you ...' Beth halted, Hattie spluttering a mouthful of cappuccino down her front. Bloody fantastic! Wiping herself with a handful of paper napkins, she gave Beth her finest 'not amused' face. Was that the best she could hope for? A man who may or may not bat for the other team with no social skills and as ancient as herself? Mind you, Beth probably thought anyone single and over the age of thirty-five was a bit of a saddo. If Roger the codger was her young colleague's idea of a dream date – well, Hattie would rather live out her days in splendid solitude. Or with a goldfish, to continue Beth's analogy.

'Sorry, Hattie. I just meant he was in his fifties and you two might hit it off. What do you say? Should I fix something up?' Beth got to her feet as an elderly couple entered, the man leaning on a stick, his other arm linked with his wife's.

He led her carefully to a chair and fussed around until she was comfortably seated. Hattie watched with a lump in her throat as the man pressed a kiss on his wife's heavily powdered cheek, then made his way to the counter.

'Two teas, please. Just plain old tea, none of that fancy Earl Grey stuff. And two slices of Bakewell tart.' He fumbled in the pocket of his well-worn tweed coat, producing a battered wallet and a handful of coins. After carefully counting them out, he made his way back to his wife. Beth followed with the drinks and cakes. Hattie had never really imagined her and Gary in their twilight years. It was something that she'd taken for granted, the two of them bickering over the TV volume, whose turn it was to make the evening cocoa and moaning that Johnny didn't visit often enough. Now it would never be.

'OK.' The word was out before she realised it. Beth looked at her blankly.

'What's OK? Oh, you mean Roger! Great stuff, I'll get it sorted. He's not a drinker – think he went a bit mental in his younger days – but he loves eating. Not in a pig in a trough way, he just likes good food. I know! You could go to that new burger place, everyone says the triple-decker with fully loaded wedges is to die for.'

Indeed, thought Hattie. She could picture the clientele now, clutching their chests as their arteries clogged with each mouthful. Still, if she and Roger had their mouths full, they wouldn't have to talk too much. Oh, why had she agreed to something she was already dreading? Gary used to say she was too nice, going along with things for fear of hurting someone's feelings. Would it hurt his feelings if she went out with another man, so soon after the Rich fiasco? Hattie didn't think so. Gary had interfered because he'd been worried about her. He hadn't said anything about future dates, and she knew from Beth that Uncle Roger didn't have a wife tucked away. As long as he didn't have anything *else* tucked away, like a blood-stained axe or collection of pickled eyeballs …

CHAPTER 26

IT HAD TAKEN Hattie longer than expected to pin down Barry for a catch-up. He'd spent time teaching in Vietnam, then been stricken by a stomach bug. He and Hattie had messaged back and forth until they settled on a date and a venue. Tonight, at eight o'clock, in The Queen's Head. Johnny was tagging along too and had promised to fork out for a couple of rounds. Hattie still couldn't believe his transformation since getting a job. He'd even put on a load of washing the other day when she was at work. Shame he'd chucked in a red T-shirt with the whites, but the sheets were now an appealing shade of sunset pink.

Hattie sat on her bed, an abandoned book by her side. Its cover blurb screamed 'Must read! Unputdownable! You won't read better this year!' Sadly, its content failed to match the hyperbole. She'd barely made it past the first chapter. It pained her to give up on a book, but this one was more insomnia cure than page turner.

'Johnny! Are you ready yet?' Hattie rapped on his bedroom door. Music blasted from within, a band she liked but whose name she could never remember. A body part.

Ankle? Kneecap? Dammit, she hated those 'senior moments' when her brain fogged over. Hattie frequently forgot things. Climbing the stairs to fetch something, then having no clue what she was looking for. Or returning from the super-market with all the ingredients for a chicken casserole, except the chicken.

Johnny's door opened, and he appeared in a fug of body spray. Hattie took a step backwards, nostrils twitching at its potency. He swivelled round and went to switch off the music.

'Who's the band again? It's on the tip of my tongue, but you know what a sieve head your old mum is,' she joked.

'That's about the fourth time you've asked me, Mother.' Johnny slung his arm over her shoulder, his still-damp hair brushing her face. 'It's Elbow, they're English, and you said the singer reminds you of some oldie.'

'Ah, yes. Peter Gabriel. He used to front Genesis. Way before your time, sweetheart. Right, let's get a wiggle on. Don't want to keep Barry waiting.'

The Queen's Head was only a fifteen-minute walk away. The rain clouds that threatened to dump earlier had dissi-pated, the sky was dark and the temperature mild. Hattie linked arms with Johnny as they strolled along, a feeling of contentment washing over her. Life might not be perfect – was it ever? – but she had her boy; Gary was still present (she'd give her last penny to have the living version back, but …) and now that Cat, Jack and Ben were in on the secret, the burden was less heavy. The one thing weighing her down was concern for her mum. Hattie spoke to her most days and saw her at least once a week. She'd pushed and prodded, convinced that Rachel was hiding something from her, but the woman had poker face down to an art. What was note-worthy was Ralph's increasing presence in her life. His name was dropped in most conversations – 'Ralph thinks this.

Ralph told me that. You'll never guess where Ralph is taking me! – and there was no denying the way her mother's face lit up when she spoke of him. Whatever Rachel was concealing, at least she had him by her side.

'HATTIE! I am so glad to see you. And Johnny, look at you. The spitting image of your dad ...' Barry's voice faltered, and Hattie hesitated before giving him a quick hug.

'You're right, he is, although he takes after me in the brains department. Isn't that so, Johnny?'

Johnny shrugged good-naturedly. 'Whatever you say, Mum. Right, who's having what? I'll get the first round in.'

With Johnny queueing at the bar for two pints and a gin and tonic, Hattie and Barry found a table with two chairs. Scanning the room, Barry spotted a spare and carried it over. They both hung up their coats on hooks behind them before settling down.

'You look great, Hattie. I can't imagine what it's been like for you – and for Johnny – and I'm so sorry again for being a useless lump.' Barry pulled a hankie from his trouser pocket and dabbed at his eyes. Hattie waited until he composed himself before speaking.

'You've nothing to be sorry about, Barry. Grief hits people in different ways, and we each have to find our way to cope with it. I couldn't have got through without Johnny, and Cat, and my mum ... they've been brilliant. I wish it hadn't taken so long for us to get together.'

Johnny returned with the drinks and some peanuts. They spent the next hour chatting and catching up with all their news. Hattie played down her epic failure of a date and the upcoming burger bonanza with Roger, unsure what Barry's reaction would be. He didn't appear surprised or upset, despite his obvious devotion to Gary. In truth, Hattie didn't really know him well. He and Gary had been a tight unit, but Barry had only been at their home a handful of times. He'd always struck Hattie as shy, although he had a dry sense of humour and was unfailingly polite.

'Great news about the job!' Barry raised his glass in a toast to Johnny, who proceeded to crack them up with stories from the shop and kids' parties.

'Old Ravenscroft is definitely a sandwich short of a picnic. Total whacko, in fact. D'you know, he reckons he's the reincarnation of some 19th-century dude? What's the name again … Robert-Houdin, a French magician. He's got posters of him everywhere; it's like a blinkin' shrine in the back office.' Johnny lobbed a handful of peanuts into his mouth, washing them down with the dregs of his pint. A short debate followed, Johnny explaining that the better-known Houdini had chosen his stage name in homage to his magician idol.

'Still, if he wants to believe in all that reincarnation and life after death crap, that's his business. I'm happy trundling along there for now. Maybe I'll get to run the place one day when he retires. That would be cool!'

Hattie flinched at Johnny's words. Not his desire to run Spellbound – if it came to be, that was great – but his dismissal of the afterlife. It didn't surprise her; she'd been knocked sideways when Gary appeared and challenged everything she'd ever believed about death. Now that others had seen him, she no longer doubted her sanity, but Hattie feared what Johnny's reaction would be. If Gary *ever* showed himself to their son, or Barry for that matter. Who knew?

It was after nine, and the three of them agreed that a takeaway would hit the spot. Unable to agree on either fish and chips or Indian, they resorted to a coin flip. Said coin produced from behind Barry's ear, Johnny's trick making Barry's face light up like a Christmas tree. Until then, Hattie hadn't realised how the corners of his mouth drooped or recognised the sadness ever-present in his eyes. He was an attractive man, she thought.

Heads it was, which meant a five-minute stroll to the chippy. Battered cod and chips for Hattie and Barry, steak pie and chips with lashings of gravy for Johnny. Clutching their steaming parcels of food, they headed to Hattie's. Seated round the kitchen table, they scoffed their feast, washed down with more beers for the boys and a mug of tea for Hattie.

Barry had said little about his job as a TEFL teacher in the pub. Hattie recalled Gary telling her he'd worked in insurance before, a high-powered role that led to the collapse of a long-term relationship. Crazy hours and little in the way of downtime had proven too much, and he'd quit. Reading between the lines, Gary reckoned he'd had a kind of mental breakdown, but it was a subject they'd never discussed.

'What got you into teaching, Barry?' asked Johnny, drenching his chips with more vinegar. 'I can't imagine a worse job, facing a classroom of bored teenagers texting under the desk while you bang on about past tenses or split infinitives. I should know; I used to be one of them!'

Barry laughed, a hearty chuckle. 'Teaching English as a foreign language is a bit different, Johnny. My students range from young kids to businessmen and women who want to learn the language. They're usually pretty motivated. Well, apart from the little ones who've been pushed into it by their parents. I've had quite a few dozing off mid-lesson. When it gets bad, I stick on an English cartoon and bribe them with sweets.'

Topping up her tea from the pot, Hattie heard the faint but unmistakable sound of a bell. She couldn't place where it was coming from. Was it possible Gary was going for a double whammy, the big reveal in front of Johnny and Barry?

Hattie wasn't sure that would be a great idea. Barry was still coming to terms with the loss of his great mate, and as for Johnny … he'd turned a corner in his life. Maybe he wasn't living his dream, but weren't dreams built of tiny stepping stones? Some you slipped on; others guided you along the way. Who'd told her that? Gary, of course. He was no poet, but sometimes he'd come out with things that were pretty profound. And not only after a potent joint.

Pulling back the curtain, Hattie scowled in disgust. Her neighbours' cat, Goebbels, was preening itself on the window sill, its collar bell jingling as it went in for a full-on bottom lick. Hattie rapped the glass hard with her knuckles. Goebbels paused mid-lick, raised its ugly mug at her with a look that said, 'What's your problem, bitch?' then disappeared into the night.

Johnny yawned dramatically, with Barry following suit. Hattie felt one creeping up on her – why were yawns so contagious? – and stifled it as best she could. Turning from the window, she saw Barry tugging on his coat.

'Hattie. Johnny. It's been great to see you both. I've an early start in the morning, so I'll bid you goodnight. I hope we can get together again soon?' Barry stepped towards Hattie, who hugged him a little longer this time. He shook hands with Johnny then departed. Hattie closed the door behind him, giving Goebbels a satisfying kick before he could strut into the hallway.

'I'll report you for cruelty to animals, Mum,' said Johnny, sloping up the stairs with another can of beer. Hattie locked and latched the door, ignoring the screech of annoyance from the cat.

'Sweetheart, that creature gives pets a bad name. I'd rather keep a rat than give house room to that feline monstrosity. Goodnight, sleep tight, don't let the bugs bite!'

CHAPTER 27

CAT HAD PICKED up her phone countless times, fingers poised to type out a text.

Sorry, Stewart, but won't make dinner after all. Something's come up. C

He'd booked a table at the Lemon Tree for this Friday evening. She'd agreed, still trying to convince herself it wasn't the stupidest idea ever. Stewart was an itch she couldn't help scratching. Each time she tried to formulate a message, said fingers failed to perform such a simple task. Her brain was screeching at them to get on with it, push the buttons instead of letting Stewart be the one to push hers.

'You are a weak and feeble woman, Cat Cooper,' she admonished herself. Hattie would be appalled if she knew her friend had agreed to meet up with her ex. To make matters worse, she'd also lied to Jamie. He'd met her at the salon as he often did if he didn't have after-school activities.

'Hey, how's it hanging, beautiful?' he'd asked, bounding in like an excited puppy. Even after all these months, Jamie's energy, zest for life and devotion to Cat never ceased to amaze her. Which made it all the worse she was planning on going behind his back. All she could cling to as a salve to her battered conscience was the belief she could set Stewart straight once and for all. Then he'd leave her alone to enjoy a life of calm and contentment.

Strolling back to her place, arm in arm, Cat listened as Jamie chatted about his day trying to generate enthusiasm among his students about the works of Jane Austen.

'I think her work is incredible and stands the test of time, but persuading a bunch of Netflix-obsessed seventeen-year-olds of her relevance today is no mean feat. Resorting to TV snippets of Colin Firth striding out of a lake might grab the girls' attention – and a couple of the boys' – but getting them to relate to the prose … nightmare.'

Reaching her home, Jamie rummaged in his pocket and produced his own key. Cat had given him one, a major step. Since she'd slammed the door on Stewart when their marriage ended, she'd regarded her house as her fortress. Impenetrable, safe and the one place she could be herself. Well, until Stewart had inveigled his way back in. That would never happen again. Ghostly Gary was always welcome – as long as he gave her some warning – Hattie had an all-access pass and her parents would never drop by unannounced. They never dropped by at all.

Once inside, Jamie had insisted on fixing her cheese on toast. Welsh rarebit without the Welsh bit. Cat sank into the sofa, unzipping her boots and wishing her guilt was as easily relieved. Sniffing a sock – phew, a bit stinky – she prepared her speech.

'Thanks so much. Just what the beauty therapist ordered.' As Cat took a bite of the snack, a strand of cheese stretched out and snagged on her chin. Scooping it up, she smiled as Jamie sat down beside her, lifting her feet on to his lap.

'So, this Friday night, a few of the crew from school are planning on hitting the high spots. Fancy joining us? They're dying to meet you. I've bigged you up, so you have to be there. Otherwise, they'll think I'm a sad fantasist. By the way, your feet are outdoing the cheese in the smelly stakes.'

'OK, much as I'd love to meet the crew, I'm going to have a late one at the salon. Tons of new stock to unpack, find homes for, and I really need an early night. Look at my eye bags. Hardly an advert for my business! I've been having really restless nights, Jamie. Sorry, think I'll have to bow out of this one.' Cat pushed her plate aside and snuggled up under Jamie's arm. She'd felt his hurt, a minuscule movement that spoke volumes. God, why was she doing this?

'Sure, I get it. I'll be on my way. Get yourself a good night's sleep and know I'm here. Cat, you know how I feel about you?' Jamie's face was a questionnaire, boxes to be ticked, answers dictating where they went next.

Cat had no answers, just a need to deal with what lay ahead and – once that was done – she could focus on the good bits. The happy bits.

'Yes, Jamie. I think I do. But I'm beyond tired. I'll call you soon. When everything's a bit more … settled.'

With a prolonged snog at the door, Cat moved to close it. But Jamie had to have the last word. Which she loved him for – oh, my God – did she just use the 'L' word?

'Sleep well. I mean it. Full-on snoring, erotic dreams, but only if they include me. Cat, just get some rest and I'll see you when you're up for it. I won't say any more, except …' Jamie pulled away, clearly itching to drop in a one-liner. 'How did the somnambulist climb Everest? She slept her way to the top.'

Friday evening came around faster than Cat would have liked. The day had been full-on with only a short break for a sandwich and a natter with Hattie. She was on tenterhooks too; burger night with Beth's uncle was fast approaching.

'I need my head examined, Cat. After the epic failure with

rotten Rich, I should just resign myself to a life of lonely widowhood.' She'd already filled Cat in on Gary's interference, and promise he wouldn't do it again. 'But I wouldn't put it past him; he's always had a wicked streak. Roger might end up wearing onion rings as earrings.'

When nudged about her own plans, Cat fudged her reply, garbling something about researching new products for the salon. Great. Now she'd lied to her best friend too. The sooner she saw Stewart and put him straight, the sooner she could get back to being her normal, truth-telling self.

* * *

'You choose, Catherine ... I mean, Cat. It's been a long time since I ate here.' Stewart was scanning the wine list and insisting she made the food selection. Out of sheer devilment – and to provoke the expected reaction – she opted for the most calorific starters and mains she could find.

'Right you are. Duck liver pâté with home-made toast, followed by gnocchi with a cream and truffle sauce. Ooh, and I could be tempted by the crème brûlée to finish. What do you think?' Cat waited for the withering look, the caustic remark. Neither were forthcoming. Stewart summoned the waiter, placed their order, and smiled at Cat. She returned the look, deep down wondering if Stewart had had a personality transplant. Or was a sociopath, something she'd looked up online during one of her darkest times post-breakup.

With the wine tasted, approved of and poured, Stewart raised his glass first. 'To us, Cat. New beginnings. And before you say anything ...' He reached over and pressed a finger against her gaping lips. 'I remember the last time we were here. How could I forget? I was a pig. Your parting speech was spot-on, even if I didn't appreciate it right away. By the time I did, it was far too late. All I can say in my feeble defence is that I loved you. From the moment I met you, dripping with rain at the bus stop. And I've never stopped—'

Stewart's soliloquy was halted by the arrival of their starters. Cat grabbed her cutlery and cut a slice of pâté, glad of the reprieve from the conversation. Not that she'd said very much, her head being stuffed with a jumble of words ranging from indignant to furious, perplexed to baffled. Don't stress, she told herself. Just get through the meal, make it clear she was happy with Jamie, and wish Stewart all the best. Job done.

'There's been no one else, a serious relationship, since we split up?' asked Cat. The waiter was now clearing away plates, ready for the mains. 'I just can't imagine you being on your own for long.' Unlike Cat, who'd taken years to contemplate seeing someone else seriously. Jamie had come along at the right time.

Stewart looked uncomfortable at her question. Seeing him squirm in his seat was akin to watching a politician being grilled about dodgy expense claims.

'There was a woman a couple of years ago, but she was desperate to start a family. Literally, within a few months she was cooing over prams and checking out good pre-schools in the area. In between, yes, I saw other women but never the right one.' There was that smile again, the one that could suck her into the abyss. Instead, Cat plunged her fork into a piece of gnocchi, letting out a low moan of delight at its decadent goodness.

A short while later, they were sharing the dessert, having decided one each was a gluttonous step too far. A spoonful for Stewart. A mouthful for Cat. Stewart signalling for her to take the last bite. All far too intimate and smacking of coupledom. Time for the bill.

Arriving back at Cat's, Stewart hopped out of the driver's

seat and hurried round to open the passenger door. He walked her up the path, waiting as she located her key.

'Thanks, Stewart. It was a nice evening. Maybe I'll see you around sometime.' Cat opened the door, then realised he was following her in. Oh, help!

'Look, just a quick coffee and I'll be on my way. Promise!' Against her better judgement, Cat nodded and went to the kitchen. *A quick coffee, then it's 'Hasta la vista, baby'.*

Seated side by side on the sofa, Cat flinched when Stewart dimmed the side light and moved inches closer to her. His thigh was now touching hers, and she hated the zing of long-buried attraction it caused.

'Stewart, I think it's time you …' Before she could continue, his arm had snaked around her neck and his mouth was hovering above hers. Damn her stupidity and double damn the fact he was kissing her. And she was kissing him back. Sliding downwards, she tried to resist but her traitorous lips were hell-bent on destruction. With some effort, she tried to push herself upright when …

'Hey, gorgeous! Just thought I'd drop by and see how my favourite lady was doing. I brought some …' Jamie's shadowy figure was freeze-framed in the doorway. He was clutching a paper bag and looked in need of blowing into it. Cat shoved Stewart aside and turned the table lamp up to its max. Catching the full extent of shock and sadness in Jamie's face, she wished she hadn't bothered.

'Jamie, I'm so sorry. It's not what it looks like, I promise!' Said every cheating, lying person ever caught in a compromising position. Stewart said nothing, just observed the situation calmly, legs crossed and arms folded across his chest.

Jamie took a step forward and placed the bag on the coffee table, along with his copy of Cat's key. He shook his head, eyes glistening, then left the room. The only sound was the front door closing behind him.

CHAPTER 28

As DAYS WENT, it hadn't been one of Hattie's finest. Maybe not on a par with losing Gary, but at least he was still around. No, the news her mum had shared with both her and Jack had knocked her sideways. Of course, she'd known deep down that Rachel was hiding something. She'd just never imagined – hadn't *allowed* herself to imagine – how serious that something was.

'Pancreatic cancer? Oh, Mum. That's not good. Oh, shit, I don't know what to say without sounding like an idiot. Come here.' Hattie had crushed herself against the woman who had raised her and Jack single-handedly, building a career and a life that ensured they'd wanted for nothing. Not just material things, but a sense of value, self-belief and that no obstacle was too hard to climb. And, most of all, a feeling of being loved unconditionally. If Rachel had ever fretted over Jack's sexuality or worried about Hattie's choices in men and career (Ha! What career?), she'd never voiced them. Now she was facing a challenge that would defeat lesser mortals, the obstacles ahead enough to defeat an Olympic athlete.

'Darling, I'm sorry I wasn't more open before, but until I had the tests, got the results … I didn't want to say what I was thinking until I knew it was real.' Rachel looked up at Ralph, who was standing behind her, hands massaging her shoulders. Hattie glanced at Jack. He was keeping it together, but only just. Rachel had already reeled off a bunch of numbers. A one-in-five chance of surviving a year or more; a seven percent chance of making it to five years.

'Yes, the odds are not in my favour. Understatement of the year!' Rachel laughed and Hattie was in awe of her resilience in the face of a brutal and unrelenting enemy within. She wasn't sure how she would cope with a similar diagnosis. Most likely by curling up into a ball and sobbing herself stupid. Perhaps her mum had already done that – comforted in privacy by Ralph – and now she was ready to face down the cancer. She explained that she'd just started a round of chemotherapy, a combination of different drugs, with the objective of shrinking the tumour.

'It's very early days, but so far I haven't felt too dreadful. Still eating well and hanging on to my hair!' Rachel patted her immaculately coiffed bob. After years of dyeing it, she'd let nature take its course, and it was now an elegant silver-grey. A perfect match for Ralph, and not only physically. Hattie didn't need to be a body language expert to see the closeness between them. The look on his face as Rachel continued explaining the treatment options was one of exquisite tenderness. *Gary used to look at me like that.* Well, he still did, but the 'being dead' part kind of got in the way of that lovin' feeling.

'What about the jaundice, Mum?' asked Jack, his wobbly voice belying his exterior calm. It was true Rachel's skin tone was yellow beneath a fine layer of make-up. 'Don't they have to deal with that first?'

It was Ralph who replied as Rachel got up and refreshed

the cups of tea she'd poured earlier. The great British cure-all. If only a pot of English breakfast could nuke rogue cells, thought Hattie. Not that the giant pharmaceutical companies would welcome that with open arms.

'Rachel has already had a stent inserted to deal with the blockage which causes the jaundice. The hope is that the chemo will eventually reduce the tumour to allow surgery to take place. So, her colour should improve, although I'm rather fond of my nickname for her!'

Both Hattie and Jack looked at Rachel, who mock tut-tutted in Ralph's direction.

'This charming man has taken to calling me "buttercup". Only in private, I'm glad to say!' She sat down again. Ralph joined her on the sofa and squeezed her hand.

'My dear, I do think it's an improvement on my first one. Isn't that right … custard face!'

A short while later, Hattie and Jack said their goodbyes. Jack started sobbing first, Hattie joined in and they wept and wailed their way along the road, ignoring the curious stares of passers-by. Hattie had just about regained her composure when they reached her home. Jack's shoulders still heaved as she went to kiss him on the cheek. Hang on a minute. He wasn't crying any more; he was laughing!

'What's so funny, little brother?' Hattie glowered at him, wondering what on earth he found amusing about the situation. Never had her own sense of humour felt more distant.

'Sorry, sis. I just thought of Ralph's first choice of a nickname for Mum and it cracked me up. Stupid, I know, but I guess a bit of levity isn't a bad thing right now. Finding some light in the darkness if you know what I mean.'

Hattie nodded slowly. Ralph's teasing manner and silly names were clearly good for Rachel. And she knew herself that seeing the funny side when life dumped on you was often the best medicine of all.

'D'you want to come in for a while? We could have more tea, or something a bit stronger.' Hattie wanted to lie down and pretend the past few hours hadn't happened, but she felt a duty to offer. Jack shook his head.

'Thanks, but I'll get going. I need to catch up on some work and fill Ben in. You know he adores Rachel, so it will be a shock for him too. Speaking of shocks, how's my other-worldly brother-in-law? When you see him, tell him we could do with another get-together. Ben's almost recovered, although I think he'll have a lifelong phobia about tablecloths.'

* * *

HATTIE SLIPPED OFF HER SHOES, pulled back the duvet and flopped onto the bed. She'd had three missed calls from Cat but didn't have the energy to ring her back. What she craved was sleep. Blissful, blackout slumber, all thoughts of illness and death set aside. To sleep, perchance to think of nothing.

'Babes. Wotcha doin' in bed with all your clothes on? Has the heating gone on the blink again?' Hattie kept her eyes closed. Death was only a heartbeat away or, in Gary's case, propped up on a pillow next to her. She loved him, always would, but there were times she needed to be alone. At least when he was alive, she knew his whereabouts. Pretty much. Now … he really picked his moments. Badly.

'Gary, it's been a tough day. I was just having a moment of introspection.' Hattie wearily turned on her side, opened her eyes and looked at the man she'd married. The one thought she'd grow old and wrinkly with. As it was, Hattie was convinced new lines were appearing on a weekly basis. The news about Rachel wasn't going to help matters.

'A moment of what? Ain't that a medical thing, like when they look up your bum?' Gary winked to show he was kidding. Hattie sighed, snuggled up closer and told him all about her mum, and what lay ahead.

'Oh, Hats. That's total crap. Sorry about my stupid joke, don't know when to keep my trap shut.' Gary smudged away a few stray tears leaking from Hattie's eyes. His touch was still fragile, like brushing against invisible cobwebs. Nevertheless, it comforted her, taking away some of the pain she felt inside.

'Let's talk about something else. Jack was asking for you, said Ben's over the shock, although it might be wise to give it some time before you pay them a visit.' Hattie gave Gary a stern look, knowing he would find it hard to resist scaring the pants off Ben again. Gary responded with his best 'I am deeply offended' expression.

'Any more exciting goings-on in the great hereafter?' Hattie couldn't bring herself to call it The Present, Clarence's preferred title. The guy sounded like a complete weirdo, judging by Gary's tales of gibberish talk and complete failure to explain anything. She hoped he wouldn't mention Marty again even though it broke her heart to think of him and his impossible request.

'Oh, sure. It's a right chuckle fest up there. Still, I've gained a couple of new mates. Not the kind I'd have chosen normally, but beggars can't be choosers.' Gary filled her in on Anna, the accident-prone granny with a never-ending supply of mint humbugs, and Bob. A builder – cue thigh-slapping hilarity – who'd met his maker when a cheaply installed section of scaffolding collapsed beneath him. By all accounts he was a miserable sod who teased Marty about his cuddly toy and derided Anna for trying to do 'a man's job'.

'Babes, I know you think the whole Marty thing is nuts, but what have you got to lose? You go there, explain things and if it doesn't work out? No harm done.'

Hattie sometimes wondered if the accident had not only

ended Gary's life but also addled his already befuddled brain. No harm done? She couldn't do it. She *wouldn't* do it. Why on earth would they believe her?

Doing that mind-reading thing again (God, she hated that), Gary rummaged under the pillow. Produced with a dramatic flourish worthy of Johnny on peak magic form a peculiar-looking object. Bloody hell, was that the President of the United States?

'This is Grump,' said Gary, looking pleased with himself. 'Take him with you and they'll believe you.'

CHAPTER 29

'IT'S a question of meeting the right one. I never did, but that's not to say she isn't out there somewhere. Probably lives in Tahiti, eh!' Roger winked at Hattie. Or maybe he didn't; one eye was constantly fluttering, a nervous tic which she found disconcerting. Not his fault, bless him. Nobody's perfect, but Hattie wished for the umpteenth time she hadn't agreed to meet him. One – she suspected she had more in common with virtually all the other men in the restaurant. Who looked vaguely normal and Gary-like. All chowing down on their burgers and swigging their drinks. And two – Roger was eyeing her like a double cheeseburger he'd like to swallow whole. With or without the onion rings.

'That was Wreckless Eric. Right? Going the whole wide world to find the person who matches?' Hattie thought that was a very expensive way of meeting The One. Circumnavigating the globe until you 'clicked'. She'd clicked with Gary when they were young, stupid and without passports. Were they just lucky? Or naïve, with no greater expectations beyond 'I like you; you like me. Let's see where this goes?' Theirs might not have been a love story worthy of putting into song, but she couldn't imagine spending the rest of her days with anyone else. Certainly not Wreckless Roger, now peeling gherkins from his burger. He'd gone for the quadruple stack with extra bacon, piquant sauce and a side of truffle-infused fries. The smell was wafting across the table, making Hattie feel queasy. Her veggie burger looked as appetising as a dried cow pat, the side salad swimming in oily dressing.

'Beth told me you lost your husband. Sorry … just thought I should get that out of the way. I think it's great you're moving on. A beautiful woman like you shouldn't be on her own for long.' Roger's eye did the faux wink thing again. Hattie attempted a smile but feared it was more of a grimace. Lost her husband? How she hated that phrase. As if she'd misplaced him, like a house key or a phone. Speaking of phones … Hattie discreetly tapped hers. Normally she hated people keeping their phones on the table when eating, but she was seriously worried about Cat. There'd been a string of texts, each one more fraught than the one before. The gist of it all was that Cat had been caught in a compromising position with Stewart – what the hell? – by Jamie. Who hadn't taken it well. Hattie hadn't taken it well either. Her best mate finds someone who worships her perfectly pedicured feet (and does a passable impression of a smitten kitten herself), then blows it by snogging her ex? Several words had come to mind when Hattie read the first hysterical message. *Idiot, moron, push-over, complete and utter marshmallow.* Then her heart had softened, like said marshmallow toasted over an open fire. Cat needed her, and much more than Roger. Despite his initial ogling, he was now intent on gobbling up every morsel of food on his plate. If she said a polite goodbye, he'd be ordering a slab of Mississippi mud pie before she reached the exit.

'Smart move, babes.'

Hattie's fingers twitched in shock as a familiar voice rang in her ear. The phone skittered across the table and landed on the floor with a sickening crunch. Roger looked up in surprise, a dribble of sauce coursing down his chin.

'Are you all right?' He eyed her warily as if afraid Hattie might leap from her chair and spear him with a pickle skewer. She didn't doubt she looked borderline deranged, with Gary hovering above the table like Tom Cruise in *Mission Impossible*. Without the wires. And invisible to everyone else.

'I'm ... fine. Just a bit of burger grease. Slippery hands. Let me clean up a bit.' Hattie cracked open a wet wipe and gave a showy display of swiping imaginary grease from her hands. She then bobbed her head up and down at Gary to signal he should join her under the table. Probably adding to Roger's suspicions that she had a screw loose.

'What are you doing here?' Hattie stage whispered, crouched uncomfortably by a table leg propped up by a folded beer mat. Luckily the burger joint piped out music loud enough to mask her mutterings. She spied her phone – the screen a mosaic of shattered glass – inches away. Roger's legs were visible too, snow-white flesh with a smattering of wiry hair peeping over the top of Bart Simpson socks.

'He's got matching Y-fronts,' offered Gary, now sitting cross-legged under the table. 'Never trust a man who co-ordinates his undies. That's just plain weird!'

And there was nothing at all weird about having a chat with your dead husband under a table in a bustling restaurant. Yep, that was normal, as was the discovery said ghostly spouse now seemed to possess the gift of X-ray vision. Hattie grabbed her phone and popped her head up.

'Sorry. Be with you in a minute. Think the battery came loose. Carry on without me!' Hattie flashed Roger her most winning smile. Part of her was cheesed off that he hadn't come to her help, but mostly she was relieved. He didn't look concerned, the lure of dessert more pressing than aiding a damsel in distress.

'Gary, I couldn't care less if he was wearing a latex bra and suspenders! You shouldn't be here. I told you; I can take care of myself.' It was Cat who needed help, thought Hattie. Time to wrap up the evening. A bollocking for Gary could wait. She cursed her creaking knees as she struggled to her feet. Roger was already tucking into a slab of pie, oblivious to all that had gone on beneath him.

'Didn't order for you, thought you might be one of those women who always decline dessert then sneak bits off someone else's plate,' he declared. 'But I asked for another spoon!'

As Hattie sat down, she felt a cool waft of air billow through her skirt. Gary had left the building. If only she could perform an equally speedy vanishing act.

'Roger, it's been lovely, but I couldn't eat another thing. And … the thing is … my best friend needs me right now. In fact, I should text her right away.' Hattie looked at her phone. Deader than dear Gary and with little chance of resurrection.

There followed a perfunctory haggle over how to split the bill. Roger caved in with what Hattie considered indecent haste when she offered to pay half (despite leaving most of her cow pat burger and passing on pudding).

'Shall we fix another date now, or wait until you get your phone fixed?' Roger did the winking thing again as he counted out notes and coins. No tip, Hattie noted. Gary had always been a generous tipper even if the service didn't warrant it.

'Erm, let's leave it for now. I've a lot on my plate but I'll be in touch.' A blatant lie, but Hattie didn't like to hurt people's feelings. There was nothing wrong with Roger; he was just a million miles from right. Maybe his perfect match was in French Polynesia, patiently weaving a hair garland and dreaming of a man with cartoon character undies.

* * *

PULLING up outside Cat's house, Hattie noted an unfamiliar car in the driveway. A flashy, expensive car with a personalised number plate. SH 1. No prizes for guessing who that belonged to. For a moment Hattie considered letting down the tyres or using her key to carve a rude message in the gleaming bodywork. No, she was an honest, law-abiding citizen. Who could cheerfully cause actual bodily harm to her best mate for letting that man cross the threshold.

Tiptoeing up the path, Hattie reached the front window. The curtains were partially drawn, only a side lamp casting scant light around the living room. She sidled closer, her heart thumping so hard she felt sure it was audible. No sign of anyone, but there were two coffee mugs on the table. Pressing her nose against the glass, she waited. Cat had been so upset; surely Stewart was only here so she could put him straight on what had been a massive error of judgement?

A minute later, and Hattie realised that Cat's slip-up was no one-off. Not unless her eyes were playing tricks on her. Nope, Cat and Stewart had wandered into the living room, looking for all the world like a loved-up couple. His arm draped around her shoulders, Cat looking completely at ease as she sank into the sofa. Now he was moving in closer, he was going to kiss her … *No! Don't do it. Abort, abort!* Unable to look away, Hattie raised her hand to rap on the window. Then lowered it again. It was none of her business. If Cat had taken Stewart back into her life, Hattie could do little. Except be there to pick up the pieces when it all fell apart again …

CHAPTER 30

THE CARRIAGE on the 9.20am train from King's Cross to Edinburgh was packed. Hattie found herself sandwiched between a beefy businessman with personal hygiene issues and a tattooed teenager engrossed in a game on his phone. His frantic finger activity was punctuated by loud cursing although he wasn't aware of the volume due to the head-phones encasing his ears. An older lady sitting opposite tutted every time an expletive burst forth and looked ready to clunk him over the head with her walking stick.

Sipping her lukewarm latte, Hattie wondered for the umpteenth time what she was doing. Heading north on a fool's errand, to persuade a grieving couple to try for another baby. A piece of paper was tucked in the front compartment of her handbag. It contained both their names and address: *Flora & David McMaster, 59 Cumberland Street.* A quick Google search revealed that their home was within walking distance of Edinburgh's main station, Waverley. Their phone number was unlisted, not that Hattie thought calling in advance was a great idea. Hell, as ideas went, the whole thing was ludicrous.

It had been a week since Gary played his trump card (oh, how he'd slapped his thighs in mirth at *that* little pun). As it turned out, it wasn't a voodoo effigy of the man himself, but Marty's favourite toy. Which was now packed away in Hattie's overnight bag, perched above her head on the luggage rack. Quite how Marty had taken Grump to the afterlife with him was something Hattie couldn't get her head around. Not that she could make sense of anything regarding Gary, Marty, Clarence and Co. She'd given up trying a long time ago.

With almost four hours until she reached her destination, Hattie had ample time to reflect on recent events. She was still processing her mum's news. Shocking as it was, she drew comfort from Ralph's presence in Rachel's life. Whatever the future held, Hattie was sure he'd be with her every painful and uncertain step of the way.

Johnny had once again showed his new maturity when she told him about his grandmother's diagnosis. He'd hugged Hattie so tightly she feared a rib would pop then rang Rachel to offer any help she needed.

'Food shopping, gardening, even toilet scrubbing. Just say the word, and I'll be there like a shot, Nan,' he'd said. Hattie felt her heart ping with pride although she had never witnessed Johnny *actually* cleaning a toilet. Leaving them a health and hygiene risk was his usual modus operandi. How he could display remarkable dexterity when shooting down villains on Play Station yet miss the toilet bowl by inches when peeing was another of life's mysteries.

'A tuna wrap, please.' She delved into her purse as a chirpy young chap appeared wheeling a trolley laden with snacks and drinks. Body odour man shrugged off his suit jacket and rummaged in the breast pocket and a wave of stale sweat assaulted Hattie's nostrils. He ordered a blue-berry muffin and a tea, and the rest of the carriage either shook their heads or ignored the steward. Hattie peeled away the cling film and picked out the slivers of cucumber. She hated cucumber, almost as much as she hated celery. Cat, however, adored both and was always trying to convince Hattie of their health benefits, particularly in a veggie smoothie …

As the train trundled along, Hattie's thoughts shifted to her friend. They hadn't spoken since Hattie had witnessed Cat getting far too intimate with Stewart. Creeping around like a deranged stalker wasn't something Hattie was proud of, or keen to confess. She'd picked up a replacement phone the day after seeing Roger and sent a curt message:

Not sure what to say. Apart from WTF? Away for a few days. H

After sending it, Hattie felt bad. Cat was her best friend; surely she should make her a priority instead of taking a trip that could only end in tears? She'd voiced her concerns to Gary, who'd argued that Cat was a grown-up and able to make her own decisions.

'I'm with you one hundred percent, babes. Stewart is a bad un but maybe she needs to figure that out again by herself. And if she loses Jamie in the meantime … that's too bad. Marty ain't got anyone else he can turn to. It's down to us. Well, you.'

Yes, it was down to Hattie. To explain the inexplicable and make the wishes of an eight-year-old come true. She'd booked herself a single room in a cheap hotel for three nights, not knowing if the McMasters would be at home but giving herself time to see them. Part of her hoped they weren't there, that she could return home with a clear conscience. *I gave it a shot, Gary, but it wasn't meant to be.* Another, painful part, wanted to see it through. Say the words, produce the evidence, and see where it led.

Hope your trip goes well. Always nice to catch up with old friends! Let me know when you're back. Seeing you was a tonic. Let's do it again soon. Best wishes. Barry

Hattie smiled at the text that had just arrived. They'd messaged a few times since their get-together with Johnny. Nothing profound, just an exchange of trivia. She'd claimed to be visiting mates from years ago. People she'd hooked up with again through Facebook, who'd begged her to come and stay. Complete and utter nonsense but how could she tell the truth? Hattie swallowed the last bite of her wrap and composed a reply:

Nearing destination. Thermal knickers at the ready! Should be fun, will be in touch soon. H x

The kiss was added without thinking. Wasn't it? She'd omitted a kiss in her message to Cat, but that was because she was mad at her. She had no reason to be mad at Barry, but did their tentative friendship warrant such a sign-off? Hattie deleted it, adding a smiley face instead.

She jolted awake as the announcement said they were approaching Haymarket station. The next stop was Waverley, and the end of the line. Hattie stretched and twisted her neck from side to side. She'd fallen asleep at an uncomfortable angle, but thankfully not on the shoulder of either of her travelling companions. Beefy man was putting on his jacket, teen gamer still glued to his screen. The train slowed to a halt, and several passengers prepared to get off. Hattie seized the chance to reach up for her bag. She let out an involuntary groan at a sharp pain in her left side, caused by her contorted snooze.

'Are you OK? Here, let me get that for you.' The tattooed one had removed his headphones and sprang to his feet. Hattie thanked him as he handed down her bag. It was a well-worn black leather number, bought in the early days of marriage. No wheels, just a shoulder strap, but Hattie was travelling light.

Minutes later, they arrived at Edinburgh's main station. Hattie stepped down on to the platform and looked right then left, unsure which direction to follow. Before she could locate the map she'd printed out from the internet, her young helper was by her side.

'Just visiting? I know the city pretty well, so if I can help …?' He had a soft Geordie accent, and a grin that put Hattie at her ease. She pulled out the map, then staggered forward as a heavyweight suitcase clipped her ankles. Righting herself, she watched as beefy man strode away, leaving a trail of BO in his wake.

'Jeez, that one was a bit ripe, eh!' Her would-be guide slung Hattie's bag over his shoulder with ease, his own back-pack already secured in place. 'My name's Tom and I'm a third-year medical student at the uni. Let's have a look.' He squinted at the map, the address circled in red ink. 'Easy peasy, a ten-minute walk and we'll be there.'

Hattie introduced herself, stammering that there was no need, she could find it herself. Tom was having none of it.

'It's a pleasure to help. I remember what it was like when I moved here. Took me ages to settle, missed my mum like you wouldn't believe. Not that I ever told her that. She's just so chuffed I'm going to be a doctor. Doesn't even mind when I bring my laundry home. And she irons it!'

Hattie couldn't decide who Tom reminded her of most. A young Gary, with his swagger and chat, tattoos and the biggest of hearts. Or Johnny, striding out into the world, making his mark. Maybe not in medicine, but by making people gasp, laugh and marvel at a bit of magic. Everybody had a part to play, no matter how small or insignificant.

'Here we are. Cumberland Street. What was the number again?' Lost in her reverie, Hattie hadn't realised they'd arrived. Now they had, she wanted to retrace her steps, board another train, and head for home.

'It's 59. Over there. The black door with the gold knock-er.' The knocker she didn't want to knock. The door she didn't want to open.

'OK. If you're all good, Hattie. Hope your friends are stoked to see you. I'll head off now. Great to meet you. Take care.' And with a wave of his hand, headphones back in place, Tom disappeared from view and from her life.

This was it. The moment she'd been dreading. Hattie cursed herself for not dropping her bag at the hotel first. If she had, she'd have bottled it completely. Plus, Grump would never have fitted in her handbag. Speaking of which ... Hattie peered inside it to check that another piece of paper was still there. It was.

Deep breaths. One foot in front of the other. She approached the door, her rational mind screaming *run, run!* It was as if an invisible force was propelling her forward, but not the ghostly hand of Gary. Terrified as she was, Hattie knew she needed to see this through. For Marty's sake.

She knocked once, very gently. There was no sign of a doorbell. No response. Again, twice, and with more force. Movement inside. Footsteps approaching. Hattie swallowed hard, her mouth dry. The door opened, and she was face-to-face with a woman she assumed was Marty's mum.

'Can I help you?' The woman was tall, slim and perfectly made up. She wore navy-blue leggings and a loose-fitting white shirt. Thick, dark hair was tied back in a ponytail. Everything shouted middle-class, thirty-something suburban housewife/ businesswoman. Except ... there were dark shadows under her eyes, which narrowed as she clocked Hattie's black bag.

'I'm not selling anything, I promise. Or spouting religious stuff. I just ... you are Mrs McMaster? Flora McMaster?' Hattie thought it wise to check she had the right person. For all she knew, Marty might have muddled up the address, and she'd make an even bigger fool of herself.

'I am. And you are …?' Flora McMaster folded her arms, one foot nudging the door towards Hattie.

'I'm Hattie Hastings. Look, I'm really sorry to bother you. Now I'm here I don't know where to begin but, please believe me, I have something important to tell you. Something you need to know.' Hattie's tongue was glued to the roof of her mouth. Her words sounded slurred. Great, Flora probably thought she was drunk.

'Listen, Mrs Hastings, I'm rather busy at the moment so if you could get to the point?' The door inched closed another fraction. It was now or never.

'It's about … I have something to tell you about … Marty.'

Beneath her carefully applied make-up, Flora McMaster's skin changed colour. From light beige to alabaster. She tightened her arms further, but the door's progress was halted.

'What about … my son? I can't imagine what a total stranger might have to say to me. I don't know you, do I? Did you work at the hospital, is that it?'

Hattie sent a silent prayer up to whoever might be listening. If it was only Gary, well, she could do with an ounce of his bravado right now.

'No, I didn't. But I know someone who knows him and I have a message for you.'

Hattie had no idea what thoughts were passing through Flora's mind at that moment. She didn't know what she looked like – deranged, deluded or desperate. There was a pause and then …

'I think you'd better come in.'

THE HAUNTING OF HATTIE HASTINGS

PART THREE

CHAPTER 31

HATTIE STEPPED over the threshold of the McMasters' home. Every nerve end was on red alert, instinct screaming at her to make an excuse and get out. Head to the hotel where she could calm herself with a strong drink before returning home.

'Come through here.' Flora McMaster gestured to an open door on the right of the hallway. Hattie entered what was clearly the main living room. Large with high ceilings and beautifully furnished, it was everything Hattie's own shabby suburban home wasn't. The McMasters weren't short of a penny, of that she was sure, but no amount of money could compensate for their loss.

'Can I get you a tea or a coffee, Mrs Hastings?' Her cheeks were now a healthier colour, but Flora was agitated, twisting her hands together in a wringing motion. Hattie was stunned that she'd invited her in, and was offering refreshments like the perfect hostess.

'Tea would be lovely, thank you. And please, call me Hattie.' The normal response of 'call me Flora' was not forthcoming. She wasn't surprised. This was hardly a normal social situation.

Left alone, Hattie placed her bags by the window and wandered over to the ornate fireplace. Traces of ash and a partially burned log suggested it had been lit recently. Lined up on the mantelpiece was a selection of photos, each displayed in tasteful distressed silver frames. Her own photo frames were more bargain basement, often forgotten completely, the images propped up on cheap cardboard mounts or stuck to the walls with Blu Tack. She picked one up. A picture of a brown-eyed boy, pulling a face. Marty. Hattie's heart tightened. She put it back, picked up another. Flora, radiating happiness, beside her a man who must be her husband, David. Their wedding photo. The two of them captured in a moment of harmony. He looked older, maybe by ten years, but his expression said it all. Devotion, maybe a touch of disbelief that this stunning younger woman had chosen to marry him? For there was no doubt that Flora was – and had been – a knock-out. At a guess, a decade had passed since the picture was taken but she still had looks that would turn heads. Whereas, David … he was pleasant enough looking, but paunchy with thinning hair and a receding chin. Hattie chastised herself for being so judgemental. Who knew what drew people to one another? Gary was an attractive man, in a grungy, 'don't care' way. Never one for fancy clothes or frippery, what you saw was what you got. Hattie fancied him rotten from the moment she met him. He made her laugh, he made her feel special and – even when he drove her up the wall – she loved him to bits. She still loved him, and whatever happened, she always would.

'What are you doing?' Flora's voice startled Hattie. She fumbled with the photo, almost dropping it. With shaking hands, she put it back in its rightful position.

'I'm sorry. I was just being nosy. That's me, always putting my foot in it. Lovely photos. I guess that's your husband, and that's ... Marty?'

Flora placed a tray of tea and biscuits on the coffee table. The rattle of cups and spoons betrayed her own shakiness. 'Yes, that's David. And Marty. But I assume you already know this. You seem to know things about us, but I have no idea who you are or why you're here. So, if you could explain?'

Hattie's mouth was still impossibly dry. She watched nervously as Flora poured the tea. If she didn't sit down, she might fall over. A moss green armchair beckoned, and Hattie lowered herself into it. She shook her head at the proffered milk and sugar. Strong and black. That was what she needed.

Flora took a chair opposite. She seemed more composed, a cup of tea in her hand. The silence in the room was oppressive. The ticking of an ornate carriage clock, the only sound. Apart from the thudding of Hattie's heart.

'Mrs McMaster. Flora.' Hattie couldn't deliver her news on such formal terms. Somehow, in some way, she needed to forge a connection if she was to have any chance of being believed. 'What I have to tell you won't be easy to hear. It's not easy to say, but I've travelled a long way to see you because I think it's something you need to know.'

Flora said nothing. Outside a car tooted its horn, and faint voices passed by the window. Hattie drank some tea. Still too hot, but it eased the dryness in her mouth.

'The thing is ... the reason I'm here is ... my husband died. In an accident. Except, he came back. I mean, he just appeared one evening. As a ghost.' Great. As openers went that one was an absolute winner. Not.

Flora's reaction was to not react at all. She sipped her tea and waited for Hattie to continue. Which she did.

'Trust me, I never in a million years expected that. I didn't believe in life after death. Nor did Gary – that's his name – but there he was. Not much different, just a bit fluffier around the edges. Squidgy, you could say.' Hattie wished she'd prepared a script, because everything coming out of her mouth was paving the way to an abrupt exit.

'Right. Let's be clear, here. You're saying that your husband died – and I'm sorry to hear that – then he returned. Forgive me, but I'm struggling to get my head around that. David and I ... well, we're occasional church goers. I should say, non-church goers now, but that's because the last time we went to church was when ... when we buried Marty.'

The mask of calm crumbled, Flora's face disintegrating piece by piece. Lips puckered, eyebrows plummeted, eyes filled with tears that battled to stay contained but lost the war. Hattie wanted to breach the space between them, hug this woman who'd lost her only child. But, she couldn't. She had to continue the story, explain the connection between Gary and Marty.

'So, up in heaven or wherever he happens to be when he's not paying a visit, he met someone. He met Marty. Not straight away, but after some time. They've, well they've kind of become friends. That's why he – Marty – asked if I would come and see you. To tell you something.'

Flora's face was a mixture of agony and incomprehension. The tears still fell unchecked, a balled-up tissue in her lap. Hattie was sure it was only her deep distress that stopped her from telling her to leave. She wanted to leave, but now she'd started ...

'Flora, I know that what I'm saying sounds insane. When Gary first came back, I thought I was losing it. No one else could see him and I couldn't get anyone to believe me. Why would they? But I swear it's true. And now my friend Cat and my brother Jack and his partner have seen him too.'

Getting to her feet, Flora walked to the fireplace and picked up the photo of Marty. She stared at it for several seconds, then put it back down. When she spoke, facing away from Hattie, her voice was tremulous but clear.

'Even if I choose to believe you – and I have every reason not to – what could you possibly have to tell me that would make Marty's death easier to bear? I don't know you, Mrs Hastings, and whatever you say can never mend the hole in my heart. In fact, coming here has added to my pain which I know will always be with me. Do you have children? Yes? Then you'll understand that losing a child is your worst fear. And when it happens, your whole world collapses. He was so little. My precious boy. He was only—'

'Eight. I know. My son, our son, is in his twenties. And there's nothing I wouldn't do to keep him safe. But terrible things happen, every day, to good people. My only comfort is to know that there's something out there, at least for those like Gary and Marty. I don't understand how any of this works, why Gary can visit me but Marty can't visit you, but I'm here to pass on a message. If you want me to leave, I'll go. But please, just let me finish.' Hattie's voice trembled. Flora turned to look at her. It was time. Hattie went over to the window and picked up her bag. Unzipping it, she pushed aside her toiletry bag and change of clothing. Nestled beneath was the one thing – or rather, the first thing – that might persuade Flora to keep listening. Carefully, slowly, she wrestled it from the bottom of the bag and brought it close to her chest.

'What's that? Wait ... it can't be. How did you get that? Tell me. How did you get that?' Flora lunged towards Hattie, who passed Grump to her. Flora seized the toy like a drowning man clutching a lifebuoy. She stroked its hair, straightening up its crumpled tartan trousers.

'This is ... was ... Marty's favourite toy. He took it every-where with him. When he ... when he died, we couldn't find it. The hospital staff searched for it, but it was gone. They said probably one of the cleaners had accidentally binned it. It's stupid, but I felt like another piece of Marty had been snatched away.' Flora cradled Grump in her arms as a mother would cradle her new born.

'Gary gave it to me. Marty wanted you to have it. To have him. As proof that what I'm saying is true. Please, Flora, hear me out. There's more—'

Before Hattie could continue, Flora tossed Grump on to her chair. She glared at Hattie, now dry-eyed but vibrating with emotion.

'There must be hundreds if not thousands of toys just like this one. How do I know this isn't a sick joke? Although why anyone would want to do such a thing ... I don't know what to think. I can't deal with this on my own. My husband, David, is at work but he'll be finishing earlier tomorrow. I need to talk to him and – if you have more to say – you can say it to both of us.'

CAT WAS HURT. She knew she should be more open with Hattie about the situation with Stewart, but her good friend seemed to be ignoring her completely. Aside from one short text – which she hadn't understood – she'd heard nothing. And where had she gone for a few days? Cat and Hattie shared everything. Well, *almost* everything.

Stewart was on his way over. A couple of weeks had passed since she'd been caught kissing him by Jamie. Much as she wanted to, she couldn't heap all the blame on Stewart. Cat had responded, common sense overruled by baser instincts. She'd told him to leave straight after and tried to call Jamie. He didn't pick up, nor did he respond to any of her messages. To make matters worse, Stewart had returned the next night. He'd apologised but the words didn't match his actions. It was clear he thought they could make another go of it.

'Come on, Cat. We had lots of good times, didn't we? I learned a huge lesson when you left me and I would never treat you so badly again.' Despite her protests, he cooked them supper and listened intently as she talked about the salon and its growing success. The only sticky moment was when Stewart put his arm around her on the way into the living room. Breathing in his familiar scent, Cat's resolve wavered again. But when he moved in for a kiss … that was too much too soon. She turned aside, his lips landing on her cheek. Unfazed, Stewart said goodnight and left. Leaving Cat in a state of inner turmoil.

'Never thought I'd say this, but you disappoint me.' Cat put down her blusher brush and swivelled round from the dressing table. Gary stood in the doorway, looking disappointed. Cat swallowed hard. Gary had always been on her side as had Hattie. Now? Was she destined to screw up her life in an endless loop of dumb decisions and wrong turns? No, wait a minute, this was *her* life and how she chose to conduct it was her business.

'Gary, good to see you. I assume you're referring to Stewart. Who, by the way, I'm not seeing again. OK, technically, I *am* seeing again, but we have a history. I'm trying to close things off but I still have feelings for him.' Which were, what exactly? If you loved someone once, if they'd occupied your every waking moment, could you switch off all your feelings just like that? Yes, it had been more than eight years since Cat took the decision to end their marriage. It was the right thing to do. Stand up for herself, refuse to be moulded into a Stewart-approved version. So why was she letting him slink back into her life?

Gary came over and placed his hands on her shoulders. Cat stared down at the patch of carpet beneath the chair where she'd spilled nail polish remover. If only she could erase her lingering feelings for Stewart as efficiently as the liquid had removed the colour.

'You were the one who said he might be telling the truth! Remember, the first time – sorry, the second time – you appeared. You asked if I was sure he was lying when he said he'd never met anyone who matched up to me.'

Gary scratched his head, leaving a tuft of hair standing on end. He looked at Cat's reflection in the mirror. Cat was relieved to see *his* reflection. Was it just vampires that couldn't be seen in mirrors? Not that vampires existed, except in folklore. Ghosts, on the other hand ...

'The old memory ain't as sharp as it used to be, darlin', but I'm pretty sure I mentioned manure. As in, old Stewie boy was talking shit. You said yourself he was lying. And what about the new kid on the block? Jimmy, right?'

Cat gave up on her make-up and nudged Gary aside. She knew that agreeing to see Stewart again this evening was a mistake. She seemed incapable of anything else at the moment.

'His name's Jamie and I'm sure Hattie filled you in on the golden moment he walked in on me and Stewart. Stop looking at me like that! We're not getting back together, it's just ... I see glimpses of the old Stewart, the one I fell in love with. Like the nasty bits have been taken away, and there's a new, improved version. Or rather, the person I thought he was.'

Her outfit for the evening lay on the bed. Gary picked up the low-cut blouse and held it against his chest. Despite her inner turmoil Cat giggled at the sight of him posing with a clingy, silk shirt against his battered T-shirt. For good measure Gary pouted like Naomi Campbell in her heyday.

'Cat, getting your bazookas out ain't entirely sending Stewart an off-limits message. More like a green light to pass go and collect whatever you get in Monopoly money these days. Is it still 200 bucks or whatever? You're worth a lot more than that, buddy.'

Cat didn't feel she was worth much right now. She'd hurt Jamie, something she deeply regretted, Gary thought she was selling herself short, and Hattie wasn't talking to her. Speaking of whom …

'Where's Hattie? I know she's pissed off at me. I got a message saying she was away for a few days, but that's been it.' If she could speak to her best friend, Cat felt she'd gain a better perspective. Or receive a tirade of abuse. Either way, she needed to talk to her.

Gary mimed zipping his mouth. God, that man was infuriating! Fine for him to drop by uninvited, but heaven forbid he reveals his wife's whereabouts.

'No can tell, Cat. She's on an important mission, that's all I can say. She'll be back in a couple of days. Anyhow, I've got that tingly feeling which means I have to love you and leave you. Behave yourself and … ditch the blouse.' Gary shimmered briefly then – whoosh – he was gone.

Cat picked up the blouse, rammed it back into the wardrobe, and pulled out a long-sleeved, high-necked T-shirt from a drawer. She got dressed, slapped on some mascara and squirted herself with perfume.

Stewart arrived ten minutes later. He greeted Cat with a kiss on each cheek and a box of baked goodies from the local patisserie. Another out-of-character gesture. The old Stewart frowned on anything sugary, so Cat had been reduced to sneaking in a secret éclair or cupcake when out with Hattie or home alone.

'Thanks. I'll stick the kettle on and we can tuck into these. How was your day?' Stewart currently worked for a small investment bank in London which he said was less pressured than his time in Switzerland.

'Somewhere between dull and boring. What about you? It's great business is going so well. If you ever want to expand – open another salon or whatever – I'd be happy to put some money in.' Stewart was completely at home, opening cupboards and locating mugs, plates and cutlery.

Cat tossed a couple of tea bags in the pot and added water. It was all too weird, the pair of them acting like an old married couple. Enquiring how their respective days had gone, sharing tea and cakes and now Stewart was offering to invest in her business. She needed to get a grip, but how? Her mother had called out of the blue the other day, her carefully enunciated words suggesting that a few gins had passed her lips. And it was just after midday. Taken aback at this rare occurrence, Cat made the mistake of mentioning Stewart's reappearance.

'Catherine, that's wonderful! You shouldn't have let him get away. A good man is hard to find. I was so lucky to meet your father and we managed to stick it out, even through the tough times. It's all very well throwing in the towel at the slightest thing but you're not getting any younger …'

Yes, Cat could always rely on her parents to make her feel worse. She hadn't told them a thing about Jamie. There'd been no point. Nothing she did impressed them. On the rare occasions they spoke, they showed little interest in the growth of the salon. Reg and Ann Cooper lived in a suburban bubble, always striving to keep up with the Joneses or what-ever their neighbours'/golf partners/social circle happened to be called. Having a beauty therapist daughter with a failed marriage wasn't something they cared to brag about.

'Stewart, I need to email a few suppliers this evening so … thanks for the offer, but I'm fine right now. If I could just get on and see you again some time.' Cat downed her tea. If he was taken aback by her abruptness, Stewart didn't let it show. He saw his own way out, no kisses this time, just another blistering smile.

Cat half-heartedly dealt with the emails, periodically checking her phone to see if there was anything from Hattie or Jamie. Nothing. She sent off another text to Jamie.

I won't pester you anymore, just wanted to say again how sorry

I am. I'm in a bit of a muddle but what we had was special. I never meant to hurt you. C xx

She didn't expect a reply. An hour later, getting into bed, her phone beeped. Cat expected it to be Stewart. It wasn't.

It's fine. I get it. You and your ex have history. I just thought ... Well, it doesn't matter now. Wishing you only good things. J

Cat put her phone on silent, thumped the pillow – hard – and prayed for sleep to come quickly.

CHAPTER 33

'WILL you two stop whispering behind my back. I have cancer, I'm not deaf!' Rachel fixed Jack and Ben with a disapproving stare. They'd taken her to the local garden centre to pick up a few plants and bits after Rachel had complained her garden was looking too drab.

'Sorry, Mum. We don't want you overdoing it, that's all. Ben can push the trolley, can't you, Ben? He's been working out at the gym recently. If you look really hard, you might spot a bicep.' Jack winked at Ben, who flexed his right arm Popeye-style.

In truth, Rachel felt exhausted, but she wasn't one for taking to her bed, apart from at bedtime. For the past few weeks she was rarely alone when it was time to sleep. Ralph hadn't moved in, exactly, but he came around most evenings. Usually they just ate, chatted or watched TV. He accompanied her on her visits to the hospital and they slept together, his arms encircling Rachel until she got too hot or uncomfortable. And they made love. Not every night, but when the mood was right, and they both needed the solace it brought. Rachel enjoyed it, but what she loved most was the feeling of joy it brought her. The sense of being alive and sticking a metaphorical finger up at the disease which threatened to end her days.

'Do you want the pink ones and the red ones? I'd go for the purple myself but I know what an old stick-in-the-mud you are.' Jack hadn't a clue when it came to flower species. When he and Hattie were little Rachel had tried to educate them, taking picnics out to the garden. She'd patiently explained the difference between annuals and perennials, the importance of pruning and fertilising. Hattie was more interested in pulling worms out of the soil and dissecting them with her trowel. Jack just looked bored and demanded more ginger beer and cake. Very Famous Five.

With the boot of Jack's car loaded, they headed back to Rachel's. A short drive, but she felt her eyes droop and did the head bob thing. In the driver's seat Jack looked across several times, until Rachel scolded him. 'Keep your eyes on the road or I won't be the only one knocking at the pearly gates!' Ben burst out laughing and Jack stuck his tongue out at Rachel. Both were familiar with her dark sense of humour, even more pronounced since the diagnosis. Hattie and Ralph were familiar with it too, but Rachel toned it down when with her lifelong friend, Alice. Any mention of death – specifically Rachel's – had her sobbing inconsolably.

'We'll stick these out in the garden and let you have a lie-down,' said Jack. Ben poured Rachel a glass of chilled water from the fridge which she gulped down gratefully. She felt slightly brighter, the cheeky banter between Jack and Ben helping to perk her up.

'I'm fine, darling. I think I'll work on a few sketch ideas and let you two get on with the rest of your day. Any plans?'

'Nah,' replied Ben, pinching a banana from Rachel's fruit bowl. 'We'll probably kick back with a couple of beers and binge-watch a box set. Jack's desperate to revisit *The X Files*, only because he fancies Scully something rotten.'

Rachel wasn't a big TV fan, preferring to read or draw in her spare time. She was familiar with *The X Files*, although anything featuring aliens, ghosts or monsters definitely wasn't her preferred genre.

'Correct me if I'm wrong, but wasn't Scully the female?' she asked. 'I thought the male lead was called – ooh, it's on the tip of my tongue – Mouldy or something like that.' Ben tossed the banana skin in the bin, and gave Rachel a hug.

'Almost. It's Mulder and Gillian Anderson plays Scully. Jack reckons she's the only woman on the planet who could persuade him to switch sides. Which would leave me bereft, but I reckon the odds of them meeting are not in his favour.'

With the pair of them gone, plants and pots lined up neatly outside, Rachel made her way to the bedroom where she worked on her children's book designs. The last one, about spiders undergoing an image revamp, had gone down well. So well, she'd been commissioned another by the same publisher. This time about the plight of hedgehogs in the UK. Once a common sight in British gardens, the prickly creatures' numbers had declined from 30 million in the 1950s to around one million today. Rachel remembered a young Hattie's excitement when she spotted one sniffing around outside. They'd fed it tinned cat food (Rachel had read somewhere that milk and bread was bad for them) and Hattie had named it Prickles.

Pencil in hand, Rachel began sketching a rough outline of a hedgehog clad in a woollen coat. Only half her mind was on the drawing, the rest was thinking of Hattie. She seemed to be coping better with Gary's death, but still Rachel worried about her. She'd been happy when Hattie went on a couple of dates – even if they'd been disasters – and delighted how supportive Johnny had become. Now, however, she'd disappeared on some mysterious trip to goodness knows where. She'd refused to discuss it, mumbled something about seeing friends, and her brief phone calls were just that – brief. Neither Jack nor Johnny had a clue what she was up to. At least, Johnny appeared totally clueless, but Jack had the demeanour of someone hiding something. Rachel always knew when he was fibbing, or not telling the whole truth. Jack would fiddle with his left ear lobe, a habit she'd first picked up on when he was a little boy, and swore blind he'd eaten his Brussel sprouts. Which she later found secreted at the back of the fridge, alongside a mound of shrivelled peas. Hattie was much harder to read. Like mother, like daughter.

Rachel scrunched up the piece of paper. Horatio the hedgehog looked more like a toilet brush than a cute animal. Was she losing her touch? She massaged her temples, the start of a headache nudging at the periphery of her vision. Going to the bathroom, she popped a couple of tablets from their protective film and swallowed them dry. Bad idea. One stuck in her throat and made her gag. Rachel leaned over the sink, turned on the tap, and scooped water into her mouth. The irony of nearly vomiting on a paracetamol when several rounds of chemo had not once made her feel sick. She knew she was one of the lucky ones, at least so far. If they could blast the tumour sufficiently to allow an operation … Rachel didn't allow her thoughts to stray along that path. One tiny step at a time. *Que sera, sera.*

The doorbell ringing interrupted her. It couldn't be Ralph; he wasn't coming round until later. Perhaps it was a parcel delivery. Some proof copies of her recent books.

'Surprise!' Johnny thrust a bunch of tulips into Rachel's hand. Slightly droopy and unwrapped, suggesting he might have pinched them from a neighbour's garden. Putting them to one side, she accepted his twenty-something version of a hug. Limp arms barely making contact, head swivelled to one side to avoid lipstick marks on the cheek.

'Indeed it is, Johnny. But lovely to see you and thank you for the flowers.' Rachel led the way to the kitchen, Johnny shuffling behind her in a pair of trainers that gaped at the toes, sole and upper separating like the mouth of a mutant fish. He was so similar to Gary, in terms of paying little regard to outward appearance. But Rachel knew that his heart was generous. Hattie and Gary had raised a son to be proud of, and she counted her own blessings having him as a grandson. So many of her friends – Alice included – barely saw their grandchildren. Or their children, come to think of it. Time-strapped, financially struggling, too wrapped up in their own world to spare much thought for those who'd brought them into it. The forgotten, neglected generation. Fumbling with smartphones and iPads, in the hope they can connect for a few minutes with their offspring, who go through the motions. *All OK? Eating well? What's new?* Then, clearly relieved when the answers are positive, shutting down their devices and moving on.

'Just wanted to check in with you, see if there's anything I can do. The boss is out of town for a few days – like Mum – so I closed up a bit early. Hey, you don't think Mum and Mr Ravenscroft are having a thing? No, that would so not be happening.' Johnny visibly shuddered at the thought of Hattie and his employer getting intimate. Rachel thought it highly unlikely. She'd met Richard Ravenscroft on a couple of occasions and found him charming but decidedly odd.

'Darling, that's so sweet. Actually, I'm feeling a bit peckish so if you could rustle up a sandwich? And one for yourself, of course.'

Rachel sat as Johnny bustled around, slicing bread and pulling out ham, cheese and pickle from the fridge. He whistled as he worked, an air of contentment surrounding him.

Rachel reflected that he'd come a long way in recent months. Stepping up to the mark after his dad's death, finding a job, carrying responsibility on his narrow shoulders. Although ... could there be another reason he seemed so upbeat?

'Delicious,' pronounced Rachel, savouring a large bite. 'I don't know why, but even the simplest of food tastes better when someone else has made it. Now, tell me what's new with you. The job's clearly going well. Running the show single-handed, and I heard from your mum that you might be going on a training course?'

Johnny nodded enthusiastically, explaining that Mr Ravenscroft had booked him on a short course in London to expand his magic skill set. 'He's picking up the tab for the lot. Including two nights in a hotel and my travel costs. Pretty awesome, huh?' Making a second sandwich – Rachel declined – he went on to say that he'd met up with Gary's friend Barry a couple of times since their get-together with Hattie. 'He's a great guy, even if he trounces me at snooker. I think he's a bit lonely, to be honest, but he has some great stories about him and Dad. Stuff that makes me smile instead of feeling sad.'

Rachel knew how that felt. Ralph had the ability to swipe away the sadness and fear with a joke, a hug, a tender kiss that said life was still worth living. Still worth fighting for. And she'd keep on fighting. For him, for her family, but most of all, for herself.

'Forgive me for being a nosy old gran, but is there another reason your smile seems more ... I don't know ... radiant?' Rachel watched as redness crept up Johnny's cheeks. Her grandson was blushing! Nail definitely hit on the head.

'Right. Well, I haven't told Mum yet. I haven't told Josh either, 'cos he'll just take the piss. Sorry, excuse my language. Anyway, I met this girl, Matilda – Tilly – when she came into the shop. Looking for a starter magic set for her little brother. We got talking; I told her how into it I was when I was young. I showed her a few tricks – Nan, stop pulling that face! – and then she paid. And asked me out.' Johnny swallowed the last bite of his sandwich. His cheeks were still flaming but his grin was broader than ever.

Rachel hand washed the plates, Johnny having gone on his way to meet Tilly after insisting he returned in a few days to do some cleaning. Her hands swirling the suds, she thought how she could never have asked a boy – a man – out on a date. The boldness of today's young women. Then she paused, laughed out loud, recalling how she'd invited Ralph into her bed. *Brazen hussy!*

CHAPTER 34

HATTIE HAD SPENT a chunk of the day hopping on and off a city sightseeing bus. Wrapped in several layers of clothing, she chose to sit upstairs which was open-top. And bloody freezing. Still, she reckoned it gave her a better perspective of Edinburgh. A visit to the castle was a highlight, as was visiting the Crown Jewels exhibition and the palace where Mary Queen of Scots gave birth to her son. She bit her lip to contain an explosion of laughter when she overheard an American tourist puzzling, 'Why did they build the castle so close to the rail line?'

Tears were never far away either. She was due to meet Flora and David McMaster at five o'clock. He had his own private dental practice and wouldn't be home any earlier. Hattie didn't know what to expect, facing both of them. She was grateful that Flora was giving her another chance. She just wasn't sure how she was going to articulate Marty's request.

After a quick lunch of square sliced sausage in a floury roll (another Scottish culinary favourite, and very tasty), Hattie rejoined the bus tour. She got off at Greyfriars Kirkyard with a gaggle of Japanese tourists, weighed down with cameras. The focal point was a small statue of a Skye Terrier. Flipping open her guide leaflet, Hattie read that the dog had been the faithful companion of night watchman John Gray. Day and night they trudged the cobbled streets together until John died of tuberculosis. For fourteen years Bobby kept faithful watch over his master's grave, until his own death. The dog's headstone read, *'Greyfriars Bobby – died 14th January 1872 – aged 16 years – Let his loyalty and devotion be a lesson to us all.'* Hattie snapped a quick photo with her phone, a lump in her throat at such a beautiful tale. If only humans could be as loyal and devoted. Not that she could complain personally. Gary had always been unfailing in his love for Hattie. Even after death. Maybe little Bobby was still trotting alongside John Gray somewhere in the hereafter. Hattie liked to think so.

With an hour to go until the meeting, Hattie decided she'd seen enough of Edinburgh. What she needed now was a stiff drink. She'd cut back recently, aware that her previous light consumption was creeping up. But faced with the task ahead, a gin and tonic (and a breath mint) might take the edge off her nerves.

Seated on a well-worn sofa in the gloom of a bar on Rose Street, Hattie stirred the ice in her glass. Its gentle clink-clink reminded her of Gary and his bell. He rarely used it now. She was used to his comings and goings. Less so Cat, Jack and Ben, not that he visited them frequently. Jack had threatened to castrate him – *cut off your ghostly goolies* was the actual phrase – when he interrupted them playing a game of naked Twister. Apparently a Friday evening favourite after a few shots.

Spinning her drink out as long as possible, Hattie checked her phone. Two messages. One from her mum, assuring her that all was OK and asking when she would be home. The other from Johnny, saying he'd visited Rachel and that he had a date. A date! Hattie never poked her nose into his love life, but she didn't think there'd been many girls in the past. Certainly not any Johnny cared to talk about or bring to the house. 'He's a late starter, Hats, that's all,' Gary would say when she voiced concern. 'One day he'll meet a girl as gorgeous as you and – boom! That'll be it. And when they get married, not that they *have* to, you'll get to wear an enormous hat and I can embarrass the boxers off him with my father of the groom speech.'

Sheltering against the drizzle with her decrepit umbrella, Hattie made her way to the New Town. Office workers, dog walkers and young couples entwined with each other passed her, all blithely unaware of the terror mounting within her. Why would they be? They had their own fears, demons to conquer, mountains to climb. Everybody did. It was just that Hattie felt very small and vulnerable, on the precipice of delivering news that would shake the foundations of the McMasters' already ripped-apart world.

'Mrs Hastings. Hattie. Come in.' Flora gestured at an umbrella stand to the right of the doorway. Hattie fumbled with the broken spokes, gave up and jammed it in as best she could. She knew she looked a mess. Hair scraped back, damp and frizzy from the Scottish weather; no make-up, bar a smidgeon of lip gloss applied before she left the bar. Sipping a coffee in her hotel room that morning, she'd stared at herself in the mirror. Somehow, applying foundation, blusher and so on seemed wrong. What she had to say was raw, bare and best unadorned.

'This is my husband. David.' The man by Flora's side stuck out his hand. Hattie shook it. The handshake was firm, but a twitch beneath his right eye betrayed his emotions. And his appearance reflected all the agony he had been through. The paunch was gone, replaced by a leanness that didn't sit well with him. As if he'd been sucked from the inside out, grief gnawing away at his flesh. His thinning hair had been shaved to the scalp, adding to the sense of a man diminished.

'Right. Let's not beat about the bush. Flora told me what you said and … well, my first reaction was to tell you to bugger off. We've had a few cranks call us up since Marty … since Marty died. It's incredible how people will latch on to loss and try to profit from it. Clairvoyants, whatever they call themselves, saying they can reach out and communicate with the dead. The difference with you is that you brought something.' David looked at Grump, who was positioned on a chair in the hallway. Looking completely at home as well he might.

'Tea, Hattie? Or a glass of wine? David, fetch something from the cellar.' Flora was composed, greeting Hattie like an early dinner guest. She'd twice addressed Hattie by her first name which calmed her nerves a little. But only a little. They entered the living room again. Hattie sat in the same armchair, her right leg jiggling up and down. She balanced her handbag on it, pressing hard on the wobbly limb. Keep it together, she intoned.

'Just some water, please. If that's OK.' Much as a glass of wine would be welcome, Hattie needed to keep her wits about her.

Flora sat opposite her, posture perfect, knees aligned and hands thrust between them. Presumably to disguise her own shakiness. She didn't meet Hattie's eyes, her gaze drifting between the window and the floor.

'Here we are.' David reappeared with an opened bottle of red, three glasses and a flask of water. He poured – wine for the two of them, water for Hattie – and stood by the fireplace. Just in front of the photo of Marty. She wanted to tell him to move, that she needed to see the boy who'd come into her life unexpectedly. But Hattie didn't need to see him. She knew him, from Gary's description. And the details scribbled on the piece of paper, now tucked in her jacket pocket.

Flora and David sipped their wine. Hattie was aware they were waiting for her to speak. To break the silence that hung over the room like a shroud.

'I know this is so difficult for you to accept. I'd feel the same if someone came and told me they had a message from the dead.' Hattie winced and grabbed her water. At the word 'dead', Flora tilted back her head and sniffed. David downed his wine and quickly refilled the glass. OK, no more procrastinating. She pulled out the folded paper – torn from one of Johnny's old jotters – and opened it.

'Hand on my heart, every word I've told you' – Hattie looked at Flora – 'is the honest truth. And Marty's toy was given to me by my husband, Gary, to prove it. Its … his name is Grump … and you gave him to Marty when he first went into hospital.' David moved swiftly from the fireplace and sat down next to his wife. She grabbed his hand, squeezing so tight her knuckles blanched.

'There's more. Marty's favourite food is beans on toast, with grated Cheddar on top. He loves Roald Dahl's books, especially *James and the Giant Peach.* He hates brushing his teeth.' David – a dentist – gave a tiny smile at that one. 'His best friend at school is called George and Marty isn't very good at sums, but he loves writing stories.' Hattie stopped. There was one other piece of information on the note. There'd been no need to write down Marty's desperate plea.

'Marty told Gary – showed Gary – the small birthmark on his chest. He said you joked that it looked like an ink splodge. And he used to try to scrub it away in the bath.'

Flora got up slowly, eyes wide and arms outstretched. She moved towards Hattie, who didn't know what to expect. A slap in the face? Being physically dragged to the door and tossed out on the street? Instead, Flora took Hattie's hands, guided her to her feet and hugged her tightly.

'Thank you,' she whispered. 'I believe you. And now I know Marty's out there, somewhere, I feel … I feel …' Flora's body trembled in Hattie's arms. David appeared by their side, gently prising his wife from Hattie and into his own embrace.

'Mrs Hastings, I mean, Hattie. I can't think of any way you could know all these things unless your story about your husband returning is true. And you don't strike me as a fantasist or a liar. What I don't understand is *why* you came here to tell us all this.' At this, Flora wriggled free and faced Hattie again.

'David, I told you that Hattie said she had a message from Marty. Something he wanted her to pass on to us. Please, Hattie, what did our darling little boy want to say?'

Flora and David looked at Hattie. This was it. Journey's end, but perhaps a fresh start for a couple shattered by their loss. Hattie drew on the last vestiges of her depleted energy reserves, and then: 'Marty wants you to be happy again. He wants … he wants you to have another baby.'

CHAPTER 35

'YOU'RE BLOODY CHEATING! Put that card back!' Gary scowled at Bob in his best 'hard man' fashion. Bob glowered back, puffing out his chest in defiance.

'You said a naughty word!' Marty waggled a finger at Gary, his own cards in danger of being crushed in his other hand.

'Bad me. Sorry, mate. Right, let's get this game over with.'

Gary, Marty, Bob and Anna were playing Old Maid. As well as boiled sweets, Anna had unearthed a pack of cards from the bottomless pit of her handbag. Gary wondered if she'd been buried with it, a bit like an Egyptian pharaoh. He remembered Johnny rabbiting on about a school project on the rituals associated with a pharaoh's burial. Food and drink were placed in the tomb for sustenance on the long journey ahead. Gary had sneaked a peek into the bag and clocked several packets of cream crackers, Mars bars and a jar of Marmite. Anna had been well prepared, but luckily not mummified. Although her tights were distinctly bandage-like.

'You lose! You lose! Old Maid!' Marty squealed with

delight as Bob was left with the odd queen. *Justice served*, thought Gary. He really was a grumpy old git, always poking fun at Marty and making 'little women' cracks at Anna. Gary liked Anna. She fussed over Marty and made him giggle with stories of the mischief her own grandchildren got up to. She reminded Gary a little of his mum, Effie. She'd always been good with children, working as a Brownie leader and running Sunday School classes when she was younger. He missed his mum and dad, Angus, terribly but hadn't tried to visit them. He feared the shock might well kill them. Hattie called them but they had made it clear they wanted little contact. Gary guessed that seeing Hattie and Johnny would be too painful for them. They'd doted on him, their only child, having believed for years that parenthood would never happen. Maybe one day they'd be strong enough …

Bob stomped off into the mist, Anna packed away the cards and Marty made himself comfortable next to Gary.

'Has Hattie seen my mummy and daddy yet?' asked Marty, accepting a sweet from Anna. He crunched away, no savouring and sucking for him.

'Biscuit, Gary?' enquired Anna, pulling out a half-knitted scarf from her Mary Poppins-esque bag. He shook his head, and she began clack-clacking away with her needles.

'I dunno, Marty. I hope so. She went to Edinburgh to see them and she's due home tomorrow.' Gary hadn't tried to follow her. He wasn't sure if he could. In any case, Hattie had been so agitated about the trip, he doubted she'd welcome his presence with open arms. She was upset about her mum, stressed about Cat and debating whether to take on extra hours at Espresso Yourself. Hattie now had access to Gary's pension and the pay-out from the life insurance, but she wasn't rolling in it. Gary wished she could find something more fulfilling. She was a bright, funny and wonderful woman but a lack of qualifications and self-belief held her back. She'd always been in Jack's illustrious shadow in that respect. Rachel was a strong, self-made woman who'd encouraged both her children to do their best. Hattie had tried, but academic stuff left her cold. Gary had seen one of her old report cards. A comment from her maths teacher. 'If Harriet devoted as much time to trigonometry and equations as she does to checking her appearance or cackling inanely with Catherine Cooper, she might achieve higher marks. But I will not be holding my breath.' Cat had found a passion – aside from Stewart – and built her own business. Hattie had met Gary and they'd muddled along, not wanting for much. Never driven by the lure of a bigger house, a fancier car, flashier holidays. Now … Gary just wanted Hattie to be happy. Johnny, too. It wasn't a big ask, was it?

'You will go and see her straight away, won't you?' Marty took another sweet from Anna. Gary nodded. He missed Hattie so much; not seeing her for a few days had nearly killed him. No, that would have been the piss head driver who'd smashed into him. And no 'nearly' about it. Still, little use fretting about the past. Jobs to do, people to haunt, that kind of thing. He was glad that Hattie had hooked up with Barry. He was one of the good 'uns. Not like those creepy twats Hattie had gone out with. Christ on a bike, if she wanted to dip her toe back in the man pool, she could do a lot better than cheating toe rags and sad singletons with underwear issues. *Wait a minute!* Surely he wasn't imagining Hattie and Barry … No. No way. His wife and his best friend. Absolutely not.

'Gary, you're not listening to me!' Marty elbowed him in the ribs. Ouch! He wrapped his arm around Marty and play-wrestled him to the ground. They rolled around, squealing and protesting, prompting Anna to gather up her belongings and huff off into the gloom.

'I was, mate. And I promise I'll see Hattie just as soon as I

CHAPTER 35   213

can. Right, let's see if we can find Clarence and annoy the hell out of him!'

* * *

HATTIE WAS on the train back to London. She felt physically drained, yet uplifted by the reaction of Flora and David. After dropping the baby bombshell, she hadn't dared to hope they would give it serious thought. Flora had fled the room, her sobs audible for minutes after. David had returned to the fireplace, staring at Marty's photo. When he spoke, his voice had been thick with emotion.

'We always wanted another child. It just never happened and when Marty was diagnosed ... well, it couldn't have been further from our minds. He was our baby, and he can never be replaced. He was always quite young for his age, slower than his classmates to pick things up. Smaller too, which made him look younger. And he didn't want a brother or sister ...'

'He wanted a dog. I know, Marty told Gary.' Hattie had tried to reassure David that these were the words of an only child, used to having his own way and the sole attention of his parents. David knew that, of course, but no doubt the words had haunted him in the days and months after Marty's death.

Flora had returned, eyes blood-shot and clutching a fistful of tissues. David had held her tightly, Hattie feeling like a gooseberry. Not an entirely unwelcome one, as they'd insisted on her staying for supper and exchanged phone numbers and email addresses.

'This has been ... a surreal meeting, Hattie,' David had said as she took her leave. 'Your message, from Marty, it's a huge shock but at the same time ... we have a lot to talk about. To think about. Keep in touch.' They both hugged her in turn, Flora's embrace lasting a little longer. 'Please, if the only way we can communicate with Marty is through your husband, it's something,' she whispered softly.

David had turned to the hallway chair where Grump still sat. He picked up the toy and handed it to Hattie. 'He belongs with Marty. I hope Gary can take him back and ... well, thank him for looking out for our boy.'

CHAPTER 36

GARY, Jack and Ben were seated at the dining table, playing a game of cards. Not Old Maid, but Beggar My Neighbour. Each had a tumbler of whisky, which Gary had almost spat across the room when he learned its alternative title.

'Also known as Strip Jack Naked,' announced Ben, winking at his partner. Jack pulled a face and turned up his top card.

'Well, I'm glad you guys have kept your gear on this time. My eyes are still bleeding from when I caught you "playing" together.' Gary grinned, placing a card in the middle of the table.

'Yeah, pull a stunt like that again and your otherworldly arse is in for a serious bruising!' said Jack.

Gary had managed to see Hattie briefly on her return from Edinburgh. She hadn't been in the mood to say much, just that the visit had gone better than expected. She'd shooed him away, complaining of a thumping headache and the need for a lie-down in her own bed. Frustrated but sympathetic – Gary could only imagine how tough it had been – he'd whooshed off. Except ... he'd ended up at Jack and Ben's. His tenuous control of where he ended up and who could see him was becoming more unpredictable. Gary half-expected to drop in to Downing Street one day and put the frighteners on Theresa May. Although he found the woman bloody terrifying. She reminded him of an old school teacher, Miss Urie (or urine, as he and his classmates called her under their breath), who they were convinced slept in a coffin and feasted on bats' blood.

'I'm bored with this,' said Ben, tossing his cards down. 'Can we play something else?'

'How about "Bugger My Neighbour"?' retorted Jack, twisting a tortilla chip into a tub of hummus. 'Don't think I haven't noticed you ogling Mike next door when he's mowing the lawn in those ridiculously tight shorts. Christ, if they were any tighter, his balls would be begging Amnesty International for freedom.'

He missed this. Gary sensed – knew – that his days back on earth were numbered. Not because of anything Clarence had said, more a creeping feeling that his mission was drawing to a close. Was it just because of Marty? That was still an open case, unfinished business unless his parents were willing or able to produce another child. Who knew? Maybe they weren't meant to do so. Perhaps it was physically impossible, or they simply couldn't contemplate starting again. How did you replace someone you loved with every ounce of your being? Simple answer – you couldn't. What you needed wasn't a replacement. You had to look at things with fresh eyes. Marty's parents might be sitting, right now, thinking of having a baby. A chain of thought instigated by Hattie. By Gary. By Marty, bless him. Eight years old and wise beyond his years.

'OK. I will love and leave you two reprobates. Promise to report back when I have the full update from Hattie on the baby situation.' Gary hoped and prayed for a speedy escape. *Need to go now. Beam me up, Scotty.*

'We did talk about having a baby, didn't we, Jack?' Ben ran his fingers through Jack's hair, retracting them when he encountered a knot.

'Yes, but you said you'd rather have a dog. No surrogates involved, and all poo disposed of externally, in little plastic bags. And dogs eat from bowls on the floor. Babies need breasts – not hairy, male ones – or bottles of formula. Ben, whenever you use the microwave, the contents plaster themselves to the walls. We would be crap parents. Let's settle for us. You and me; just the two of us.'

As Gary shimmered and shimmied his way back to his spiritual home, the last words he heard were Jack and Ben serenading one another. He was glad his departure was rapid; they couldn't sing for toffee.

* * *

'Feeling better, babe?'

Hattie switched off the TV she'd barely been watching.

'A bit, thanks.' An hour's snooze had taken the edge off her headache, helped also by a couple of paracetamol. A quick shower, then she'd put on her beloved Pokémon pyjamas. Just as well she didn't have a new love interest. Any man would run a mile at her choice of nightwear, and her undies would score even higher in the passion-killing stakes. Lucky it was only Gary and Johnny who saw her in her jim-jams. And Cat too. She'd threatened to burn them on several occasions, and for Hattie's last birthday she'd bought her a slinky camisole with matching frilly knickers. Not wanting to appear ungrateful, Hattie had taken the outfit upstairs and tried it on. She'd swirled and twirled in front of the mirror, sucking in her stomach and rearranging her boobs. Why did the left one never co-operate with the right? They were separate entities, lopsided and hell-bent on doing their own thing. Just as Hattie wrangled them into position, there'd been a rap on the window. Geoff the window cleaner – who came the first Friday of every month – had given her the thumbs up and a quick flap of his chamois cloth.

She'd messaged Cat to say she was back. That was all. Hattie wanted some time to process the whole Edinburgh trip before she could face her best friend and the reality of her renewed relationship with Stewart. She needed to see her mum too, as she'd undergone another round of chemotherapy during Hattie's absence.

'Up to talking about Marty's folks now?' asked Gary. He was leaning against the wall, the swirling paintwork visible through his body. Hattie shivered as she realised he was becoming a little less substantial every visit. Fading from view, bit by bit. Did this mean his time was running out? She couldn't bear the thought that one day – perhaps soon – he might vanish forever.

'It wasn't easy, Gary. If it hadn't been for the list of things about Marty and Grump ...' Hattie dashed out of the room and thundered up the stairs. She returned pink-cheeked and panting moments later with Grump in her arms. Dammit, she needed to up her fitness level. Serving cakes and coffee or mopping the kitchen floor wasn't exactly boosting her cardio strength.

'They believed me. I went twice – the first time it was just Flora, Marty's mum, and she insisted I came back when her husband was there. When I told them what Marty wanted ... oh, Gary, they'd tried for another baby in the past but with no joy. And Marty's illness meant they couldn't think about it anymore. But now ...' Hattie passed Grump over to Gary. He ruffled his tousled hair affectionately, much in the same way he used to ruffle Johnny's. Until their son discovered hair gel/putty and freaked out if either of them dared to touch his carefully coiffed spikes.

'D'you think they'll try again? What should I tell Marty? Hats, the wee fella deserves some good news.' Gary paced around, nervous energy radiating off him. 'You know what, I think this is my mission! Or part of it. I dunno, does just passing on a message to Marty's parents count, or do we need an actual bun in the oven scenario?'

Yet again, Gary's turn of phrase made Hattie smile. And cringe. He'd always spoken first and thought later. Often much later, when those he'd upset had stormed off, delicate sensibilities bruised. But nobody stayed mad with Gary for long. His generosity and kindness far outweighed his ability to cause lasting offence.

'They're going to keep in touch. Beyond that, it's down to what they want, and Mother Nature. I did my best, Gary.' Fresh tears pricked at Hattie's eyes, and she pulled out a tissue tucked in her sleeve. 'Sorry, it's so hard to think of what they've been through. If they do have another baby ... will that make things better, or just serve as a constant reminder of Marty?'

Gary plonked Grump down and took Hattie's hands. Now, they weren't only opaque and insubstantial, they felt icy cold. She tried not to shudder, or think what that might mean.

'Babe, we've done our bit. Or rather, *you* did something amazing and I couldn't be prouder. They'll never forget Marty, and the wee fella has me twisted round his little finger. Even if another baby doesn't come along ... what you told them will give them comfort. Trust me, you did good.'

CHAPTER 37

'I LOVE fajitas but I'm rubbish at putting them together.' Barry raised his tortilla wrap, blobs of sour cream, salsa and guacamole dribbling onto the plate. Hattie was impressed with her own construction skills, the contents neatly contained in a well-folded parcel. She took a bite – delicious – and smiled at Barry.

'Erm, you've got a bit of salsa on your chin.' He leaned across and dabbed it away with his napkin. Maybe not so well-constructed after all. It was nice of him to point it out although removing it himself felt a bit … intimate. Gary had never been great at letting Hattie know about things like that. The one and only time they'd tried skiing in Aviemore, before they got married, it had been blowing a blizzard. Finding the goggles more hindrance than help, she'd stuffed them in her pocket. Gary had followed the instructor's lead with confidence, Hattie valiantly slipping, sliding and eventually careering into a fence. No damage done, apart from a bruised bum and the giggles of a group of five-year-olds who'd all mastered the snow plough with irritating ease. A nice lunch and a hot spiced wine helped alleviate her embarrassment. Until she visited the ladies' and discovered her mascara was liberally plastered around her eyes. Storming back into the restaurant, she'd yelled at Gary for not telling her. He'd simply shrugged, claimed he hadn't noticed, and said, 'Who wears make-up on a ski slope anyway, Hats?'

'Did you have a nice time with your friends?' Barry topped up Hattie's wine glass, his pint glass still half-full. She'd let him know she was home after a week or so, needing time to process all that had happened, and he'd quickly replied inviting her out for a meal.

'Yes, it was … nice. To see them again. But I mainly did some sightseeing on my own because they had to go to work and things.' If Barry was surprised at Hattie's 'friends' inviting her to stay then leaving her to her own devices, he said nothing. She hated lying to him, but what was the alternative?

'I've never been to Edinburgh, or anywhere in Scotland,' confessed Barry, now on his second wrap and still making a pig's ear of it. 'Which is a bit strange because my fiancée was from Glasgow.'

Hattie tried not to look shocked at this snippet of personal information. Barry had never revealed that much to Gary. Well, he had *alluded* to a relationship, but not one that was supposed to lead to wedding bells. 'Oh, I'm sorry, Barry,' she said, 'I mean – not because you've never been to Scotland – you can go there any time, not that you have to, of course …' *Enough already*, she told herself. The poor man opening up about his private life, and she was twittering on like a mad woman. 'Carry on. I'll just shove a fajita in my gob and listen.'

Chewing away, Hattie heard that Barry had met Lorna through the insurance company they both worked for. She'd been sent down south for training, Barry being one of the team responsible for the week-long programme. They'd hit it off straight away, and she'd subsequently left her native country to relocate at head office.

'I'm not the most outgoing person on the planet, Hattie, whereas Lorna … she walked into a room and within minutes she was surrounded by people. I didn't know what she saw in me, but I couldn't have been happier. She was smart, funny and beautiful in a quirky way. Not like you …'

Great. There she was, liking Barry more and more for his honesty and openness, and now he hints that she'd turn milk sour with her ugly mug. Gary'd always teased her that she 'scrubbed up well' and she thought she was reasonably attractive …

'Hattie, your face is a picture! I didn't mean for one minute that you're not beautiful. Because you are.' Barry had the grace to look contrite, mingled with a smidgeon of embarrassment. His second beer had just arrived, and he swallowed a mouthful. 'What I meant was … Lorna wasn't a classic beauty. Her features individually were ordinary but somehow they worked together. God, that sounds terrible. As if I'm a bloody oil painting. It's just, she didn't blind you straight away with that drop-dead gorgeousness that makes men like me shake their heads and retreat. I got to know her, and realised she was a good person, and I fell in love with her. I'm sure lots of men fell in love with her but … she chose me.'

Hattie didn't know if she wanted to hear how the story ended. Not well, that much she'd figured out. But if Barry wanted to keep talking …

'We started living together as soon as she moved down. At first, it was an arrangement of convenience. I had a spare room, rent was expensive elsewhere and we agreed it was nothing more than colleagues looking out for each other. Head office didn't need to know, not that they gave a toss as long as employees turned up and did their jobs. Anyway, within a few weeks we were a couple, and I couldn't have been happier.' The smile on Barry's face as he described Lorna melted away like wax on a long-burning candle.

'How long were you together?' asked Hattie, deciding that a third fajita was a Mexican mouthful too far. Barry had stopped eating and was fiddling with the frayed strap of his watch.

'Almost two years. We got engaged after six months. And you're no doubt wondering why, in all that time, I never went to Glasgow with her. Lorna visited her family there every few months, but she made excuses why I shouldn't join her. Said her parents were very strict, and wouldn't approve of her "living in sin" with someone. I went along with it, but in my darker moments something didn't ring true.'

'So, what happened? I thought you told Gary that it was the stress of your job that caused the break-up?' Hattie hoped she wasn't speaking out of turn, but Barry seemed keen to continue. His fiddling ceased when the strap broke and the watch landed on his plate.

'I figured something was wrong when Lorna would be texting, then break off immediately when I came into the room. Or she'd be chatting on the phone, then put on a different voice if I appeared. Like … she was talking to someone else, then pretended it was her mum or a girlfriend. It was in the last couple of months. I knew something wasn't right, but she kept saying everything was fine.'

Hattie had no idea where this was going, but she felt so sorry for Barry. Why did nice, decent people like him and Cat attract the wrong kind of person? Not that she'd heard the Lorna punch line yet, but it wasn't going to be a hearts and flowers moment. Barry rubbed his face vigorously, his eyes downcast. When he looked up, the pain in his expression was palpable.

'One day I came home from work – Lorna had taken a

sickie, said she had a bad stomach – to find she'd packed up and gone. She left a letter, a Dear John, saying she had a boyfriend back in Scotland, and they'd decided to have another go at it. Turns out they'd split up and that was why she'd taken the job at head office. To get over him, except … she never did. He'd got back in touch and they'd been calling and messaging and she'd seen him a few times in Glasgow. I guess that was the real reason Lorna never wanted me to go there. It wasn't because of her parents; it was in case we bumped into *him*.' Barry emphasised the last word, his hurt laid bare in three letters.

Assuring the waiter that they were finished – Hattie didn't want a dessert or coffee and Barry needed a hug – she shuffled her chair around until close enough to do so. He accepted it, squeezing Hattie back forcefully. She counted to ten, then drew away, feeling again that sense of intimacy that unnerved her. Was it because he was Gary's dearest friend, someone she absolutely couldn't get involved with? Why was she even thinking of such things? Hattie didn't need another man in her life, particularly one as vulnerable as Barry. She liked him, and he clearly liked her, but … that was it. Wasn't it?

They left the restaurant arm in arm. Hattie's concern about where things were going subsided as Barry filled in the rest of the story. He'd started having panic attacks after Lorna left, bad ones that gave him heart palpitations and sleepless nights. His work suffered and – unable to cope with the ten-hour days and well-meaning comments from colleagues – he'd quit. Barry told Hattie he hadn't had a mental breakdown, but he'd teetered on the brink.

'I couldn't do it anymore. I thought I had the perfect life, the perfect woman, but it was just a badly built game of Jenga. One shove and the whole thing came crashing down.'

Lying in bed, Hattie wondered why any woman would

get engaged when she was still clinging to another relationship. She'd strung Barry along, then did a runner without a
backwards glance.

Spritzing the pillow with lavender spray in the hope of
nodding off quickly, Hattie hoped she wasn't inadvertently
stringing Barry along. He'd kissed her on the cheek when
they parted, nothing unusual. It was just the way he looked at
her – just a moment longer than was necessary – that made
her uneasy.

CHAPTER 38

'So much for bloody lavender spray as a sleep aid! I should have squirted some Mr Sheen on the pillow; at least I might have woken up shiny instead of shagged out.' Hattie stomped around Cat's kitchen looking for the strongest coffee she could find. Green tea, decaf and something unpronounceable – rooibos – taunted her from the shelves. She finally located a jar of what appeared to be instant granules. Peering inside, she recoiled at their sticky remains. Still, it was coffee.

'So, where have you been and why have you and Gary been acting like you're an MI5 agent?' Cat stood with hands on hips, indignation oozing from every pore. Hattie scraped a spoonful of the gravy-like substance into a mug and sniffed it. Just in case it *was* gravy.

'Don't get narky with me, Cat. I'm not the one who's been getting all cosy with their ex. And don't deny it because I saw you—' Oops. Hattie hadn't meant to let that slip out. Now she'd have to come clean about snooping around outside Cat's house after her date with Roger.

Cat's expression changed to one of disbelief. She opened

the fridge, grabbed a milk carton and slammed it onto the table.

'What do you mean, you *saw* me? No, wait, it was Gary, wasn't it? Floating around, sticking his ghostly nose into other people's private lives. He gave me a right telling-off for seeing Stewart again, but he didn't admit he'd seen us together. I'll bloody kill him!'

It wasn't the first time someone had threatened to kill the already-dead Gary, and it probably wouldn't be the last. Hattie poured boiling water on her granules and took a deep breath.

'No, it was me. I went on another date – not a success – and you'd been texting me about Jamie finding you with Stewart. I wanted to throttle you, and the only way I could do that was by dropping by. Which I did and … I happened to see you with him through the window … and you kissed him. Again. Eurgh!' The last comment was a reflection of the drink rather than Cat's actions, although Hattie felt queasy at the thought of what she'd witnessed.

'You were spying on me?' Cat shook her head. 'Not so far off the mark with the MI5 stuff after all! Well, Mrs bloody Bond, you'd better get down to Specsavers because I didn't kiss him. Ha! Put that in your Sherlock Holmes pipe and smoke it!'

As well as muddling up fictional spies and detectives, Cat looked ready to combust with indignation. OK, maybe Hattie *had* misread the situation when she'd saw them together, but …'

'All right, all right. I'll take your word for it but … **but** … you texted me to say Jamie'd caught you and Stewart getting up close and personal. I have proof, right here, on my phone so don't you go acting like little Miss Innocent all of a sudden.' Hattie glowered at Cat, Cat curled her lip in defiance and the only sound was the thump-thump of the washing machine. And the tiniest tinkle of a bell.

'Ladies, ladies. Don't tell me I'm going to have to referee a full-on, hair-pulling argument. Not that it wouldn't be entertaining. Maybe if I hosed you down a bit; wet T-shirts might add to the fun ...' Gary stood there smirking and stuttering like a failing light bulb. *On, off. On, off. Now you see him, now you nearly don't.*

'Gary, first of all, Cat and I are grown-ups who're just having a little disagreement. Secondly, if you think we're going to fulfil your sad male fantasies you can dream on. And lastly ... are you feeling OK?' Hattie's outburst at Cat was forgotten as she watched him flicker in and out of focus.

'Feelin' grand, babe. Nice to get away from clueless Clarence for a while. You know, I asked him if helping Marty was my mission.'

Cat looked puzzled. 'Who's Marty when he's at home?'

Hattie and Gary exchanged glances before Hattie spoke.

'It's a long story. I'll fill you in later. What did Clarence say?'

Gary rolled his eyes in disgust. 'Something about me being relatively efficacious, but with – blah, blah – another task to undertake. The dude thinks he's an enigma. More like a friggin' enema, the amount of crap he spouts.'

Cat had stomped out of the room, reappearing with her coat on and jangling her car keys.

'Right, seems like I'm being kept out of the loop here so I'll leave you two to carry on the secret chit-chat. I'm off to the dump. Slam the door behind you when you leave.'

Hattie felt a rush of guilt. She hadn't given Cat a chance to explain what was going on with Stewart, or revealed the reason for her sudden trip. Not that she was sure she wanted to share Marty's story.

'Listen, Cat, we'll catch up soon, OK? I'll call you, I promise. Johnny's bringing a friend home for dinner but I doubt they'll want to hang around after they've eaten.' She pulled a 'forgive me' face and Cat gave her a squeeze.

'Sure, chat soon. See ya, Gary.' Then she was gone.

'A *friend*? Would that happen to be a girlfriend, by any chance?' Gary wiggled his eyebrows suggestively, prompting Hattie to thump him on the shoulder. A thump that was more like tickling jelly.

'Yes. I don't know a thing about her, but I'm looking forward to meeting her. Let's change the subject. How did Marty react when you told him about my meeting his folks?' Hattie absent-mindedly downed the rest of the coffee, shuddering as the foul liquid assaulted her taste buds.

'He was over the moon, Hats, and then some. Positively jigging with glee until that miserable sod Bob stuck his oar in and said babies don't grow on trees. Poor wee mite burst into tears and started talking about seeds and tummies. I guess they hadn't got around to the full sex education talk before Marty ...'

As always, the thought of Marty's too-short life rendered them silent for a few moments. Gary found his voice again first.

'I know it's a long shot, babe, but you never know. Anna's already started knitting bootees, just in case!'

CAT PARKED up by the bottle bank and started tossing empties into it. She got a certain grim satisfaction at the sound of shattering glass even if she was conscious of the volume of bottles in the boot of her car. Since Stewart was dropping by more and more often, her alcohol consumption had risen exponentially. Cat wasn't sure which worried her more – his stealthy infiltration into her life, or an increased likelihood of liver failure.

Done with the bottles, Cat moved on to newspapers and magazines. She hated binning magazines, watching their glossy covers featuring miracle diets, life-changing hacks and age-busting serums slide into oblivion. Ooh, there was one promising to drop a dress size in a week! Dammit, it slipped from Cat's grasp, she dived after it and ... ended up doing a virtual headstand. Fantastic. Legs flapping in the air, knickers on show to the world. Why had she worn a short dress to go to the dump? At least she had tights on and no one would see her bum as her knickers were full-on, hide-all numbers.

'Need a hand?' As Cat grunted her way upright, a familiar voice interrupted her progress. Followed by a pair of familiar hands grasping her firmly by the waist. Ooph! Cat steadied herself, dizzy after the sudden rush of blood to her head.

'Hi, Jamie,' she mumbled, tugging the skirt into place. Sod's law that she'd bump into him again at the dump, the place where they'd first met. Cat tried her best to organise her recycling for the street collection, but sometimes she got the dates mixed up.

'Hi, Cat. It's not every day I get to rescue a damsel in distress. Or should I say, *dat* dress?' Jamie grinned as Cat tried to untangle part of the hem that had become snagged in her knickers. Trying to look on the bright side, she reckoned it was better Jamie – who'd seen her in and out of underwear – than some stranger who'd come to her aid.

'Were you randomly foraging, or did you bin something by mistake?' His question was an innocent if cheeky one, but the words *like me?* flashed through Cat's mind. Not that she'd binned him, just that being caught in a clinch with your ex-husband didn't do much for a new relationship.

'It's fine. There was a magazine I wanted to keep ... an

article on … twenty things to do with a lemon.' Cat wasn't about to divulge the truth. Jamie didn't need to know she'd gained a few pounds in recent weeks. Another side-effect of Stewart, now that he'd stopped being the calorie police.

Jamie rubbed his chin in a contemplative manner. He had a fine coating of stubble which wasn't unattractive. And his eyes were still ridiculously sparkly. Of course they were! Cat might have let him down, but she wasn't arrogant enough to think she'd dim his inner glow. Another woman would snap him up sooner or later … if they hadn't already.

'Hmm. I can think of a few. Stuff one up a chicken's rear end. My mum taught me that one. Slice it and add to a gin and tonic. Oh, and make lemonade, because that's what you do when life gives you lemons.' Again, Cat's internal voice shrieked, *Your fault! It's all your fault!*

Whatever Jamie had been dumping, he was all done. As was Cat, who wanted to say something but had developed a serious case of verbal failure. Even 'Bye then, see you around' was beyond her capability.

Luckily, Jamie wasn't a man often stuck for something to say. He always had a quip to suit the occasion (apart from the time when there'd been no words to express how he felt). Cat accepted his gentle kiss on the cheek and pushed down the feeling of loss that kicked her in the stomach.

'See you, Cat. Take care. It was funny meeting you here, brings to mind the time a man stopped me in the street and said he was looking for a rubbish tip. I said to him, "Arsenal to win the league."'

And with that Jamie got in his car, waved and drove off. For a moment Cat kicked around the joke – football wasn't her thing – until the penny dropped. Then she laughed and laughed some more until she started to cry.

CHAPTER 39

'DARLING, I'm fine. The doctors say the chemo is going well. They're cautiously optimistic that I might be able to have the surgery in a few months.' Hattie had stopped by at her mum's on the way to the supermarket. She'd promised Johnny not to embarrass him in front of his new girlfriend. Ways to embarrass him, according to Johnny:

• *Bombarding Matilda (Tilly) with questions about her background, education and political leanings*

• *Bringing out Johnny's 'Early Years' photo album and showing the one when he pooped in the scales just after birth, and the classic image of him pirouetting in a tutu at play-school*

• *Serving sliced Battenberg cake and mini sandwiches on her best china in a bid to look 'posh'*

• *Opening her mouth pretty much at all*

Rachel looked better. Her colour was back to normal, and she insisted she was eating well, although more weight loss was evident. Also evident was a stack of suitcases in the hallway, topped by suit carriers, CDs and books. Either she was going on a long holiday or ...

'Hello, Hattie. Lovely to see you.' Ralph appeared from the

lounge, balancing more books in his arms. They exchanged an awkward kiss over the pile, the top one teetering precariously. Rachel intervened, a coy smile playing at the corner of her lips.

'Right. I'm guessing this lot isn't destined for the second-hand shop,' said Hattie, nodding at the miscellaneous items in the hallway, 'which means—'

'Yes, darling. Ralph is moving in. It's silly paying the upkeep on two houses when we spend most of our time together here. Ralph has put his place on the market to rent although we might sell it at some stage.'

Hattie hoped her face conveyed the right message. Pleasantly surprised instead of slightly stunned. Her seventy-something mum was shacking up with a man? Mind you, not just any man but the adoring and erudite Ralph. He was poles apart from Rachel's previous posse of male admirers, none of whom Hattie could ever imagine getting their slippers under the bed. Or their leg over, not that she wanted to imagine what her mum and Ralph got up to in the bedroom.

'That's great!' Hattie's voice came out high-pitched and overly enthusiastic. Not that she wasn't happy for Rachel; she'd spent too many years living alone and knowing Ralph was going to be close by was a great comfort.

'Have you told Jack yet?' Hattie dreaded to think what her brother might have to say on the subject. Something crude, no doubt. Involving jokes about matching Zimmer frames or recommending lubricants.

'No, darling, but I'm quite ready for his witty riposte. Now, let me stick the kettle on and you can tell me how your trip went.'

Left alone with Ralph, Hattie felt unusually tongue-tied. Luckily, Ralph put her at ease with chitchat about the weather (unseasonably warm), his favourite show on Netflix (gruesome but gripping) and other innocuous topics. He leapt to his feet when Rachel returned, taking the tray from her and planting a kiss on her cheek.

'Now, let's hear all about where you went and what you got up to. We were joking that you'd hooked up with a mystery man and gone off for a few nights of passion!' Rachel stirred two sugars into her tea, one eyebrow raised in question. Ralph mock-frowned, his underlying look one of devotion. Hattie garbled her well-rehearsed story of catching up with friends – 'No, Mum. No one you know,' – and was grateful that her propensity for telling porkies hadn't resulted in a Pinocchio-style nose.

They talked about Rachel's impending operation, which would go ahead if the tumour shrank sufficiently. The Whipple Procedure, which Hattie thought was too pretty a name for something so unpleasant, involved removing not only part of the pancreas but potentially other organs. It sounded gruesome but Rachel remained upbeat.

'Maybe I'll be one of the lucky ones. In the meantime, life is for the living and I fully intend to make the most of whatever I have left.' She leaned into Ralph, who squeezed her hand. Hattie blinked hard, determined not to cry. If the unthinkable happened – if Rachel died – would she be able to come back like Gary? If not, would they find each other wherever he happened to be? Gary hadn't hooked up with anyone he knew in the kingdom of Clarence. No deceased grandparents or other long-gone relatives. Not even his boyhood mate, Kevin, who died after smashing his motor-cycle into a wall.

'I so admire you, Mum. I don't think I would have your strength if I was faced with something like this.' Which was true. Hattie didn't cope well with illness. Even a touch of a cold had her huddled up in bed, mired in misery and awash with Night Nurse. Gary – unlike many men who complained of 'man flu' and were on the verge of calling 999 – had always been the tougher one. Soldiering on and never complaining. Apart from the odd gripe at the mountain of sodden and snotty tissues Hattie would leave strewn around the bed.

'Darling, you've coped so well since Gary died. I knew you would, but you've rallied much faster than I thought. I know Cat is a great support and Johnny … well, he's turned into a fine young man.' Rachel related how he'd dropped by unannounced and made lunch, as well as offering to come back and help with some household chores. 'And he's got a girlfriend! Oops, have I let the cat out of the bag?'

After assuring her mum that she knew about Tilly – was in fact off to get some food for the three of them that evening – Hattie headed to the shops. Basket in hand, she looked forlornly at the fancy cakes and pastries, before snatching up a tub of mini chocolate rolls. For herself, not for sharing. A large lasagne, ready-made mixed salad and some assorted chips and dips would do the job for dinner. Johnny didn't know much about Tilly's eating preferences, but at least she wasn't a vegan. What *did* they eat, anyway? Hattie enjoyed a decent diet with plenty of fruit and veg, but giving up meat, fish, eggs etc. was akin to torture. No more bacon butties? No bloody way!

'THIS IS FAB! Did you make it yourself?' Tilly forked up another mouthful of lasagne, her slight frame belying an appetite worthy of a starving lioness. She was on second helpings, having devoured most of the chips and dips single-handedly.

'Erm, no. Sorry, it's shop-bought but I'm glad you like it.' Hattie looked at Johnny, who was drowning his salad in Dijon mustard dressing. Ninety percent dressing, ten percent leaves. He'd taken a tiny sliver of lasagne, apparently content to let his girlfriend scoff the rest. Hattie wasn't hungry. A handful of mini rolls before their arrival had given her a sugar high and a sore stomach. She'd deliberately not pictured what Tilly might be like (although tattoos, piercings and Doc Martens had fluttered across her imagination). Instead, the girl wore a floral dress, her hair a dirty blonde scraped up into a messy bun. She was make-up free, her skin that enviable porcelain Hattie could only have dreamed of in her youth. Her teens had been plagued by spots, the hideous blighters regrouping during the night. *Right, guys, you take the cheeks, we'll cover the forehead and – yes – let's zap one on the nose. Full-on, glow-in-the-dark beacon!* Much to her disgust she still got the odd one as did Cat. Johnny had escaped unscathed, inheriting his dad's blemish-free complexion.

'Well, my mum can't cook to save her life,' continued Tilly. 'She actually burnt spaghetti once and nearly blew the door off the microwave baking a potato.'

'Mum's a good cook,' added Johnny. 'She does a mean chilli and her slow-cooked leg of lamb is legendary.' He grinned at Hattie, who blushed and apologised for resorting to a ready meal.

'No worries. If it wasn't for stuff like that, me and my brother would have died of starvation years ago!'

Over bowls of ice cream Hattie learned that Tilly was nineteen, and lived at home with her twelve-year-old brother, Robin, and her parents. She was in her second year of studying graphic design and planned on taking a gap year at the end of the course to travel to Asia. As she chatted, Johnny looked at her with an expression of sheer adoration. Hattie was happy for him. Tilly was smart, funny and very likeable. Gary would love her too, not that it was likely he'd ever meet her. Or show himself to Johnny. With each passing week, Hattie feared that Gary's time on earth was ticking away. His visits were less frequent, his appearance more fragile each time. The flickering wobbliness reminded her of the Princess Leia hologram in *Star Wars* as she begged Obi-Wan Kenobi for help.

'I'm so sorry about your husband. Johnny told me what happened. I can't imagine … well, it's just horrible.' Tilly's pale eyes filled with tears. At a loss what to say, Hattie dolloped another helping of ice cream into her bowl. That did the trick. God, the girl could eat, spooning it in so fast she must surely have brain freeze.

As Johnny and Tilly got ready to leave – 'We're meeting Josh and some of the crew for beers,' said Johnny – Hattie's phone pinged. A text from Cat. Asking if they could meet up soon. She fired back a rapid *Sure thing. Will be in touch* x Quick hugs from both, then she closed the door and took a deep breath. Time to get to the bottom of the Stewart situation. And hopefully find a way to consign him to history permanently.

CHAPTER 40

'WOAH, MAN. WHY THE LONG FACE?' Clarence was never a bundle of joy, but right now he looked like a lottery winner who realised they'd torn up the ticket.

'I have experienced an epiphany, Gary,' intoned Clarence solemnly, hands clasped and wringing together in internal turmoil.

'Oh dear, was it painful?' asked Gary. He knew – sort of – what the word meant, something about a sudden realisation. But winding up Clarence was one of the small pleasures he had in The Present.

Clarence scowled, then returned to his hand-wringing. Gary decided to leave him to his thoughts and try to track down Marty. He'd only taken a few steps when …

'Tis better to have loved and lost than never to have loved at all.' Gary halted and turned, stunned to see Clarence hunched over, head drooping. He backtracked and knelt down beside him.

'Wanna talk about it, dude? Cos something's on your mind, and I'm willing to listen. Maybe we can swap stories. You share what's bugging you and I'll tell you what I think my mission is. But I ain't sure I've got the whole picture yet. Part of it is to do with Marty, right? But there's something else …'

Clarence wiped at his eyes with the sleeve of his black cloak-thing. Heck, the dude really *was* having a bad day. Gary went to give him a man hug, then thought better of it. To his relief, he saw the unmistakable figure of Marty approaching through the shifting mist, Grump tucked under his arm.

'Why is Clarence sad?' asked Marty. He fumbled in his pocket and produced a handful of sweets, no doubt purloined from Anna. 'Would you like one?' He held out his hand to Clarence who hesitated before taking a striped mint. He sucked it tentatively, his expression alternating between puzzlement and cautious enjoyment. Gary took one too, and he and Marty waited, mist swirling around their feet.

'I am beholden to you for the unfamiliar confectionery,' said Clarence finally. 'The sweetness offsets the inherent melancholy I must carry for all eternity. As a guide, my time here is infinite, whereas others … they will pass on to The Next Realm. But only when their mission has been effectuated. Your time is drawing near, Gary. And Marty too. Soon our ways will part and deliverance to a higher plane will complete your journey.' Clarence sniffed loudly, before tapping his lips with a finger. When neither Gary nor Marty responded, he stuck out his tongue. Marty did the same, crossing his eyes for good measure. Gary laughed at the absurdity of the situation, his spectral companion and little dead friend pulling faces at each other. It was only when Clarence impatiently pointed at Marty's shorts he realised the old sod was after another sweet.

'OK, are you going to spill the beans or just chomp your way through Marty's bonbons?' Gary's irritation at Clarence was growing, as was his sense of unease at what happened next. What in the name of the wee man was 'The Next

Realm' and what did it mean for him and Marty? Would it be like moving from economy to first class on a plane: comfier seats and more legroom? Not that he'd come across any seats where they were now, and the smiling cabin crew offering hot flannels and refreshments were also conspicuous by their absence. No, it was probably more like going to the gate and waiting grim-faced as the information boards promised updates, hours ticking away with no news and only false promises. Except in their case, the wait would last an eternity.

'The Next Realm is a special place where the chosen ones find ever-lasting peace. I have assisted many in their transition from this world to the next. I have been fortunate to encounter some inspiring individuals who moved me with their intellect and mastery of the English language.' The look Clarence gave Gary suggested he wasn't included in this elite group. Not that he was bothered; he just wished misery guts would get to the point.

'Alfred Lord Tennyson was one such fellow. It was he who penned the exquisite line you heard me utter. The eloquence of the words, conveying the bittersweet agony of finding love and knowing it can never endure.' Clarence dabbed at his eyes again. Marty passed him another sweet, his face a perfect picture of bewilderment.

'I remember little of my time on earth, Gary,' Clarence continued between loud crunches. 'The centuries have passed, each one bringing other souls in search of solace and understanding. One was a lady whose brilliance and beauty captivated me like no other. Indeed, I lost my heart to her and I believe the feelings were reciprocated but ... my dear, beloved Jane was always destined to progress to a higher level. Yet, it is only now as I ponder on the vagaries of love, that I realise I was blessed. As you were, Gary, to have loved and been loved by your fair spouse.'

How Clarence knew that Hattie was indeed a looker and not a wizened old hag was anyone's guess. Gary had given up trying to fathom the ins and outs of the afterlife. All he wanted now was to figure out the final piece of the puzzle and hope that Marty got the news he so desperately wanted to hear. In the meantime … 'That's a bummer, Clarence, pardon the expression. Who was this Jane chick and what made her so special?'

Clarence frowned, either at Gary's choice of language or because Marty had turned out his pocket to show all the sweets had gone. 'I am unfamiliar with the term "chick", although I can surmise from the context that it is some modern – and I feel rather unbecoming – word relating to the fairer sex. Jane was a remarkable woman, well read and with a lasting legacy of literary works which endure to this day. Why, another fellow – a recent arrival – informed me that her books had been translated into motion pictures. A concept I struggle to process, yet there is so much on earth I feel is beyond comprehension.' Clarence sighed heavily. Marty looked bored out of his skull and had resorted to a bout of nose-picking. Gary, however, was dumbstruck. He might have got a D in English, and several detentions for covertly panting over a copy of Playboy instead of studying Chaucer or some other mind-numbing text, but—

'Are you seriously telling me you had the hots for Jane Austen? As in, *Pride and Prejudice? Sense and Sensitivity?* OK, not sure about that one, but even I've heard of her!' Hattie had watched the TV version of the former at least half a dozen times, always pausing for a little too long on the scene when Colin Firth emerged dripping from a lake. Gary had tried to mimic the scene once after indulging in a few too many pints. He'd stripped off, waded into a duck pond and strode out covered in algae, his boxers weighed down so much his knackers were on show. Hattie hadn't looked at him with lust; no, she'd wet herself laughing, filmed the whole episode and posted it on YouTube. It received over two hundred views, several obscene comments and gained Gary the nickname of Saggy Bollocks.

Clarence's expression brightened dramatically. Thoughts of his lost love might have temporarily given him an even bigger dose of the glums, but bragging about his famous sweetheart was clearly an ego boost. Crikey, he looked in danger of cracking a smile!

'Indeed, Gary. I was smitten by the wit, intelligence and allure of Miss Austen. It was an honour and a privilege to spend time – albeit fleeting – in the company of one so exquisite. To paraphrase another fine gentleman, "Parting was such sweet sorrow."'

OK, Gary recognised that line too. At least some English lessons he'd yawned and fidgeted through had made a lasting impression. What he didn't get was why clever clogs Clarence had been appointed his guide when his previous line-up included bloody Shakespeare?

'Gary, can we go and see Anna now?' Marty tugged at Gary's hand. 'She promised we could play cards and that Bob wouldn't be there cos he's disappeared.' Really? Gary wondered if pain-in-the-arse Bob had ascended to The Next Realm. More likely, he was stuck in transit somewhere between here and the hot burny place. Not that he was evil, just a jumped-up no one who got his kicks out of being nasty.

'Sure thing, buddy. I just need to ask Clarence … ' Oh, effing brilliant. His so-called guide had sailed off into the mist, leaving Gary's question about his mission unanswered. Again.

CHAPTER 41

'DO YOU BABY-OIL YOUR SPLASHBACK?' enquired Cat, rubbing
cream into the liver-spotted hands of regular customer Joy
Carter. Making small talk was all part of the job, and
normally Cat enjoyed it. Having a bit of a laugh, exchanging
random thoughts and – like now – household tips. Except—

'Do I what?' Joy recoiled, her demeanour one of a woman
who'd been asked if her bedside cabinet was bulging with sex
toys. Snatching her hands away, she glared at Cat indig-
nantly. Cat bit her lip in an attempt not to giggle. The daft
old biddy clearly thought she'd been referring to the lubrica-
tion of her private parts. Somehow she couldn't imagine Joy
getting herself greased up and ready to roll with husband
Ernest, who'd probably drop dead on the spot. He was a
meek and mild little soul, booze his only pleasure (although
he'd been spotted entering the local betting shop on a few
occasions). Possibly dreaming of winning big and escaping
the tyranny of joyless Joy and her ninety-denier nylons.

'Sorry, I wasn't being rude, Mrs Carter. I read somewhere
that using baby oil on stainless steel in the kitchen gave it a
shine and stopped it getting stained.' Cat gave her best 'the

customer is always right' smile and resumed the pre-manicure treatment.

An hour later, and she was on her way home. Her appointments diary was packed for the next two weeks, leading Cat to think again about expanding the business. Bigger premises meant she could take on extra staff, but did she really want to accept Stewart's offer? The more she thought about it, the more anxious she felt. Tentatively rebuilding a relationship with him was one thing. Being financially beholden was quite another.

IN THE SHELTER OF SEMI-DARKNESS, Stewart peeled off Cat's clothes. His hands were everywhere, still so familiar after all these years. She raised her bottom from the mattress, allowing him to ease her knickers downwards. All the time he was kissing her, caressing her, Cat's fingers stroking his silky chest hair. It was good, it was fine, it was *right*. Wasn't it? Cat had crumbled at last, when Stewart turned up with a bottle of vintage champagne, flowers that must have cost a bomb and assurances that she could pay a loan back in her own time and without any pressure. When he'd kissed her, she'd responded with passion and it seemed natural for them to go to bed. And it had been as wonderful as she remembered, until … the flinch was tiny, barely there. Another woman on a close encounter of the first kind probably wouldn't have registered it but … Cat's brain cells regrouped, shouted orders and formed orderly lines. Stewart's lips travelled south and – there it was again – hardly perceptible but a definite shudder as he traversed her stomach. Cat had gained a few pounds in recent weeks, due mainly to being wined and dined by her ex. Fully dressed, the weight gain was negligible, but stark naked Cat knew there were more lumps and bumps. And Stewart's reaction was all-too familiar, even if he was trying to mask it with murmurs and moans.

'Oh, Cat.' Stewart edged further towards his target, his fingers teasing their way along her thighs. And there it was again. She counted down inside her head. *Ten, nine, eight, seven, six —*

'Stop. Now.' Cat wriggled out from under Stewart, pulling the duvet over her chest and sitting upright. Stewart sat up too, his face a carefully constructed picture of hurt and miscomprehension. He did it all so well, but Cat wasn't fooled. She *had* been, stupidly sucked back into his vortex of charm and charisma, but he hadn't changed. She'd wanted to believe he had, because then she could forgive herself for marrying him in the first place. Dumb then, dumber now, but Cat's self-worth was clawing its way out of the mire.

'What's the matter? I thought you wanted this. You know how I feel, Catherine. Why else would I have come back?' Stewart reached across to kiss her, but Cat pulled away.

'You say all the right things, Stewart, but actions speak louder than words and ... you flinched. Don't deny it, you think I'm fat and at some point you're going to *help* me lose weight. Or *advise* me on how to dress. Or try to interfere in how I run my business. Well, guess what? I don't want any of that. I am what I am, and what I am ...' Cat stopped talking, afraid she might burst into song. Although she did feel like singing, and maybe tossing in a few dance moves too. Not naked, however. She embraced her jiggly bits, but Stewart clearly didn't.

'Don't be silly, Catherine ... Cat. I've tried my best to be the man you want me to be and I've said I'm sorry about the past. If you're happy a bit – heavier – then that's fine. We could try the keto diet together but if you'd rather not ...' Stewart's words tailed away, as Cat scrambled out of bed and retrieved her undies. She got the thong on back to front and took several attempts to hook up her bra, but she didn't care. All she wanted was for Stewart to leave her alone and to be with a man who loved her unconditionally. Someone who made her feel comfortable in her own skin, who looked at her and saw only good things. Someone who made her laugh and never, ever put her down. Someone like ... Jamie. But that ship had sailed, and Cat had well and truly scuppered it. Ran it aground, and for what? A man who was unable to change, who was choking down his true feelings. She could never be herself with Stewart. He would always find a way to diminish her, intentionally or otherwise.

'Please, leave now. And ... don't come back.' Cat's voice trembled but her resolve was strong. Issuing the ultimatum without pubic hair on display would have been better but ... at least she hadn't slept with him. Her grey matter had won the day, even if was too late to salvage what might have been.

'You don't mean that. Come on, Cat, we're meant to be together.' Stewart reclined in bed, showing no intention of moving. Cat stood her ground, her robe hanging feet away on the door, but she didn't budge. She maintained eye contact and pleaded with her brain to override all lustful thoughts. Stewart was incredibly easy on the eye, he just wasn't any good for her as a person.

'No, we're not. That's why we split up and I'm sorry I let it get this far but ... it's over, Stewart. Once and for all.' This time Cat grabbed her robe and opened the door. Stewart reared up, like a cobra ready to strike. His mesmerising eyes, which had gazed adoringly at her minutes before, glinted with steely disdain.

'Oh, really? So you've just been leading me on all this time, playing a little game? Seriously, Cat, it's not as if you have a lot of choices. I mean, in all the years since we divorced, how many men did you see? Hmm, let me think ...

a couple, if I recall correctly. And as for the latest one – whatever his name is – he hardly looks your type. What is he … a librarian or something?' Stewart gave a derisory snort. Hot, angry tears filled Cat's eyes. Both for putting herself in this position, and in response to Stewart's sneering dismissal of a man who was superior in every way.

'Jamie is a teacher, and he is … was … the best thing to happen to me until you appeared and screwed it all up. Yes, I take part of the blame but I'm not going to let you ruin the rest of my life!'

Stewart cocked an eyebrow, the oh-so-familiar but carefully hidden sneer of old distorting his face. 'Sweetheart, if you kick me out I'm afraid that's exactly what you'll do. I doubt lover boy will have you back, and if you don't take care that middle-age spread will—'

Tinkle, tinkle. The unmistakable sound of a bell, and then …

'Out! Get thee out!' A voice boomed around the room, bouncing off the walls and causing Cat to tip backwards and clunk her head on the half-open door. Ouch! Rubbing her skull, she saw that Stewart was pinned to the headboard by an invisible force, eyes now wide with terror.

'I will release you, but cross this threshold again and you will regret it for the rest of eternity,' the voice intoned, menace dripping from every syllable. For a brief moment there was total silence, bar Stewart's gasping breaths and Cat's strangled giggles. Fighting to keep her composure, she watched with silent delight as Stewart dressed at breakneck speed. As he legged it out of the room, he couldn't resist a pause in front of the mirror. Yes, once a vain bastard, always a vain bastard.

'Gary, I know it's you, despite the weird talk. *Get thee out? Have you been hanging around with Shakespeare or some-thing? Come on, you daft bugger. Let me see you!' Cat heard the roar of Stewart's car engine and the squeal of brakes as he exited stage left. Christ, now *she* was getting all Bard-like.

'Sorry, darlin', but that needed to be done. Saved by the bell, and all that. I don't think he'll be back any time soon.' Gary came into focus, but he was – literally – a shadow of his former ghostly self. Cat gulped and moved towards him. Hattie had said he was gradually disappearing; now the evidence was right in front of her. Like an ageing photograph, Gary's edges and colours were fading away.

'From the look on your face, I know I don't look so hot and my time's running out. It's just … I've still got a job to do, and it's about Hattie. It has to be. I've done all I can for Marty but there's something else.'

Cat's heart went out to Gary. He looked so forlorn, even in his diminished state. 'Maybe it's making sure she's happy before you … before whatever happens next, happens. Like, finding her another man?'

Gary's expression grew glummer. The thought of his beloved Hattie being with someone else was bound to hurt, but Cat knew he wouldn't want her to stay a grieving widow forever. OK, he'd meddled in her dates, but neither of them had been ideal candidates for a lasting relationship. Was there someone else out there, Hattie's perfect match?

CHAPTER 42

Pulling up outside Espresso Yourself, Hattie felt exhausted. She hadn't slept well for what seemed like weeks. Her brain constantly bounced between her mum, Gary and Cat, with concerns about Barry also interfering with her shut-eye. And it had been over a month since her trip to Edinburgh. Hattie hadn't heard a word from the McMasters, not that she expected to so soon. Why was life so blinking complicated? Her only consolation was that Johnny seemed content both with his job and the delightful Tilly. And she'd remarkably found an accessible parking spot which was like finding gold at the end of a rainbow.

Bending over to grab her bag from the foot well of the passenger side, Hattie bounced forward and bashed her head hard on the dashboard. Yelping in pain, she straightened up, unsure what had happened. A sharp rap on the window provoked another yelp. Struggling to focus – her vision was blurred with agonised tears – she looked over to see a man gazing in at her. Oh, help. Was this one of those car robberies she'd read about, when defenceless women were rammed then their handbags snatched? Should she put down the window, or drive off in search of a police officer?

'Are you OK?' The man's voice was muffled by the glass between them. Now that she could see a little better, he didn't *look* like someone to be afraid of. Then again, thieves didn't necessarily wear balaclavas or stockings over their heads. Nope, even some of the world's most notorious serial killers had looked like Mr Joe Average. Praying that she wasn't making a huge mistake, Hattie pushed the button, and the window glided down.

'Gosh, I'm so sorry. I was trying to manoeuvre into the space behind you and I completely cocked it up. Sorry again, my reverse parking skills leave a lot to be desired.' Sombre grey eyes looked at Hattie with concern. She couldn't help notice little white creases fanning out, stark against the smooth tan of his skin.

'Um, it's fine. I mean, I'm fine. Apart from ...' Hattie rubbed her forehead, wincing as she touched a rapidly swelling lump. 'I guess I should check out the damage to my car, if there is any.' She pushed the door open, and the culprit moved aside, taking her arm as she swayed slightly. Allowing him to help her to her feet, Hattie tottered to the back of her car and squinted at the bumper. A minor ding, to add to the others she'd accumulated over the years. Her car was approaching vintage status but only in terms of it being ancient, not collectable. She loathed reverse parking herself and would rather drive another mile than attempt to squeeze into a space designed for a Little Tikes toy car. Still, he must have been gunning the accelerator to force Hattie's face into the cheap plastic fascia.

'Look, you're a bit shaken, and that's a nasty bump on your head. I can take you to A & E ...' Hattie shook her head vigorously at the suggestion, then regretted the sudden movement. Ouch! Her rear-ending assailant took her arm again and gestured towards the door of Espresso Yourself. 'How about we go in there and ask for some ice for your head? Then I can try to make amends by buying you a drink and something sweet for the shock.'

It wasn't as if Hattie had anywhere else to go, so she nodded in agreement. Locking their cars, they headed inside and up to the counter. Beth was slicing a lemon drizzle cake, and there were only a handful of customers dotted around with their coffees and pastries.

'Hiya, Hattie. Jeez, that's either one cracker of a spot or you've done something nasty to your forehead!' Beth hurried round the counter and tentatively touched the bump. At the same time she looked Hattie's companion up and down with an accusing air. He raised his hands in a 'guilty as charged' expression, Hattie quickly explaining about the car incident in case Beth thought he'd physically attacked her.

'Here, pop this on your head and go sit down.' Beth produced a makeshift ice-pack wrapped in a tea towel. 'Don't worry about your shift, I'll cover it if you need to go home. It looks like a quiet one today and Miriam's due in so I'll explain what happened. Now, what can I get you and …?' They both looked at mystery man, who was clearly unsure whether to hang around or simply hand over his insurance details and scarper.

'I'm Laurence. Laurence Jones. And I'm sorry I've mucked things up for you at work too. Look, I'd like to hang around to make sure you're really OK. And a coffee and slice of that cake would go down well.' He smiled, revealing slightly crooked but white teeth and held out his hand. Hattie shook it. Beth was otherwise occupied fixing their order.

Finding a corner table, Hattie introduced herself and they chatted about her job and other mundane things. She kept the ice-pack clutched to her head, although the pain had quickly subsided. Laurence explained he was an optician –

'although you might be thinking I need my own eyes testing if I can't judge parking distances!' – who'd recently set up a practice in the neighbouring town.

'I'm from Wells in Somerset originally, but decided I needed a fresh start after my wife died.' Hattie mumbled the usual platitudes, reluctant to share her own status. Was he telling the truth? She'd been stung by ratbag Rich's blatant lies, not that she thought Laurence was chatting her up. Although she could easily listen to his gentle West Country lilt for hours …

Twenty minutes later and Hattie's head felt much better. Their drinks and cakes were finished and there was no sign of Miriam. A gaggle (or should that be a giggle?) of teenage girls had burst through the doors, chatting excitedly about the end of exams and bombarding Beth with complicated coffee requests.

'Listen, I'd better get to work before my colleague's head explodes,' said Hattie. 'Honestly, I'm good and I don't want to take up any more of your time.'

Laurence insisted on exchanging details, including their mobile numbers. Hattie assured him there was no need; she had no intention of visiting the garage. A new – or marginally less beaten-up car – was on her wish list. There were still a couple of small investments Gary had made that could soon be cashed in. They might not see her living the champagne and caviar life, more 'fur coat and no knickers' as Gary would say, but every bit helped.

Shaking Laurence's hand, Hattie batted away further apologies and watched as he left. No sooner had she reached the counter and started helping out with the orders, than Beth waggled her eyebrows suggestively.

'What? Stop giving me that look. You know what happened so let's not go down the "he fancies you" road again. Because he doesn't, and even if he did … well, I'm done with men.' Hattie bit down her irritation, both at Beth's smirk and one of the teenage customers demanding to know if the brownies were carb-free. She smiled sweetly and suggested carrot cake instead. Still carb-loaded but their vegetable content seemed to satisfy Miss Picky Pants.

'I wouldn't kick him out of bed for eating crisps,' declared Beth, as the mad rush subsided. 'He's got a bit of Richard Gere about him, although not quite as old. More *Pretty Woman* days, but a few more wrinkles. God, didn't you just fancy the pants off him in that movie?'

Privately, Hattie preferred him in *An Officer and a Gentleman* and she hadn't clocked the resemblance. Now, come to think of it ...

* * *

'So, it's over? Really, *really* over?' Hattie tried and failed to keep the cynicism out of her voice. She'd felt guilty at not seeing Cat sooner, but her best friend had gone to ground. Just a short text saying she 'needed to sort her head out'. Hattie had given her space, praying that meant she would see sense and kick Stewart into touch. Much as it pained her to admit it, she'd felt sure that Cat would never shake free of him. She knew how hard it had been the first time around. This time? She'd doubted Cat would have the emotional strength to send him packing. Except ... by some miracle, she had.

'Yes, it's over.'

Hattie had found Cat sitting on her doorstep when she got home after another exhausting day at work. Her face reminded Hattie of a happy/sad theatre mask, split between joy and despondency. The joy, she knew, was because Stewart had finally exited stage left and wouldn't be back for a bow. The sadness – hazarding a not-too-wild guess – was to do with Jamie. The one who got away. Or rather, slipped away when a determined ex-husband stuck his oily oar in.

Cat was sipping a large whisky. Visibly shaken by her final encounter with Stewart, she pulled no punches detailing what had happened. Crikey! At least Stewart hadn't *actually* stuck his … Hattie shuddered, both at Stewart's below-the-belt words and her own tiny measure of the Scottish stuff. Even drowned in Diet Coke it tasted vile. Still, solidarity and all that. It was when Cat revealed Gary's part in Stewart's Olympic-worthy departure that she almost choked.

'I can't believe he did that! No, who am I kidding, I can *totally* believe he did that. Go Gary!' Hattie punched the air and whooped. Cat followed suit, then they hugged each other and did a little happy dance around the kitchen. Tears were mixed with more whoops, both of them bordering on hysteria. Cat seized the whisky bottle and necked it, Hattie opting to pour a glass of white from the fridge she'd opened two nights before. Calming down, they toasted the future. A Stewart-free one. Yeah! More happy dancing. Then … the upbeat tempo turned to a slow melody. A tune that spoke of heartache and loss. There wasn't any music, of course, just the rhythmic realisation that things were changing. Nothing lasted forever. No one lasted forever.

'How … how did he seem? Gary, I mean.' Hattie's lip trembled, and they squashed together in a sombre embrace.

'Fragile. Like he was splintering before my eyes. Oh, Hattie, he was so amazing with Stewart but he said … he thought maybe he had one last job to do. And I wondered if he can't rest in peace until he knows you've got somebody else by your side.'

Hattie pushed away thoughts of earlier in the day, and the person who'd bruised her head and bashed her bumper. Besides, she had dinner tomorrow night at Barry's who she regarded firmly as a friend. Nothing more, no need for any complications. She could be happy *without* a man; of course she could!

'What about you, Cat? Are you OK or is there someone you should call? Jamie, perhaps?' She held her best friend in the world at arms' length and fixed her with the sternest of stares. 'You don't know if it's completely broken unless you try to fix it. Call him. What have you got to lose?'

CHAPTER 43

As HATTIE ENTERED Barry's house, she detected the distinct whiff of air freshener. The perfume was verging on sickly, tickling her nostrils as she allowed Barry to take her coat. They'd exchanged kisses on the cheek, all fine and dandy although he gave her that look again as he drew away. Was she imagining things? This was Gary's great mate, and she was very fond of him. That was all. End of story.

In the living room, Hattie realised her version of the story might differ just a little from Barry's. Unless a linen-clad table resplendent with candles, elaborate place settings – four courses, by the looks of things – and lighting dimmed so low she might need a miner's helmet was the norm for visitors. Hattie half-expected to see rose petals strewn across the shag pile which – oh, help! – made her wonder if they were strewn somewhere else.

'Gosh, you've gone to a lot of trouble, Barry,' she stammered, accepting a glass of something fizzy with a flower in it.

'It's hibiscus,' said Barry. 'They add a touch of flavour and it looks pretty, doesn't it?' He clinked his glass against

Hattie's, and she gulped down a large mouthful to steady her nerves. Her expectations had been nothing more than spaghetti Bolognese and a bottle of plonk. Judging by the setting, she was in for a romantic *dinner à deux,* which filled her with dread. She glanced around the room, wondering if a string quartet would pop up and serenade them. Or if Gary would appear and send Barry shrieking into the night.

'Sorry, it all looks a bit OTT,' said Barry, who'd gone into the kitchen and returned with two plates of salad topped with strips of smoked salmon. 'I wanted to impress, but my cooking skills are limited so I resorted to cheating. Everything's pre-made, but I did open the salmon packet myself!'

Hattie smiled, inwardly cringing at the whole set-up. She hadn't sent the wrong message to Barry, had she? Yes, he was a nice man, and they'd leaned on each other, shared their grief but … nothing more. She looked at his kind, open face and wanted to weep. If life was simple, they'd skip off into the sunset, holding hands and making plans. But, life wasn't simple. She loved Gary, and replacing him would never be a cut and paste job. Barry wasn't The One. Did he even exist? Hattie hoped that Cat could make up with Jamie because he was one of the good ones. And although she'd only met him briefly, Hattie felt sure he was the forgiving type.

They ate their way through all the courses, chatting away as normal. Barry was planning another trip to Asia, possibly Vietnam, to help a colleague set up a new language school. Hattie expressed her relief at Cat escaping the clutches of Stewart, and her delight at Johnny's fledgling relationship with Tilly. They talked about Rachel, and how well she seemed, even more so now that Ralph had moved in.

'They're thinking of taking a holiday soon,' said Hattie, drowning her strawberries and shop-bought meringues in cream. 'Maybe a week's cruise around the Mediterranean.

They can't go away too long as Mum'll need more treatment in the run up to her operation. Fingers crossed.'

Barry started clearing away the dishes, urging Hattie to stay put when she offered to help.

'I'll fix us a nice coffee then we can get more comfortable,' he said, stacking the bowls and spoons. Her sense of foreboding returned. What exactly did he mean by 'comfortable'? Hopefully just a seat on the sofa and not a trip upstairs to a rose-petal-festooned bedroom. With Barry fussing away in the kitchen, Hattie took out her phone. Two messages and a new email. The first was from Cat. *Messaged Jamie to ask if we could meet, and he said yes! Probably doesn't mean anything but ... Thanks, Hat. Love you xxxx*

The second was from Jack. *Hey, Sis. How's it hanging? And I don't mean your double chin, arf, arf! Got some news for you, but better if you see for yourself. Buzz me when you can come over. Xx*

She opened her email and saw immediately who it was from. Flora McMaster, Marty's mum. Her finger ached to open it, but at that moment Barry returned with a tray of coffee and petits fours. Hattie stuffed the phone in her pocket and smiled. She'd read it later, not trusting what her reaction would be depending on its content.

Barry had set the coffees out on the table and gestured for Hattie to join him. She moved to sit on the solo armchair but Barry patted the seat next to him. Swallowing her anxiety, she sat as close to the edge as possible.

'Oh, I forgot to say! Someone crashed into my car today. Well, not exactly crashed, more like shunted me forward when I was parked. I've got quite a bruise on my head but I covered it up with some amazing concealer Cat gave me.' Hattie knew she was babbling, her nerves forcing words out in a garbled rush. Her anxiety levels shot up as Barry leaned over and gently touched her forehead, concern laced with something deeper – more intimate – writ large on his face.

Hattie flinched, not through pain but fear that Barry was about to kiss her. He withdrew his hand quickly and, as he did, Hattie's mind flashed back to the cause of her injury. Not the car, but the driver. Just for a moment Laurence Jones's handsome face came into view and Hattie felt a frisson of something. Attraction? Which was ridiculous as she would most likely never see him again. Maybe she had a mild concussion, causing her to imagine things. Like Barry being interested in her in *that* way ... Oh, no. He'd shuffled up closer and taken Hattie's hand. She had no choice but to face him, and hope that she really had got the wrong end of the stick.

'Hattie, I hope I'm not speaking out of turn, but you've come to mean a lot to me. Without you ... well, you know how much I loved Gary, and that I didn't cope well.' Barry's eyes filled up, and he squeezed her hand. Hattie fought the temptation to snatch it away. All she could do was listen and muster the courage to say what needed to be said.

'I know you still love Gary and miss him every day, but I feel we've become close and ... the truth is I've fallen for you. Some people might think that's wrong but I believe – if Gary was out there, looking down, he'd give us his blessing.'

Would he? Hattie didn't know, and she wasn't going to ask. He probably already knew and might give his opinion at some point. What she did know was that Barry could only ever be a friend. There was no physical attraction, at least on her part, and even if there was ... Hattie still couldn't picture a future without Gary in it, even if all the evidence suggested his time on earth was tick-tocking away. And if there *was* another man out there, it needed to be someone new. With no shared history or emotional baggage. A fresh start.

'Hattie? Please say something.' Barry's watery eyes met hers, hope gleaming through the tears. Hattie wanted to sprint out the door, maybe invent a fast-acting bout of

260 THE HAUNTING OF HATTIE HASTINGS

gastroenteritis (the salmon had been a bit grey), but she couldn't. Sometimes, you had to be cruel to be kind.

'I'm so sorry, Barry, but it's a no.' Where the heck did *that* come from? Hattie had no idea why she'd come out with such a callous turndown. Possibly too much time spent watching Dragons' Den, squirming as enthusiastic entrepreneurs were rejected in a similar style. She tried again. 'It's not you, it's me.' Great, from cutting to clichéd in a heartbeat. Barry now looked like a Death Row inmate who'd heard his final appeal had been rejected. Come on, Hattie! Say something to make him feel better!

'What I mean is … what I'm trying to say is … you're a lovely man and you'll always be part of my life. And Johnny's too. But I'll always be reminded of Gary when I see you. And that wouldn't be fair on you, knowing that I picture him every time we're together. You'll meet someone else, someone who doesn't mess you around like Lorna did. And you'll be happy, Barry, because no one deserves to be more than you.' Phew, that sounded better. Barry gave a weak smile and let go of Hattie's hand.

'Deep down I knew this would happen, but you can't blame me for trying!' Barry pushed the plunger down on the forgotten cafetière and poured them both a cup. 'You're a beautiful, smart and caring lady, Hattie, and way out of my league.' Before Hattie could protest, he continued, 'Gary was the best mate a bloke could have, and I count myself lucky to have known him. And having you as a friend … well, I'll always be here for you, Hattie. And Johnny.'

Hattie left a short while after. They hugged by the door, the embrace of two people united by a common love for a special person. They'd never be a couple, but Hattie knew Barry would be part of her life forever. However long that might be.

CHAPTER 44

STILL UNABLE TO BRING HERSELF TO read the email, Hattie texted Jack to see if she could drop by on the way home. She was curious as to what the 'news' might be. Maybe they were getting married? Hattie doubted it. Jack had once quipped that, 'Marriage is an institution, and I don't want to be an inmate.' Although he'd kindly added that as both she and Gary were barking mad, the state of matrimony suited them perfectly.

It was Ben who opened the door, his words of welcome drowned out by squealing and whimpering as a solid ball of fluff tangled itself around Hattie's ankles. Bending down, her face was enthusiastically licked from top to bottom. At least Barry hadn't got *that* far.

'Down, girl! Come on, heel!' As Ben dragged the fur ball away, its claws scratching on the expensive wood flooring, Jack appeared, looking more dishevelled than usual. He was holding a cloth that appeared to be covered in …

'She pooped again. On the kitchen floor. Thank God those tiles are easy to clean. How can something that little be so full of shit?'

Ben stroked the puppy's head, and its whole body quivered with excitement. 'Oh, I don't know, Jack. You're not exactly a man mountain yourself, yet you contain a fair amount of doo-doo. Now, darling Doris, say a proper hello to Auntie Hattie.'

The chocolate Labrador pup went in for another lick of Hattie's face. She ducked and ruffled its ears. *Doris?* Quirky name, but no less than she'd expect from her brother and his partner.

'Sorry about the face-licking, but we have her booked in for doggie training so she'll soon be perfectly behaved. Won't she, Ben?'

Ben rolled his eyes, perhaps not so enamoured with their bundle of joy. Yet, he'd been the one who said he'd rather have a dog than a baby. Reality was clearly biting, as was Doris, now chewing away at Ben's designer shirt. 'Bad girl! All I can say, lover boy, face-licking is one less personal chore *I'll* have to undertake!'

* * *

THE TIME for stalling was over. Hattie sat at her laptop, knowing she had to read the email but feeling sick in case the content wasn't what she wanted to hear. She'd dodged it for a week, unable to open it by herself. She didn't want to do this alone. There was only one person she needed by her side right now. Her rock, the man who'd given her so many happy years and was still doing so, long after he was supposed to.

'Babe. I'm here.' His voice was weak, diminished, as feeble as a whisper carried away on a breeze. Hattie looked up and gasped. Gary was hardly visible, a shadow of his former ghostly self. Not even a shadow, just a vague imprint. A footprint in the sand, washed away by the ebb and flow of the tide. It was almost time.

'Read it, Hats. Whatever it says, we need to know. Marty's been bending my ear and now the answer's right here. Good or bad, we gotta do this.'

Hattie could barely see the screen for the tears coursing down her face. A song kept playing in her head. Something about *the end is near*. Of course it was. Gary had always been living – or dead – on borrowed time. But why was that particular tune bugging her right now?

'It's Clarence,' said Gary, tapping into her thoughts again. 'We finally got a proper chat and I know my mission was twofold. Helping out Marty – duh, we figured *that* one out – and making sure you were OK. And you will be, Hats. I know there's someone there for you. And you've already met him.'

Hattie blinked hard, her mascara stinging like hell. She tugged a tissue out from her sleeve and swiped at her eyes. Who was Gary talking about? Surely not Barry, or one of her best-forgotten dates?

'I believe his name's Laurence, and he's a good 'un. Don't ask me *how* I know, but when he asks you out … say yes.'

It was beyond surreal, her already-dead and soon-to-be-departed again husband recommending a new partner. Laurence. Oh. My. God. A thought suddenly struck Hattie. What if he called himself Larry? *Gary, Barry and Larry.* It would be like a warped version of The Marx Brothers.

'He doesn't, babe. Stop stressing and start living. Can we check that bloody email now?'

'Hang on a sec.' That song was still buzzing around like an annoying mosquito. 'What's with Clarence and that partic-ular number? I recognise it now, "facing the final curtain", and all that. Was he doing the Sinatra version or Sid Vicious?'

Gary laughed, a sound she'd always loved. Now, it only reminded her of the past, and nudged her into a future she had no idea how to navigate. He was leaving, and Hattie didn't know if she could say goodbye again.

'Hell, no. It was definitely the Clarence version. Gloomy as fuck and as uplifting as a trainer bra. I won't miss him when we move on to The Next Realm, except Marty hopes it'll be like Disneyland. All spinning teacups and rollercoaster rides. Hate to break it to the wee fella, but I hurl on that stuff.'

Hattie opened the email. Her heart was in her mouth as she began to read.

Dear Hattie. I hope you're well. Gary and Marty too. That is such a strange thing to write, but I've clung on to what you said, and it's kept me sane. Made me sane, to be honest. I never thought I'd get over Marty's death, but I have. He will always be my precious, beloved boy but your visit made me see that grief is something you can drown in, or rise above and learn from. Marty wasn't with us for long, but he taught us to love, be loved and to value each day. His were too short, but I treasure all our memories.

Anyway, I won't keep rambling on. I just wanted to tell you that I'm pregnant. I can't quite believe it after all these years, but three home tests and a visit to the GP confirmed it. We're having a baby! David's over the moon, we both are. I know it's still very early days but nowadays I believe in miracles. If I can accept that ghosts exist, I can believe in just about anything.

Thank you, Hattie, for coming to see us and helping us to move on. We hope you can pass on this message to our darling boy through Gary. And we wish you only happiness in the future.

All our very best wishes. Flora and David.

PS. We'll let you know when the baby arrives!

Hattie looked up from the screen, shoulders heaving as she sobbed uncontrollably. Gary moved to touch her, but she could no longer feel him. Only a slight movement of air indicated there was anyone else in the room.

'Babe, that's brilliant! I can't wait to tell Marty. Oh, Hats, please stop crying. You'll short circuit the computer with all those tears.'

Gary was disappearing, bit by bit, and there was nothing either of them could do about it. Hattie wanted to scream and howl and beg for him to stay, but she knew it was no use. 'There are so many things we never got to do,' she wept. 'Like ... like celebrate our silver wedding anniversary. I always thought we'd throw a big party then go on an amazing holiday.'

Gary briefly came back into focus. 'I know, babe. But the years we had were the best. And you've got so many more to look forward to. I know it.'

Hattie reached out to take his hand, but it was impossible. The tears were flowing so fast she could barely see. 'And we never got to go on a cruise. Mum and Ralph went on one.'

Gary chuckled, a sound as delicate as wind chimes in a gentle breeze. 'Hats, you know you get seasick on a pedalo.'

Hattie half-sobbed and half-laughed. Gary tried again to comfort her, and this time she felt the faintest of touches. An oh-so-tender and light- as-a-feather kiss.

'I think it's time, darlin'. I don't want to leave you, but I ain't got a choice. You're gonna have a good life, Hats. A *great* life. Take care of our boy and always remember that I love you.'

'I love you too, Gary. I always have and I always will,' she whispered. 'And I will miss you so, so much.'

A second later Hattie thought he'd gone. Then, as she succumbed to another bout of sobbing, she heard his words one last time.

Never forget. Just cos you can't see me no more ... doesn't mean I'm not there.'

* * *

'Mum! Mum! You won't believe what's just happened ...' Johnny bowled into the room at top speed, dragging Tilly

behind him. 'Old Ravenscroft has had a heart attack! It's brilliant!' Tilly let out a shriek of horror and punched him hard
on the arm.

'Fuck. Sorry. That came out *totally* wrong. What I meant
to say …'

Johnny ground to a halt as Hattie raised her tear-stained
face from the cushion she'd been clutching for over an hour.
If she wrung it out over the sink, she was sure gallons of
water would be produced.

'Oh God. What's happened? Is Uncle Jack OK? Is it to do
with Cat? Oh, no. Please don't tell me that Nan has…'

Hattie shook her head. There were so many things she
wanted to say; so much she would love to share with her son.
Their son. But she couldn't. Not now. Gary had gone and all
she had left were memories of their time together, both in
life and in death.

'Sorry, Johnny. Tilly. I was just having a moment. I sometimes think of your dad and it just gets me right *here.*' Hattie
clapped a hand to her chest, never one hundred percent sure
where the heart really was. Or the liver, kidneys or pretty
much any internal organs. Apart from the brain. She knew
where that was. Rattling around in her skull, woefully under-
used. Hattie knew she didn't want to spend the rest of her
days working at Espresso Yourself. But what else could she
do? Maybe take a course in something, but Hattie had no
clue in what. She'd speak to Cat, who might have an idea
or two.

'Anyway, sorry to be such a pig about Ravenscroft but he
had a minor heart thing. Not his first, by all accounts.'
Johnny looked at Tilly for reassurance, and she smiled. 'Anyway, he's taking partial retirement, which means I'll be pretty
much running the shop single-handed. Ace, isn't it?'

Hattie did her best to look pleased, but the tears kept on
coming.

'Oh, Mum.' Johnny and Tilly plonked down on either side of her. Johnny hugged her tightly, Tilly whispering that she'd put the kettle on. She left the room, and Hattie leaned into the comforting arms of her son.

'I know I don't ever say it, but I miss Dad terribly too,' said Johnny. 'I s'pose I didn't want to upset you, bringing it up all the time. But, the thing is ...' He hesitated, twiddling with a loose thread on his baggy jumper. 'Sometimes I get the feeling that Dad's still around. Like, he's watching over me.'

Hattie's eyes widened. Gary had desperately wanted to show himself to Johnny, but he'd never been able to. Now it seemed that his presence had been felt. *Just cos you can't see me no more ...*

'And it's not just a feeling,' Johnny continued. 'I swear I've smelled his aftershave. Sensed he's right there when I'm getting into bed or brushing my teeth. Sounds mad, but it's like he's still looking out for me. D'you ever get that too, Mum?'

Hattie brushed away another onslaught of tears. Eyes stinging and heart aching, she nodded. 'All the time, love. All the time.'

CHAPTER 45

'I THOUGHT about having a picnic at the dump, seeing as it's our favourite meeting place, but ...' Jamie's eyes danced with mischief. Instead, they'd met at a popular tapas bar in town. Sautéed baby chorizo, salt cod croquettes and a platter of Serrano ham with Manchego shavings lay before them. Along with a jug of sangria packed with chunks of chopped fruit. A picnic anywhere would have been a no-no, the steady drizzle showing no signs of relenting.

Cat forked a few pieces on to her plate. It looked and smelled delicious, but her appetite was fighting a losing battle with the butterflies in her stomach. Seeing Jamie again in all his twinkly, good-natured glory made Cat realise what a complete idiot she'd been. Choosing Stewart over Jamie? She deserved a plague of pus-filled boils for being such a pathetic pushover. Although Cat prayed that she'd escape that particular punishment. She was here to try to salvage what she could even if it was only friendship.

'Erm, how's school? It must be coming up to half-term soon,' asked Cat, despairing at her deadly dull conversation skills. They'd always been able to make each other laugh, or

Jamie was cracking her up with another of his one-liners. At this rate he'd be face down in the tapas having died of boredom.

'Yeah. In a week's time. The forecast says we're in for a mini heatwave then, just as the kids break up. I'm hoping to escape to the beach for a few days. Fancy joining me?' Jamie sliced a croquette in half and waggled it at Cat's mouth. She accepted, the process of chewing allowing her time to digest what he'd just said.

'Are you asking me to go away with you?' Cat swallowed, a lumpy bit sticking in her throat. A glug of sangria freed her vocal cords, not that she knew what else to say.

'I was thinking Cornwall. My folks have a small cottage on the coast which they hardly use. And, yes, I think the clue was in the "fancy joining me?" bit.' Jamie rested his chin on his hands, sighing in dramatic fashion. 'Look, I called Beyoncé and Gwynnie but they blew me off, so you're my last hope. Can you take a few days off from the salon, or will the wrinkly clientele attack you with pitchforks and vats of serum? I think you should be impressed, by the way, as I've swotted up on all things anti-ageing and beautifying. Not that you need any of it. Because you're perfect, just as you are.'

Cat gulped, unable to believe that Jamie was giving her another chance. Did she deserve it? She hadn't even explained what had happened between her and Stewart. How easily she'd been sucked in by his lies and superficial charm. 'Jamie, do you believe in ghosts?' Cat wasn't sure where the question came from, only that Gary had come to her rescue and somehow hearing Jamie's answer was important.

Jamie looked puzzled as well he might. 'I've never given it much thought, to be honest. Why, did you murder your ex and bury him under the patio?' Cat gasped, then realised – as usual – Jamie was joking. At least, she *hoped* he was joking.

'It's all over, I promise,' she said. 'Not that it was ever truly *on* again. I just got sucked back into something I'd worked so hard to get out of before and …'

Jamie pushed the food to one side and took Cat's hand. His familiar touch soothed her nerves and reminded her of how good they were together.

'I already knew that,' said Jamie. 'Otherwise, you wouldn't be here, would you? And I'm so glad you are. I'd love to take you to Cornwall and feed you fish and chips and ice-cream and go skinny dipping in the sea. Depending on the temperature, of course, and if you're willing to entertain onlookers with your nakedness. Or we can save that for indoors.' His look of mischief was mingled with such longing, goose bumps broke out on Cat's arms. She had a second chance, and she wasn't going to blow it. The salon could close for a few days; she'd reschedule her clients and come up with a plausible excuse.

'Shame you didn't dispose of Stewart under the patio,' Jamie continued as they settled the bill and headed for the door. 'He might have come in useful after all.'

It was Cat's turn to look puzzled. 'Useful for what?' she asked, as Jamie draped an arm around her shoulders.

'Well, if you'd left his bum sticking out, you'd have somewhere to park your bike!' He gave Cat an almighty squeeze, as she collapsed into giggles. 'Sorry, not one of my own. Stolen from the legend that is Billy Connolly.'

Minutes from Cat's house, she remembered that Jamie hadn't answered her question about believing in ghosts. She repeated it, recalling all the time she'd doubted Hattie. And the comfort they'd both gained from his unexpected return.

'I guess the jury's out for me,' said Jamie, stopping to look at Cat. 'I've never seen one, but that doesn't mean they don't exist. There are a lot of things we don't understand in this world, never mind any other, so I'll keep an open mind. Although...'

Cat knew what was coming, and it couldn't have been more welcome. Jamie's warmth and good humour were a breath of fresh air, compared to Stewart's buttoned-down and bullying ways.

'If Death set up a sewing business, there could be some serious reaper cushions. Oh, and you know those glass coffins? I would be seen dead in one of those. And here's another—

Cat seized Jamie by his jacket lapels and pulled him towards her. 'I love your one-liners but – for now – can you just shut up and kiss me?'

* * *

'HE'S GONE, CAT. FOR GOOD.' Hattie's tears had dried up, but she felt emotionally wrung out. Never had she been more grateful to see her best friend, especially as Johnny and Tilly had gone out for the day and she wasn't working until mid-afternoon. She clutched her mug of tea, its heat providing scant warmth for her icy fingers. She'd lain awake most of the night, hoping Gary would reappear. When he didn't, Hattie had kicked off the duvet and spread-eagled herself across the bed, remembering the heat of his side and how she'd snuggled into it when he'd got up before her. There she'd stayed until dawn broke, along with her heart.

'Oh, Hattie. I'm so, so sorry.' Cat hugged her tightly. She wept openly, grieving for Gary all over again. Hattie was heartbroken, yet she knew she had to move on. Their extra time together had been bittersweet, but she was grateful for every precious moment they'd been given. *Til death do us part* was one of their wedding vows, and they'd managed to cheat it, at least for a while.

'We knew this was coming, Cat,' said Hattie, passing a box of tissues across the table. 'Now, blow your nose and tell me what happened with Jamie.'

As if by magic, Cat's mournful expression changed to one of joy as she related how she and Jamie were firmly back on track. Hattie felt her own spirits lightening, Cat's happiness clearly infectious.

'We spent all night talking – well, not *all* of it! – and here's the thing.' Cat rummaged in her bag and pulled out a folder. Hattie looked on as she produced a glossy brochure and spread it out in front of them. 'I picked this up a few weeks ago when I was thinking about bigger premises. OK, Stewart stirred up the idea in my idiotic brain, but he might just have done me a favour. Both of us, to be accurate.'

Hattie's sleep-deprived state meant she was struggling to make sense of what Cat was rabbiting on about. She peered at the brochure which showed some kind of café premises along with detailed floor plans and lots of statistics. Still none the wiser, she waited for Cat to continue.

'Stewart offered to splash some cash if I wanted to expand or whatever. Which is obviously not going to happen now but … I came across this place a while back and I think it would be perfect. I've already drawn up a rough business plan and spoken to the bank and … Hats, it might seem crazy but why don't we go into business together?'

Hattie's slouched position became more and more upright as she listened to Cat's excited chatter. The premises were a run-down café that had been on the rental market for almost a year. They comprised a main dining area on the ground level and several rooms upstairs which had been used for storage and basic accommodation.

'What I'm thinking is, I turn the upstairs space into a couple of treatment rooms and we transform the café into a trendy juice and coffee bar serving healthy snacks and light meals for my clientele. Customers can come in for a drink or whatever and see all the amazing stuff I offer. We'll have signs and blackboards up with deals of the day and maybe a loyalty card giving discounts on treatments and drinks and things. We'd need to sort out the finance bit between us, but I know you're fed up with Espresso Yourself and this way we'd be our own bosses and … best of all … work together!' Cat clapped her hands together like a demented seal. Hattie looked again at the brochure, then back at her friend. Could it really work? Was this a heaven-sent opportunity to do something different, reinvent herself and find a new purpose in life? Did Gary somehow, in some way, have anything to do with this? Hattie had some money put aside, and if it wasn't enough … she could always take out a small loan against the value of the house. *You're gonna have a good life. A great life.* Maybe it was time to 'seize the day' or – as her mum once put it – 'squeeze the day'. Hattie could picture the moment, when she was around fifteen or sixteen and struggling with school, boys and life in general. Rachel had made her favourite hot chocolate with squirty cream on top and stroked her hair as Hattie ranted about teenage injustices.

'Darling, my philosophy has always been to treat life like a lemon. You can choose to squeeze it gently and release a little juice and a lot of pips or you can squeeze it hard and get every last drop. A half-squeezed day is a half-lived one. And we never know how many days we'll get.' Rachel might be living on borrowed time, but she was still a full-on lemon squeezer.

'So, what do you think? I know we can do this, Hats. Please, please say yes!'

Left alone to think about it, Hattie desperately wanted to run the idea past Gary. Except, those days were over. She had to stand on her own two feet now. Make her own decisions and face the consequences, good and bad. Picking up her phone, Hattie scrolled through the saved numbers until she came to the newest one. Laurence. When he asks you out … Who said anything about *him* asking *her* out? Suddenly filled with a steely resolve, Hattie hit the 'call' button.

'Hi. Laurence? It's Hattie here, from the café … thank you, nice to know I'm not instantly forgettable! No, it's not about the car. The car's fine; I just wondered if you'd like to meet for a drink sometime? You would? Great! Let me just grab my diary and we can fix a date …'

CHAPTER 46

EIGHT MONTHS LATER

'HAVE THEY HAD THE BABY YET?' Marty asked for the umpteenth time. It was the equivalent of 'Are we there yet?' on a long car journey, but Gary couldn't be annoyed at his little friend's persistence. His days on earth were long past, but he was still able to pick up signals. Little snippets of news that seemed to seep into his head, unannounced and sometimes tricky to decipher. What he did know was that Flora was due to give birth any day now, and that they were having a boy.

'Mate, it won't be long now. Babies have a habit of coming out when they're ready, even if it takes longer than their mum and dad would like.' Gary thought wistfully of how Johnny had been two weeks' late putting in an appearance. Poor Hattie had waddled around the house sipping raspberry leaf tea and giving Gary 'come hither' looks as a roll in the sack was another alleged way of kick-starting labour. They'd given it a shot, but settled for a cuddle when Hattie complained she felt as sexy as a beached whale.

Both he and Marty were now in The Next Realm which was a step up from The Present. Marty was miffed that they hadn't come across any rollercoasters or water slides, but the feel of the place was … lighter. Instead of the swirling dark mist, it was more like being enveloped in a cloud of fluffiness. It even *smelled* better, less sulphur and more strawberries and cream. Although the unpleasant pong might have owed more to Bob's flatulence problem. Gary didn't miss him one bit, but he hoped that one day they'd meet Anna again. As it was, The Next Realm was a friendlier, more sociable place. There were a lot more people – OK, ghosts – around and everyone seemed jolly. Gary hadn't bumped into anyone famous yet, not even Clarence's beloved Jane. Mind you, he was pretty sure he wouldn't recognise her. Jeez, he wouldn't recognise Shakespeare unless he was spouting a few lines from Hamlet and carrying a skull.

'Do you miss Hattie?' Marty's question brought Gary up short. He had no idea how long it had been since they moved to a higher plane. There were no clocks or calendars around and his wristwatch had stopped at the exact moment of his death. All Gary knew was that Hattie was well and happy with her new man. A bittersweet thought, but it was the right thing. Gary also knew that Rachel was on the road to recovery, and Cat had found her soul mate in Jamie. As for Johnny, Gary's heart swelled with pride at how his boy had turned his life around. He was running Spellbound now, Ravenscroft fully retired and spending six months of the year in Tenerife. Johnny was looking into franchising the business, as well as expanding on the children's party side of things. Would Gary's updates on earthly goings-on last an eternity? Snippets of information floated into his head at random times, as if he was picking up rogue radio signals. Who knew, but he'd be grateful for the afterlife news feed as long as it lasted.

'Course I do, Marty.' Gary finally replied, gently cuffing his young companion around the ear. 'Just like you miss your mum and dad, but we're lucky. We were so, so loved and we get to carry that love around with us always. Some folks never have that even if they live to be a hundred.' He hoped Hattie lived to a ripe old age and was always surrounded by love.

Marty snuggled into Gary's side, Grump dangling from his other arm. 'I'm so glad I met you, Gary. And I don't think I'd like to be one hundred cos that's really, really old! Even older than my teacher Mrs Wicks, and she was all wrinkly and super grumpy and … Ooh, look!' Marty bounced up and down, pointing frantically into the distance. Gary followed his gaze. Through the fragrant fluff he could make out a vague shape in the distance. It couldn't be, surely … but it certainly looked a lot like …

'It's a bouncy castle!' Marty squealed with delight, doing his own little bounce on the spot. 'Ooh, let's go and get on it. I tried one on my birthday, and it was brilliant!'

It might not be his choice of entertainment, but Gary allowed Marty to lead him by the hand to the unexpected inflatable. Still clutching Grump, Marty scrambled up with some help from Gary. He followed, the wobbly surface already crowded with excited children.

'Come on, Gary. Let's bounce!' And they did, higher and higher, faster and faster.

'Wee hee! Don't you just love this?' And, to his surprise, Gary did.

'It's great, mate. A total blast.' They slowed down for a moment, Marty carefully placing Grump at his feet. 'We'll be friends forever, won't we, Gary?' he said, eyes wide and solemn. 'Pinky promise?' Gary smiled and held out his little finger, entwining it with Marty's.

'Pinky promise. Friends forever.'

* * *

CAT and the Hat had been open just over a month, but business was going well. They'd struggled with the name, before settling on the one given to them by their English teacher. Their logo was a cute cat wearing a floppy pink hat and preening itself, set against a coffee cup background. Hattie loved the relaxed vibe of the place, serving freshly squeezed juices and smoothies, alongside hot drinks – all organically sourced – and food with the emphasis on healthy and nutritious. Cat's loyal clientele had followed her to the new premises, and the café side had attracted even more customers seeking treatments. With a second treatment room ready, Cat had advertised for an assistant and Hattie was confident she'd need an extra pair of hands soon herself.

'Two kale, apple and beetroot juices coming up.' She smiled at the young couple, both looking at leaflets detailing all the massages and other therapies on offer.

'Can we have two slices of the black bean brownie as well?' asked the woman. 'Hey, Mark, do you think we should book a his and hers hot stone massage for our anniversary?' Mark, bless him, looked underwhelmed at the suggestion but gamely nodded when Hattie pointed out the salon entrance.

Taking a breather a few minutes later, Hattie was joined by a flushed Cat, who gulped down a bottle of mineral water in one go. 'I have never seen so many blackheads on a nose before! The room was like a hammam by the time I steamed the buggers out!'

Fixing them some green tea, Hattie glanced at her watch. Only another hour until they closed up and headed back to Hattie's to get dolled up for a night out. A double date, no less. Not the first one and – judging by how well the four of them got along – definitely not the last.

'Jamie said he'd swing by in a taxi and get Laurence first, then come to us,' said Cat, blowing on her tea. They were going to The Lemon Tree, a place of mixed memories but now a firm favourite with the group. Hattie and Cat treasured their memories of good times, but had jointly resolved to keep making new and equally happy ones.

* * *

'Does my bum look big in this?' Cat stretched around to check out her rear, encased in skin-tight faux leather trousers.

'Bloody enormous. Like something you'd see wallowing in an African river,' retorted Hattie, wriggling into a body con dress Cat had persuaded her to buy online. 'Is breathing optional when you wear stuff like this? And how the hang do you pull the zip up without dislocating a shoulder?'

Cat stuck out her tongue before lending a hand, zipping up the dress in one expert move. She looked Hattie up and down appraisingly before giving a double thumbs up. 'Not bad for a couple of old dears. Right, let's have a wee glass of fizz before they get here.'

Hattie hung back as Cat clomped downstairs in her sky-high heels. She sat at the dressing table and stared at her reflection. What she saw was a forty-something woman, all made-up and ready for a night out with the man she'd been seeing now for eight months. Laurence, the man Gary knew she'd go out with. *A good 'un.* And he was, he really was. Kind-hearted, funny and completely on Hattie's wavelength, he'd also met with approval from Johnny and Rachel. They'd visited Rachel together when she was recuperating at home after surgery. Hattie had been a bag of nerves, but Laurence immediately hit it off with Rachel and Ralph. She'd introduced him to Johnny and Tilly at home one evening, Laurence admitting he used to dabble in a bit of magic himself. They'd tried to outdo each other in the tricks stakes,

Johnny winning hands down. Tilly had taken Hattie aside and muttered, 'I think he's a keeper, Hattie.'

Gathering up her hair to fix it in a topknot, Hattie felt the slightest waft of air on the back of her neck. Turning round, she saw the window was half-open, curtains flapping in the breeze.

'Hats! Your drink's going flat, and the lads are here and raring to go!'

Hattie picked up her jacket and bag and headed downstairs. Laurence greeted her with a kiss on the lips, Jamie with a kiss on the cheek. She took a mouthful of her drink, before following them to the front door. 'Go ahead and get in the taxi. I won't be a minute.'

Standing in the hallway, keys in hand, Hattie looked at the well-worn tweed jacket still hanging on a peg. A second-hand shop purchase, Gary had loved it and worn it all the time, despite its shabbiness. Hattie couldn't bear to throw it away. Not yet. 'Miss you,' she whispered, stroking a sleeve. She stepped outside, pulling the door closed behind her. And – just for the briefest moment – Hattie could have sworn she heard the faint tinkle of a bell …

THE END

ACKNOWLEDGMENTS

I can't quite believe I've reached the end of this story. Writing The Haunting of Hattie Hastings was a journey into the unknown – and the afterlife – with no idea how it would go down. Thankfully, the public response has been hugely positive and I hope you've enjoyed your time with Hattie and friends.

A huge thanks to the talented Lisa Firth at Oliphant Author Services for the stunning cover. Big thanks too to Nick Jones for allowing me to steal hilarious one-liners from his Gagged and Bound book series.

Proofreading is vital to ensure a book emerges into the world in the best possible shape. Thanks to Marion Adams at Full Media for casting an expert eye over the manuscript and picking up all those pesky errors that slip through the net.

Once again, I'd like to thank The Book Club (TBC) for introducing me to so many wonderful authors and dedicated book lovers. Reading other people's work is so important to the process of writing. Thanks also to Shona, Jane and Lindsey for helping identify the odd boo-boo and giving me so much encouragement.

I'm already working on something new, and perhaps a little different. The fabulous thing about being a writer is allowing your imagination to take flight …

If you haven't already read my other books, please check out my debut novel, A Clean Sweep and its short prequel, A Clean Break. Finally, if you could spare a few minutes to post a review on your preferred platform, it would be so appreciated. Reviews mean the world to authors and can be as short as a few words. Thank you! ♥

ABOUT THE AUTHOR

Audrey Davis is the author of romantic comedy A Clean Sweep and its short prequel A Clean Break. She originally released The Haunting of Hattie Hastings as a novella trilogy between November 2017 and July 2018. Audrey lives in Switzerland with her husband and enjoys shopping, cooking, eating and drinking red wine. And – of course – reading and writing. She gets quite giddy with excitement when readers make contact, so please feel free to get in touch through either Facebook or Twitter.

Printed in Great Britain
by Amazon

27626268R00169